CLOUDLAND

CLOUDLAND

Joseph Olshan

ARCADIA BOOKS

Arcadia Books Ltd
139 Highlever Road
London W10 6PH
www.arcadiabooks.co.uk

First published in the United Kingdom by Arcadia Books 2013
Originally published by Minotaur Books, St Martin's Press, New York, USA 2012

ISBN 978-1-906413-92-7

Typeset by Anna Gorovay
Printed and bound by CPI Group (UK) Ltd, Croydon CR0 4YY

Arcadia Books supports English PEN *www.englishpen.org* and The Book Trade
Charity *http://booktradecharity.wordpress.com*

Arcadia Books distributors are as follows:

in the UK and elsewhere in Europe:
Macmillan Distribution Ltd
Brunel Road
Houndmills
Basingstoke
Hants RG21 6XS

in the USA and Canada:
Dufour Editions
PO Box 7
Chester Springs
PA 19425

in Australia/New Zealand:
NewSouth Books
University of New South Wales
Sydney NSW 2052

in South Africa:
Jacana Media (Pty) Ltd
PO Box 291784
Melville 2109
Johannesburg

For Lynn Darling

On n'aime bien qu'une seule fois: c'est la première . . .

Jean de La Bruyère

(The first love is the only love.)

PART ONE

ONE

I T WAS UNDER AN APPLE TREE that I saw her—up the road on the walk that I've taken hundreds of times in my life. I noticed her pink parka and thought: she's out here drinking in the un- usual warmth of late March; her face to the sun, hardy soul she must be, sitting there tanning in a crater of melting snow. I didn't have my dogs with me because they're older and arthritic and because the muddy road was deeply rutted, slippery with glare ice.

I usually go a half mile up the road to the red farm with a glass greenhouse where my painter friend raises orange trees that bear fruit all winter. Then I make a slow turn and wander back. I'm usually thinking about my deadline; that day I was grateful that a trusty reader from Mississippi had sent me a formula for ridding white T-shirts of armpit stains. When I passed the or- chard, there she was again: the pink parka, the face still canted to the sun at the same angle, and—I realized for the first time— completely still. Now I stopped, partly because of how motion- less she was, but also because I could hear Virgil and Mrs. Billy barking back at the house. The shift in wind direction had prob- ably brought them her scent.

Sinking into the soft, crusty snow, I took wobbly steps toward her, somehow knowing not to call out, but still not knowing how she might be. Ten feet away I saw the depression of snow around her, soaked in rusty brown. Now certain she was dead and the stain was blood, I made myself march on until I stood before the pale gray face, the slight double chin. I turned away for a moment, overcome with nausea. When I forced myself to look at her again I noticed beads of ice melting on her brow. I was thankful that her eyes were closed. Her parka was pretty well zipped up, but her throat was exposed and blotchy and eggplant purple, her lips bruised and black. I knew it was Angela Parker, a nurse who had disappeared in mid-January from a rest area off Interstate 91 and whose blood was found all over the inside of her car.

When she'd first gone missing and her picture was published everywhere, I actually thought I recognized her as someone who'd taken my blood several times at the hospital. I remembered the kind manner distracting me from the needle, nimble fingers making the draw much less of an ouch. She was the sixth victim in two years.

Long before Angela Parker was buried in the orchard snow, I'd imagine all sorts of marauders: hunters heading home from a day in the woods; drug runners from Canada on their way down through Vermont toward Boston or Providence. My driveway is just a quarter-mile long, so the rumor of passing cars filters through to me, especially when leaves have fallen and there is no buffer to the sound. I hear most of everything that passes.

And motorists have always mistaken this road for a more popular thoroughfare another half mile down Route 12. They usually recognize their error by the time they're cresting the first long hill, which is precisely where my driveway begins. Often at night I've been sitting at my writing desk, sifting through correspondence from people who read my advice columns, when a pair of headlamps telescopes through my rolled-glass windows. Somebody will have made a wrong turn onto my land, their car paused, its lighted eyes staring and blinding. Sometimes a car has ventured close enough to the house that the motion detector lamps have switched on. I've stopped working and waited until the vehicle began moving again.

But after the discovery of her body was reported all over the northeast, I found myself wondering if the killer would read the article, would learn that I was a forty-one-year-old woman living alone up here on Cloudland. I began to worry that each wandering tourist was the man whose DNA the police had been unable to detect—always the killer in my mind's eye, never some flatlander looking for Advent Road, whose famous B & B has been written up in all the travel magazines.

A few years ago, my editor at the newspaper syndicate said to me, "I can't imagine anyone would dare to bother you when you have dogs and a domestic pig no less."

"Why would a bunch of animals stand in the way?"

"Because they'd protect you."

I looked at my babies and thought: Would you? Could you? My house pig, Henrietta, often got angry and territorial. She'd rush the dogs and knock them over. I always wondered if she had it in her to take out a murderer before that murderer could stick his knife into her heart.

The night Angela Parker was stabbed and dumped unceremoniously in the apple orchard, there were no lost tourists, no invasion of headlamps; we had a snowstorm with blizzard conditions. The flakes were funneling down like pestilence, stinging my nineteenth-century windows. The wind was howling, its drafts seeping through the old bony rafters of the house. I was trying out a recipe for marble cake that somebody from Omaha had sent me, mixing white flour with cornmeal and threading dark chocolate into the batter. I heard the town truck dredging through, its yellow wing plow carving the fresh snow up into waves. The plowman remembers a single pair of virgin tire tracks winding along the deep drifts, tracks that, in his estimation, miraculously made it up Cloudland Road's first big hill before they vanished.

Earlier that day Angela Parker had met some of her hospital coworkers at a ski resort in southern Vermont. Driving home she stopped at the Hartland rest area on Interstate 91 sometime between five and seven P.M. She called her husband from a pay phone to say she'd made it that far in the storm. But she never turned up at home, and the following day her car was found in the parking bay of the rest area. By then she was already ten miles away from where she was abducted, just up the road from me. And to think that each time I went for a walk I had passed within fifteen yards of this mother of two lying in a vault of snow that would entomb her for the rest of January and February and most of March. Her husband grew so distraught when she disappeared that he ended up begging his parents to move up from Tewksbury, Massachusetts, to take care of him and his children.

When they finally brought her down from Cloudland, the road was so clotted with spring mud that the funeral home had to borrow a four-wheel drive. I couldn't help but watch them load her rigid body onto the stretcher, just the way I couldn't help watching when Hiram Osmond, our local "knacker man," arrived with chains to winch my dead farm animals up into his pickup truck, taking them home to hack and boil. I also watched hunters lug their quarry out of the forest: dead bucks with glazed, opaque eyes and huge pink slits in their bellies. I watched the seasons blend: a spike of warmth in midwinter, then a venomous cold that gave rise to the frost heaves that sent cars careering off the road. But when the ice finally thawed and the ponds caved in with a bellow, those apple trees where I found her had begun to throw their buds.

TWO

ANGELA PARKER WAS MURDERED on a Saturday, the holy day to Seventh-Day Adventists, who were among the first settlers of New England. If you comb my forest you'll find abandoned homesteads with remnants of stone foundations that look like walls built to nowhere. In one of the interstices my daughter once found somebody's notebook, moldering yellowed pages of faded cursive recounting Bible stories: David and Goliath, Ruth and Boaz, Naaman's little servant girl, and the fisherman Peter learning how to tend sheep.

The Seventh-Day Adventists believe that after death every soul sleeps until the Day of Judgment, that the departed can slumber for millennia until they are finally wakened to stand judgment with the rest of the living and the dead. Even those long dead will feel upon resurrection as if they have been sleeping scarely one minute.

The afternoon I discovered Angela Parker's body and raced back to the house, I dialed 911 and reached the local dispatcher, a temporary I didn't know, who actually disbelieved me when I said, "This is Catherine Winslow up on Cloudland. I'm pretty certain I just found the body of Angela Parker, the nurse who's been missing."

"And how would you know that?" asked the surly woman.

I ignored her attitude. "Why don't you patch me through to Nelson?"

"It's Sunday. Chief O'Reilly don't come in on Sundays."

"Okay, well, I'm just outside town, so you probably should send a Statie."

I undoubtedly sounded sure of myself because she asked, "Do you work for us?"

"No," I said, and then reminded her to tell the Staties that I was the first house on Cloudland Road.

Chief O'Reilly told me subsequently that for some reason the dispatcher's caller ID read out the same exchange as the mental hospital in Waterbury; the poor woman probably imagined that I was a loony.

The state police barracks in Bethel sent Leslie Fullerton, a doughy young man who'd been unmercifully teased at Wood-stock High for his unfortunate name and his weight problem. The torment he endured probably inspired him to become a Statie in order to pull rank on all those who once abused him. I'd been waiting for his arrival at the end of my driveway, and when the green cruiser finally showed and the window rolled down, he looked apprehensive. "Hello, Mrs. Winslow. I heard you think you found the . . . *nurse.*"

I nodded and told him I believed I had.

"Well, hop on in." Together we drove up the rutted, muddy road, the bare trees bowing against the sharp, late-March wind, ravines and streams surging wildly with runoff, little craters of brown peeking through the diminishing snow mass on the broad fields. The cruiser bounced and skidded in the mud as we climbed the short distance to the orchard. I was asking Leslie why the state didn't equip more of their vehicles with all-wheel drive when the two-way radio blared a burst of loud static. He never bothered to answer me. When we finally arrived, he looked toward the body leaning against the apple tree, shook his head, and almost seemed hesitant.

"You stay here," he said.

Glad that I didn't have to lay my eyes once again on Angela Parker, I watched Leslie, all 230 pounds of him, struggling across the orchard in two feet of soft corn snow, sinking down in places I'd glided over. He suddenly tripped and fell forward. "Fuck!" I heard him say. He got up again and approached the dead woman. He leaned toward her for a moment, shook his head, and then began shambling back, his face crimson, his eyes dazed. He climbed in next to me, winded. "There's a big tree down. I fell over it." He grabbed his heart-shaped dispatch radio and called in a code. The immediate response was garbled to me but intelligible to Leslie, who said, "Affirmative . . . to what the coroner says." Then to me, "Dr. Stern crossed Lake Champlain and is out of range. So we've got to get the local deputy coroner."

Leslie completed a three-point reverse on the tight road and we began driving the rutted throughfare back to my place.

"Dr. Malcolm Banfield," I said after a few moments of gloomy silence. "Good luck on Sunday. That's the day he goes around euthanizing people."

Leslie shook his head and said, "Oh great." With a glance in the rearview mirror back toward where Angela Parker lay, "Means I'll probably be there all night securing the site until they can get down from Burlington."

Imagining the desolate task of guarding the body, I shivered and said, "Well, I can offer you plenty of coffee and homemade doughnuts. I don't sleep much most nights anyway, so I may as well drive up and bring you refills."

Leslie grunted and thanked me for the offer.

Back at the house Virgil and Mrs. Billy greeted us with howling barks, Henrietta oddly absent. When I led Leslie into the kitchen I could see that my 250-pound potbellied pig once again had gnawed through the childproof plastic lock on the garbage cabinet, rummaged through the bin, and was lying on her side, scarfing a bunch of lemon rinds. "Look at you!" I scolded, and she stopped and peeked at me with a familiar craven glint in her eye. I was too rattled by now to care.

"Holy shit," Leslie said when he saw Henrietta. "She doesn't bite, does she?"

"Do you?" was my answer.

My calendar was lying on the kitchen counter, and I saw my own notation that Malcolm Banfield and his wife (who substituted for me at the local prison where I taught a writing class) were actually away on vacation. When Leslie learned this, he began radioing for the name of the deputy assistant medical examiner. I interrupted to say it was Brenda Moore and that I also had her phone number. "You're sure on top of things, aren't you, Mrs. Winslow?" he said with a sarcastic edge.

"Well, I don't feel like it," I said, blinking and seeing afterimages of pink.

Taking in the room with a glance, noticing the piles of books and magazines on the dining room table, Leslie said, "Man, you got lots of reading to do."

"I collect information for my column. And for my column I've interviewed both Malcolm Banfield and Brenda Moore. That's why I have their phone numbers. Brenda also deals with the prison."

"Yeah, that's right. You teach at the prison, don't you?"

"Every other Monday."

"Anyway, not to contradict, but the barracks will have to be the ones to call her."

A moment later the dogs went crazy barking again, and I went to look out my study windows. Several state police cars had swerved into my driveway, as well as an unmarked Jeep Cherokee, enough commotion so that even Henrietta left her snack of lemon parings and barreled ahead over to the sliding glass door to survey the new arrivals.

"Your buddies are here," I informed Leslie, watching men in starched uniforms emerging from their vehicles. He hurried outside to join them, and I numbly followed and stood just outside the door. I immediately recognized Detective Marco Prozzo, in an ill-fitting sharkskin suit, getting out of the unmarked car. Prozzo was the Springfield-based detective running the serial murder investigation from the Vermont side of things. On local television I'd seen this New Jersey transplant meandering around with volunteer crews searching for missing bodies. A short, squat man with a wide nose and full, asymmetrical lips, Prozzo gathered the group together in the driveway, presumably to discuss investigation strategies. I assumed he would have to honor the protocol of steering clear of the victim until the coroner's own personal Statie could arrive. "Yeah, well, guess what," I heard the detective say. "He didn't answer his page or his cell. We can't wait too long. There could be something crucial here."

"Won't be a happy coroner," one of the Staties warned him.

"I'll take the heat," Prozzo said.

The reprieve of the unseasonably mild temperature was quickly fading as a northern chill knifed through my cardigan. I pulled its flaps around me.

The detective turned toward me and called out, "You must be Catherine Winslow, hello there. I need to ask—" The conversation was interrupted by the arrival of the county sheriff in his white SUV. Leslie had been telling the others about the sorry state of Cloudland Road, and it was quickly decided that they should pile in the all-wheel-drive car to travel the short distance to the site of the body. As the men began squeezing in, Prozzo took a few steps closer to me. "What time would you say you first saw her?" I checked my watch and estimated that I'd made my first pass around 2:30 P.M. He thanked me with a wink and joined the others.

Three days later, my Cloudland neighbor, Anthony Waite, invited me to lunch at Joanie's Café in Hartland Three Corners. Anthony, a doctor from Canada, came to live on Cloudland when his wife was offered a college professorship at Colby-Sawyer College in nearby New Hampshire. He worked at the psychiatric hospital down in Springfield, the only place that was hiring when they moved to the area. Anthony also had invited one of our only other Cloudland residents, Paul Winter, an internationally recognizedp ainter.

We chose a secluded, tattered vinyl booth facing a horseshoe-shaped counter. The moment I sat down all eyes in the restaurant were fixed on me, looking concerned; after all, this was a local café and I knew most of the patrons. One by one folks began rising from their places, leaving their half-eaten breakfasts to tell me they were sorry I had to witness what I did. One or two even dared to gently suggest that I consider renting out the studio apartment that I'd fashioned out of an extra sitting room—so I'd have another presence in the house. Living in rural New England and dealing with people on a daily basis requires a certain kind of protocol, a "what do you think of the weather we're having" sort of preamble before business is done or opinions are delivered with reticence and sometimes even wry humor. Some of those who left their meals to come over made a few moments of small talk before asking if I owned a gun. I assured them I had a rifle. One young electrician I'd watched grow up informed me that the sale of firearms had skyrocketed in recent days, particularly to women like me who were living alone. That doors, forever left unsecured, were being bolted. That Home Depot over in West Lebanon kept selling out of security locks. People paid their respects and went back to eating, but I could read in their faces that they were wrestling with the reality of a series of brutal crimes that remained unexplained and unsolved.

I automatically ordered scrambled eggs, knowing I'd probably have no appetite. Since discovering Angela Parker's body I often felt queasy whenever I smelled food, imagining her gelid gray flesh, what little blood that remained in her body frozen in her veins, its deep rusty stain like Italian ice in the orchard's snow, her neck purpled from strangulation.

Combing his thick, shiny auburn hair out of his eyes, Anthony said, "I guess I should have realized you'd have to receive people here. Hope that's not too uncomfortable for you."

"It's okay. I actually appreciate all this concern. Let's face it, everybody is freaked out."

Glancing around the room, Anthony said softly, "I asked both of you to lunch to let you know that I've begun working on all the cases, going over the evidence that has come in."

We stared at him for a moment and then Paul said, "Working on the cases? I thought you were down in Springfield dealing with all the schizos."

"Do you know anything about forensic medicine?" I challenged.

"Back in New Brunswick, forensic psychiatry was one of my specialties. I offered to work on these murders when I heard Dr. McCarthy"—he paused respectfully—"was unable to."

We'd all heard that Dr. McCarthy, Windsor County's forensic psychiatrist, had been diagnosed with Alzheimer's. Anthony turned to me. "The police don't want anyone to know I'm working for them until I get up to speed."

"So you invited us here to tell us to keep our mouths shut," I pointed out.

"No, just a request. I'm actually concerned about how everybody is doing." Anthony was looking meaningfully at Paul, a short and gnomelike seventy-five-year-old with prominent, questioning blue eyes. "Let's face it, the two of you, Wade, my family, and myself are the only full-time residents on Cloudland. It's pretty desolate up where we live. The perfect place to leave a body that won't be found for a good while."

There was a gnawing silence between the three of us. Finally, I said, "So you're working with that guy Prozzo?"

"Directly."

"He seemed to know me."

"I've spoken of you. He told me his wife and his daughter read your column. Anyway, Marjorie Poole, the woman who got away from our killer last year, is a bellwether." Anthony was speaking of the only woman attacked who'd managed to escape. "Most of the other women were pretty badly decomposed by the time they were found, whereas Angela was frozen for nearly three months. The strangle marks on her neck and Marjorie's are pretty identical, as well as the stab wounds. It's a certain kind of knife."

"A filleting knife," I said. "Deep-sea fishermen use them."

"So could he be a fisherman who came inland?" Paul asked. He was looking at me oddly. I'd been inadvertently tracing my finger along a scar on my neck. The moment I realized he was peering at me I could actually feel the pressure of sadness that had been chasing me for the last two years, reliving the alarm of having my windpipe blocked, my breathing thwarted by a man I loved.

"It's a common enough knife, really," Anthony said, adding that as in the other murders, there had been no handling that suggested sexual intent; and that this could mean the killer himself was sexually impotent.

"One thing that continues to amaze me," I said, "is that Marjorie Poole has been such a terrible witness. You would think she'd be able to give enough detail so that they could nail this guy."

Anthony looked from one of us to the other. The rolled-up sleeves of his shirt had slipped down his forearms, which were covered with golden hair. As he rolled them up again, he said, "I'll explain, but once again, it can't go beyond this table." He looked around to make sure our waitress, an inveterate gossip named Sheila, was out of earshot.

He reminded us that Marjorie Poole, a twenty-seven-year-old potter, had been attacked outside her studio loft in Claremont, New Hampshire. At seven o'clock one winter evening, carrying two plastic bags of groceries she'd been keeping in a small refrigerator, Marjorie began heading along the row of deserted offices and studio spaces. The building had originally been a wool mill, whose oak floors creaked and sighed when you walked along them and whose ceilings rose high up into an industrial cathedral. Out of the corner of her eye she claimed to have seen a densely built man sitting on a bench in front of one of the refurbished offices. Head in his hands, he was wearing a camouflage army jacket and a Boston Red Sox baseball cap. She sensed an air of distress about him and almost stopped to ask what was wrong. But a glance down the long, empty corridor was enough to make her wary. Later on she swore that he never looked up at her, that she'd never been able to see his face very clearly. A few moments after she passed him, he leapt off the bench and attacked her from behind, jamming his jacket sleeve into her mouth.

He ringed her throat with fingers encased in woolen gloves. Then she felt a sharp, stupefying pain in the small of her back; he'd pulled up her soft down jacket, her striped jersey, and found bare skin. That winter Marjorie Poole had been going to a tanning parlor in West Lebanon, in anticipation of a holiday with her boyfriend in the Lesser Antilles. There was a tan line between her lower back and the top of her buttocks that was adorned with a discreet shamrock tattoo. With his long blade, the killer aimed for it, and the knife drove in halfway, piercing the shamrock, just missing her spleen, the tip barely nicking the wall of her bladder. She managed to backhand him with a grocery bag lined with large pouches of frozen strawberries, striking him forcefully on one side of his head, stunning him into momentary submission. He let go of the knife and she foolishly but instinctively reached around and yanked it right out of herself. While she bled her pain distilled into fury. She took a savage lunge between the flaps of his camouflage jacket, jabbing an inch into his gut, mixing her blood with his before fleeing and, unfortunately, leaving the knife behind.

Anthony leaned forward. "What you don't know is that Marjorie Poole was high when she ran into this guy."

15

"How high is high?" I asked.

"They found traces of cocaine and Vicodin and alcohol in her blood."

"That's *really* high," I agreed.

"She was so high that she couldn't really give the police any details about his face or how old he looked."

"So that's what it was," I said. "Not traumatic memory loss."

"Correct." Anthony leaned back and crossed his arms over his chest. "But here's the thing," he said. "Being high probably saved her life. In medical school they say, 'God protects the inebriates and the babies . . .' Basically she was too stoned to panic. And really fought back hard with everything she had. Even though she couldn't give us any particulars about his face or his age, she does remember one very significant thing." Anthony paused, scrutinizing Paul and then me. "When he was trying to kill her he told her about 'The Day of Judgment' and that she'd sleep until then. And when she was on the way to the hospital, they found a few Seventh-Day Adventist pamphlets shoved into the pocket of her peacoat."

"And the connection?" I wondered aloud.

Raising his ginger-colored eyebrows, Anthony said, "It hasn't been reported and it won't be reported, I don't think, but a similar pamphlet was actually found in Angela Parker's ski jacket."

Shuddering, I said, "What about the rest of the women?"

"We're checking through the files, but as far as I can see, nothing like this has been linked to any of the other bodies. But we have to take into consideration that every other victim was killed when it was warmer, so the bodies had decomposed and were picked over by animals by the time they were found. Had it been left, printed matter might have been scattered."

"Or depending on the weather, decomposed or dissolved in the elements," said Paul, who, being an artist, knew about the durability of paper.

"How about the one killed in her home?" I said.

"Janet Tourvalon?" Anthony said. I nodded. "Nothing printed

found anywhere near her. However." He held up a finger. "Everything else matches, the strangle marks, the knife wounds."

"Maybe he found God and His literature more recently," said Paul, a lapsed Catholic.

"I think he's just trying to mix it all up, red-herring style," Anthony said.

"Or maybe just getting bolder," I said, "and taunting us with clues."

Sheila, our waitress, arrived with more coffee and refilled Anthony's cup and mine. "Whatya up to these days?" she said to everyone. "You doing all right, honey," she addressed me, and then was uncharacteristically direct for a Vermonter. "Talk about one crazy day, going for a walk and finding a stiff in the snow!"

"Not one of my better ones."

She grimaced. "I can only imagine."

Sheila was a tough-talking, rail-thin blonde who was rumored to have been a partner in a crystal meth lab that was run out of an auto body shop attached to an old, degraded farmhouse. The local scuttlebutt claimed that she was out of town when the operation was raided and shut down.

Glancing at Paul, who knew her a lot better than Anthony, I said to Sheila, "I'm coping. And *you*?"

"Oh, keeping my thoughts and deeds pure," she said with a saucy smile. "Be a lot happier when the weather perks." We all reflexively glanced out the window across the parking lot and past the drive-up bank teller to a short field where the snow had melted down to stubbled grasses that were a monochrome, mud-seasonal brown. "Dreary, isn't it?" Sheila remarked. I looked back and saw her winking flirtatiously at Anthony, who waited until she drifted over to the next table of customers.

"I think she *likes* you," I said.

Ignoring my remark, Anthony said sotto voce, "Angela Parker was an atheist . . . according to her husband."

"Well then, slim chance she'd be carrying around inspirational literature in the pocket of her ski jacket," said Paul, who tore his last piece of toast in half and tossed it on his plate. He unfolded his paper napkin and laid it on top so that it spread over his unfinished omelet like a funeral shroud.

On the way out of the restaurant, Paul stopped to chat with our local state representative, who was dining alone at the counter. As Anthony and I walked to the parking lot, he asked how I'd been feeling day to day. "You're looking a bit slimmer than your usual svelte self," he said.

I told him I'd scarcely eaten in the seventy-two hours since I'd found her, my thoughts still hounded by visions of pink parkas, a lacerated neck, and melting ice on her forehead.

I told him that over and over again I'd been imagining myself in my last day of life, leaving my family for an outing with friends, the ozone smell of snow in early hours, sweet wood smoke, the feeling of a solitary adventure on the horizon, driving with my skis in the back of the car, and then, after a long day on the slopes, legs and thighs burning from all the exertion, heading home cozy and warm as the snow begins to ping the windshield. I'm gripping the steering wheel tightly, peering out into diminished visibility, holding the road carefully, afraid of veering off the highway, just wanting to make it back to my family safe and sound.

"I feel disconnected and vague," I admitted. "All the time. I usually have trouble sleeping. Now it's worse than ever."

"Do you take anything for it, the insomnia?"

"On and off. Basically just live with it. Stay up late at night reading."

Raking his heel across a loose patch of gravel as though to get a cake of mud off of it, Anthony said, "I'm surprised Breck hasn't offered to come and visit."

My daughter was living five hours away in New Jersey. I hadn't seen her since early January. "Breck's caught up in her girlfriend right now," I explained with a pang of missing her. "But she calls fairly frequently. When I told her what happened she offered to come . . . halfheartedly."

He fixed his pale eyes on me. "Why don't you drop by the house. I'm happy to give you a script . . . for your sleep."

I hesitated.

"Seriously. When is good for you? How's tomorrow morning?"

"Tomorrow morning's fine."

"Come by around . . ." He thought a moment. "Ten o'clock. . . . Now, just one more thing, Catherine," he said, looking toward Paul, who was standing well out of earshot. "You're not going to write about anything we spoke of, are you?"

This puzzled me; he was well aware that I no longer did investigative journalism.

"I never knew you gave that up forever," Anthony said when I reminded him.

"Never say forever . . . but for the most part, anyway. Not that I think that you read my columns, but FYI: the only thing that might be usable from what you told me would be 'how to stop a killer with a bag of frozen strawberries,' which I honestly think my syndicate editors might sneer at."

He laughed and then said, "I know you've done a lot of true crime reporting. And I know you've been following this investigation. . . ."

"Meticulously," I told him.

"I'd like to be able to discuss . . . certain findings with you from time to time to get your take on things." Glancing at the restaurant, where Paul was just beginning to make his way toward us, Anthony said, "I think you could be helpful to me. But it would just have to be between us. And there will be certain things that I might not be able to divulge."

"I understand. I'd be happy to assist."

"Great." He gave me a bone-breaking hug, approached Paul and squeezed his shoulder, then trotted off to his red pickup truck.

Paul and I climbed into his vintage Saab and drove a mile homeward down Route 12 as it opened onto a piebald landscape of snow and brown. It was April 1, still many weeks away from any hint of green.

"You're awfully quiet, dearie," he said to me.

"That's because I'm feeling *queerie.*" I managed to smile.

"How come?"

"I keep thinking about her, poor soul."

"Angela, you mean?" Paul said.

"Of course Angela! I'm sorry, I don't mean to sound so impatient."

"It's okay . . . Oh now, *Jesus!*" Paul exclaimed, and pulled over to the side of the road.

"What's wrong?"

"I forgot to pick up a dozen eggs."

"You just had them . . . for breakfast."

"Not for eating," he snorted. "For mixing tempera."

Then something occurred to me. "Tell you what, leave me at Wade's office, go get your eggies, and I'll make Wade give me a ride home."

"Fine," Paul said, but then went ruefully quiet as he carefully made a U-turn and drove us back toward Hartland Three Corners. "When you go in there, tell my . . ." He hesitated and then said, "*Son* he owes me a call."

"Before I leave, I'll pick up the phone and I'll put it in his hands."

Paul finally stopped the car in front of the town clerk's office, turned to me, and said, "I was watching you while Anthony was talking. I saw you touch your neck like that."

"Yeah?"

"Well, of course I was wondering—"

"I figured you were wondering."

"That boy," he said with a dismissive tone.

"Yeah, I was thinking about *that boy,*" I said with the bitter taste of longing.

"Still away, though, isn't he?"

"Yup. Says he's never coming back."

"I certainly hope that's true. . . ."

"You do, huh?"

"I hope *you* do!"

I didn't answer.

THREE

H E WAS A STUDENT OF MINE who strategically waited until the class was over before approaching me. I used to call him a boy; however, he was very much a man in every way except perhaps in his unbridled idealism. And I guess in the end that idealism came between us but it didn't kill us. Youth that is as yet unbroken allows the young to believe that if they set their mind, most of what they desire will be within their grasp. He was no different.

I don't believe in love at first sight. I do believe that some people dazzle you at first glance; however, who they really are never catches up to how they first appear. In my experience the ones who crawl under your skin and stay there like stubborn splinters are those who might put you off at first with, let's say, nervous arrogance or something physical such as pinched and narrow shoulders. But then they begin to grow on you slowly, insidiously, until you realize they somehow know you without knowing you, that their body fits yours perfectly, that their touch and their words have set your whole being burning on some kind of crazy high flame. And no matter what happens, that flame continues to burn. It burns even after you've reached the sad and disillusioning moment when you realize the complications greatly outnumber the virtues, it burns when you know you're sinking into a terrible, tortured darkness.

I was thinking this while walking into the Hartland town hall, thinking that if you hate longing and pain you can choose to live on the outside of things and not let them or anyone in. As much as I had suffered over him, I was still glad that I loved him, glad that I'd allowed myself few delusions about the relationship.

But, ironically, I had deluded myself about Vermont. About all the years I spent here *part time* thinking I was woven into the local fabric, believing that I was passionate about the rural conflicts, that I cared about the disputed rights of public passage over class 4 roads, or even that I grieved over reckless rural tragedies such as when four high school kids driving at eighty miles an hour in a fifty-mile-per-hour zone hit black ice and thundered into the bedroom of a local veterinarian, killing everyone involved but the doctor, who luckily was out in her barn feeding farm animals. It was only when I began living here full time eight years ago that I really began to cleave to the placid, lovely landscape, that I truly felt the resentments between the landed gentry and the tradespeople forced to rely upon them, that I became embroiled in the disputes about architectural integrity. But most of all I entered deeply into the lives of Paul (whom I'd known for years) and his adopted son, Wade.

Their relationship began in a most usual way. At one time Wade and his parents lived down the road from Paul in caretakers' quarters; Wade's father used to manage the one-thousand-acre farm that still belongs to the CEO of a biotech firm who lives primarily in Boston. Wade's father was annoyed that his son shied away from helping him take care of the vast tracts of land and cattle, whereas Wade's mother, who worked as a part-time dressmaker, was horrified and embarrassed by her son's fascination with fashion patterns. Both parents called him "lazy" and "girly." He despised them so much that he ended up venting his rage on Paul, the "rich" artist who lived nearby.

One winter evening while Paul was in Florida, Wade broke into the artist's home and went on a rampage. He demolished crystal goblets and Windermere porcelain plates. He shattered pre-Columbian vessels and, with an ax he'd found in the barn, splintered ancient African masks. He tore down curtains, flung books from the shelves and scalped them from their bindings. He found an heirloom strand of *peau d'ange* pearls that he snapped, loose baubles bouncing and scattering over the wood floors into nooks and crannies and taking forever to find. At least he had the presence of mind to leave Paul's canvases alone, as well as those of some of his contemporaries, including a Robert Motherwell.

When Wade was suspected and finally tracked down by the police, the priest of the local Catholic church intervened. He contacted Paul, described Wade's miserable home life, and managed to bring the two of them together. Wade offered a sincere apology and proposed to atone for the damages by doing odd jobs around Paul's house for a year. After some careful consideration, Paul decided to accept Wade's offer. Soon he began to feel compassionate toward the young man, insisted on paying him for household chores, and, after Wade learned how to drive, to run errands. As their unconventional friendship solidified, Wade eventually learned everything he could about Paul's art: how to stretch canvases, to make tempera, and soon began keeping track of all the paintings for cataloging and exhibitions. His work was meticulous and it served him well when eventually he was elected to be the town clerk.

The closer the two became, however, the more Wade drifted away from his family, who were repulsed by his innocent friendship with Paul. This happened to coincide with Wade's father being laid off by the Boston CEO. When his parents ended up taking another job and moving to a neighboring town, Wade began living at Paul's house. Ten years later Paul adopted him, and from then on they'd lived together as father and son in an uneasy alliance. As though having never quite recovered from that strange initiation, their relationship, though close, had always been marked by a certain tension. They reminded me of two lovers who'd become strictly platonic and who'd been living together for far too long.

Wade was sitting at his desk, perusing a stack of revised tax bills, one of his early spring tasks. Thirty-eight years old, he was dressed in neatly pressed blue-collar Carhartt jeans and a bulky sweater, which I knew he wore to give padding to his scrawny upper body. His mustache was pencil-thin, but it was as much of a mustache as he could muster.

"You wanted to see me?" I said to him.

He looked up and smiled sardonically. "Hiya, Catherine. Give me a sec, will you."

Across from Wade, sitting at a long, scarred banquet table, was John Dutton, a nonagenarian historian for Windsor County. He was scrutinizing record books and reading aloud the details of land records and property transfers, road construction and subdivisions to a transcriptionist that Wade used from time to time. John was a deliberate man with a face that showed its age like dried, cracked earth. Entries handwritten a hundred years ago are difficult for most people to decipher; John Dutton, with amazingly sharp lucidity, was able to read the faded sepia-colored ink in the old ledgers. He declaimed names aloud with beautiful cadence and deliberation, and they were invariably proper English names: Evangeline Peabody sold 6.2 acres to Lawrence Saunders for sixty-two dollars; William Mathews subdivided a five-hundred-acre parcel of woodlands and wetlands and sold a seventy-five-acre meadow to Alida Buchanan; a class 4 road runs across the northern ridge of Robert Bacon's land one hundred yards from the property line. Seeing that John was in the midst of his stentorian declarations, I suggested to Wade that we talk in the records room.

He gestured his assent, and I followed him into an adjacent office with one entire wall neatly filled with dozens of green and red leather binders. The room smelled like glue and carbon paper. We sat down opposite each other at a rectangular monk's table.

He scrutinized me. "Miss Rural Elegance, you look tired."

"I'm a wreck. Can't sleep. Nightmares."

"Maybe you should read two books at night instead of one."

"I do. Last night I started with a Josephine Tey mystery and then around three I switched to this book about what the world would be like if none of us were in it." I paused and ran my hands over the table bearing the scars of what was probably life at the mills in the nineteenth century. Thinking for a moment of all those hardscrabble lives, I said, "I just keep seeing her. I keep seeing Angela where I found her. It was like he . . . it was like he dug up the fresh snow so he could lean her against that tree. So that somebody like me would find her propped up and bright pink when the melting began. When the sun was thawing her face."

"So you think he thought about it, that he planned it . . . how she was going to look in three months' time?"

"I do."

I heard a gust of early-spring wind slamming against the town hall, the rafters creaking. Wade had a lost look on his face and for a moment he reminded me of an emaciated, contemplative figure in one of Paul's better-known paintings, owned by the Whitney Museum. And then I remembered.

"Before I forget, Paul wants you to call."

Wade hunched down in his chair. "Yeah, I know, he left one of his frantic messages. Worrying about something insignificant."

"Worrying about you, mostly, I would say."

"What's to worry? I have no other life. No lover. He sees me every day and night."

"That's just it. Maybe he thinks you will . . . go off eventually and leave him."

"How could I do that? He needs me. I've repeatedly told him

that I'm terminally single." Wade paused thoughtfully. "He's just generally afraid of things."

"Elderly fright, I think they call it."

The biographical content on Wikipedia and other Internet sources gave conflicting information about Paul's actual age. He claimed to be seventy-five, but both Wade and I hedged that he was closer to eighty—Paul guarded his real age as zealously as an over-the-hill starlet. The wind had brought with it a raw draft of cold that seeped into the room. I rubbed my hands together. "Jesum . . . chilly in here," I said.

Wade indicated all the leather-bound folders of land transfers, of births and deaths and marriages. "It can get a bit breezy from all the ghosts trafficking in and out of this place," he remarked.

"Come on!"

"I'm telling you. It gets really weird in here sometimes when you're alone. Winter nights especially. I often think I hear people whispering—"

"Whispering words of the dead," I said. "And I wonder what they're saying to each other."

"How about what they're saying about *us*," Wade amended. He crossed his legs at the ankles and looked at me appraisingly. "Okay, so what did Anthony want from you two?"

I shook my head. "Not supposed to tell anybody."

"You don't think Paul's going to blab as soon as I get home?"

"So let *him* break the confidence."

"You're being ridiculous. I'm going to know by nightfall so you might as well just spill it now."

He was right. And so I explained that Anthony had just become an unofficial psychiatric consult for the serial murders.

"So that must mean Doc McCarthy is officially gaga."

"Apparently so." And then, knowing that he'd soon hear it from Paul, I relayed the gist of the breakfast conversation: that, according to Anthony, the potter, Marjorie Poole, was drunk and high when she was assaulted, and a religious pamphlet was stuffed into her pocket as well as in the pocket of Angela Parker.

Wade bunched up his lips so that one side of his flimsy mustache touched the tip of his nose. "But how was that kept out of the newspaper?"

I told him what a journalist knows: that investigators filter what goes public; presumably, the killer will be out there reading whatever is written and published. That there are details they don't want him to know they know.

"So now they think this guy is some religious freak?" Wade was incredulous. "Anybody buying that?"

"Not yet."

"How about you?"

"Me? What do I know to think?"

Through the closed doors we could make out John Dutton's mellifluous droning of the names of people who, by all accounts, had finer handwriting and more hours of the day to devote to the inscription of ledgers with painstaking, calligraphic flourishes, when families tended to settle in one home and stay put for the rest of their lives and even when death itself didn't seem like such an anomaly.

Wade remarked, "In this day and age you'd figure they could get some of his DNA off of Marjorie or Angela or any of the others."

"He wears gloves, Wade."

"Still . . . something . . . hair or fibers." He paused for a moment. "Catherine, it amazes me we had no idea somebody drove up our road and dumped a body."

Even though he appeared concerned, he sounded oddly flat and dispassionate, and I took dutiful note of this. "We're hardly clairvoyants," I told him.

"No, we're certainly not. And that's why I called you. Because there is something else going on that I think you should know."

"Shoot," I said.

"I was fixing a leak in the greenhouse over the weekend. I saw

Emily Waite driving down the road like a bat out of hell. Bouncing over potholes."

"She's usually such a careful driver," I noted.

"Well, obviously in a state. When she glanced at me, she looked, pardon the expression, dead," Wade said, pausing for effect. "Then five minutes later I saw Fiona, Fiona Pierce, driving up the hill in her Volkswagen Beetle."

"And?"

"That's the third time I've seen Emily leaving and Fiona arriving," Wade said with no inflection in his voice.

Fiona was one of my fellow volunteers at the prison. "Maybe she knows one of the weekend people," I made myself say, even though I sensed where he was heading.

"I also saw them early in the winter, Anthony *and* Fiona walking in the snow at the tree line way behind Paul's house—Emily and the girls weren't home."

"How come you never told me *then*?"

"Because *then* I didn't know for sure what was going on." Wade leaned back in his swivel chair. "And because I knew it would bug you."

"So you just wait until I find somebody murdered and *then* tell me?"

"Hey, I can't help . . . the timing of certain things."

"Okay, let's go slow. So they were walking out in the open?"

"Yes, Catherine, in the open."

"And they seemed . . . *together*."

"Holding hands together."

I knew that Wade needed to get back to work, but I wanted to sit there in his vault of deeds and land records, the moldering smells of nineteenth-century documents, letting the news settle in a bit more. I wondered whether Emily had any idea about Fiona. Finally I said, "The Waites have always seemed . . . relatively content together."

"I won't disagree," Wade said.

"But people should realize that if they do something on the QT around here, more often than not somebody in this town will find out about it."

Wade looked at me warily. "Except of course if they happen to be a serial killer."

The following morning the temperature had remained unseasonably mild. Rather than drive the mile and a half up the road to Anthony's house, I put on a black cashmere turtleneck and a loden wool vest that my daughter, Breck, and I found on sale at a local clothier called Ibex and walked.

Cloudland Road is flanked on either side by tall oaks that in the summer cast a lovely drape of cooling shade. Wide-open meadows and pastures gently undulate as they stretch far back to forest, the land itself slowly rising to an elevation of 1,900 feet and opening to a view of the Green Mountains that to the north end up at Camel's Hump, and in the blue, hazy southern distance are framed by Mount Ascutney. Growing up, I'd spent summers and holidays in Vermont, and when I got married, my husband and I bought my 1800s Cape on Cloudland and continued commuting from New York City until we got divorced. Within a year of our split he developed an aggressive form of throat cancer and died, and I then began living here full time with my daughter. That was eight years ago (when Breck was fourteen) and Paul and his adopted son, Wade, were the only other year-round residents. Anthony, his wife, and their two daughters arrived a few years later.

Paul and I bought our parcels—mine fifty acres, his twenty—before property values skyrocketed. Anthony inherited approximately forty from his American grandmother. The rest of the pristine land is owned by the biotech CEO out of Boston who spends little time in his picturesque *Architectural Digest* farmhouse but who has nevertheless stockpiled a thousand acres, installed Scottish Highland cattle, and built Cape-style guest-houses for his friends and caretakers along the road and on several pinnacles of carefully cleared hillside. He'd had one of the ponds dredged in a perfect hourglass shape to please his reputedly implacable wife. My favorite house of his that he built and rarely uses is graced with a widow's walk that gives a commanding yet lonely vantage point of the land with its swales and distant woods. Cloudland has always been largely uninhabited. When you drive along the road itself, it's a rare thing when another car passes in the opposite direction—in short, a perfect location to excavate layers of deep snow and trundle a body.

Spring comes relatively late to northern New England: early April often feels like dead of winter. Leaves generally don't even bud for another six weeks; you never see croci until at least the third week. That day I set out into a landscape that was still largely snowbound. At the fringe of a sloping pasture stood a copse of sumacs whose vermilion leaves of the previous autumn still clung to the branches and looked like drops of blood holding fast to white fabric. I was passing the orchard for the first time since finding the body and saw that it was cordoned off, yellow police tape spooled from tree to tree, sometimes angling sharply to circumscribe its boundary. In places where the tape had been tied off, extra pieces hung like dead appendages fluttering in the wind. I could see pock-marks where the snow had been scooped up for lab sampling—all in all, an eerie scene like something out of a TV police drama. This was the sort of disturbance I thought I was moving away from when I finally left New York City.

I walked past Paul's house and noticed a front loader pawing at a bunch of tree stumps, the freshly spaded earth a rich terra-cotta brown. I remembered him mentioning a plan to expand his vegetable garden, but the ground, in my opinion, was still too frozen to excavate. I continued another half mile to Anthony's, set at the back of gently sloped snowy fields, a two-hundred-year-old Colonial, stained a deep Delft blue, with an unattached barn that is painted pristine white, and, like many of the old Vermont barns, is slowly caving in on itself.

The fact is I knew the Waites somewhat, but not nearly as well as I might have. Up until now I'd kept a bit of a distance from them because of a strange coincidence. Anthony had done his medical residency at a hospital in Saint John, New Brunswick, near to Grand Manan Island, where my family had kept a summer residence since 1865. The first time we were introduced I quickly figured out that he was the young doctor who'd come over from the mainland to attend to my stubborn, domineering grandmother, who'd been having trouble breathing but refused to be hospitalized. Once we established that I was one of the Grand Manan Winslows, Anthony recounted his first glimpse of Granny sitting on the porch facing the lighthouse on Bancroft Point and saying, "I'll be right here plugged into this chair when I go," as he pulled a glittering vial and a needle out of his black bag. "But not yet," she told him with wide-eyed trepidation. "Don't worry, I'm not euthanizing you," he joked, preparing the injection, dosing her with a steroid that made her a lot more comfortable. Granny was amused by Anthony's comeback, and subsequently, whenever something ailed, she'd call and request him. Despite his crippling schedule, he would show up; the old lady apparently intrigued him.

Even though I wasn't by birth a New Englander, I adopted a bit of a New England attitude toward Anthony in that I found it awkward that he actually knew my grandmother. Then, too, I happened to remember a negative remark Granny once made about the young physician who had tended to her, specifically about a relationship that he'd been in which he'd ended "cruelly"—that was the word she used.

I knocked on the sliding glass door that led to his kitchen and he opened it with a grand gesture, hair tumbling into his eyes, a dishcloth balanced on his broad shoulder. He told me to come on in, "Just pulling a few more pancakes," returning to an old, enameled, wood-fed cookstove, beige disks of batter smoking in a black skillet. The kitchen smelled of yeast and coffee, and his two young daughters were sitting quietly at the table, elbows planted on vinyl place mats decorated with huge green frogs. Because their maternal grandmother was black, they had wonderful clear and dusky complexions. They were staring at me in such a way that I almost felt foolish for intruding.

"Good morning," said the eldest, twelve years old, whose eyes looked huge behind the lenses of her large round tortoiseshell glasses.

"Hiya, Mrs. Winslow," said the slightly younger and more striking of the two, with carrot-red hair and lots of big, dark freckles.

"I told you before you can call me Catherine," I said to them.

Glancing at her father, who was ladling more batter into his skillet, the youngest said to me, "Dad says we're supposed to call you Miss or Mrs."

I turned to Anthony, who said, "Until you are given permission otherwise. She'd like you to call her Catherine," he told his girls, laughing to himself while I looked around the kitchen.

"So where's Mama hiding out?" I wondered.

"Grading final exams," the three of them said in unison. Emily was a professor of botany.

Anthony was born in 1967, the same year as I; he looked youthful and fit flipping pancakes with a happy, jaunty air, still wearing his plaid pajama bottoms. You would never guess there might be marital strife lurking behind this happy scene. His domestic ease momentarily put my own slapdash housekeeping into relief. Despite the fact that I wrote a household hints column, my place had always been chaotic: dishes stacked up to a tilting mass; mismatched socks stuffed into drawers, orphan shoes; sludged coffee cups; and too many animals roaming around—and not always in harmony. By comparison, Anthony's house seemed orderly and clean, and the few times I'd visited them I imagined that he and Emily created a seamless, choreographed domesticity graced by all of Emily's hothouse plants—orchids and anthurium and Hawaiian lava and plumeria, tendrils of vines strangling banisters and book-cases and support beams.

While Anthony was changing out of his p.j.'s, I went to say a quick hello to Emily. I found her surrounded by what looked like a stack of term papers, sitting at a long green table in the sun-room, which smelled of humid earth and fertilizer. The room was chilly and she was wearing an ecru-colored angora sweater. She seemed deep into her work; I didn't want to disturb her and told her so.

"Don't worry. I can take a short break," Emily said, putting down her yellow highlighter pen. She had light tan skin, a curly mass of black hair with a radiant, natural streak of white running along the top. Looking at me over half-moon reading glasses, she said in her slight delicate drawl, "We need to see you more often. Drop in anytime, there doesn't have to be a reason."

"Same goes for you and the girls," I said. "*Chez moi.*"

Her brow furrowed. "There is one thing I keep meaning to ask: in your column have you ever written about how to get wa-termarks off of wood furniture?"

"I covered that about a year ago. It depends on whether they're light or dark marks."

"They're light."

"Okay." I thought for a moment. "So you take two small dishes, one of table salt and one of mineral oil. You dip your finger in the oil first and then the salt and you rub them into the wood. When the spot is gone then you wipe with a soft, dry cloth and polish it.

"If that doesn't work, you can try cigar or cigarette ash and boiled linseed oil. You follow the grain of the wood and wipe the ash lightly into the spot, then wipe with the linseed oil."

Emily laughed. "Now I just have to find some ash and linseed."

"I'd start with the salt and mineral oil."

"I will." She hesitated. "May I ask: how come you write your column under a pseudonym rather than your real name?"

I got this question a lot and it made me uncomfortable. "Because I don't consider it serious journalism. Like the major pieces, exposés, profiles for national newspapers and magazines I used to do. I got offered the household hints gig after my ex-husband died. A paradox, really. My readers should only know what a bad housekeeper I am. But the pay has been steady and handsome. And I've managed to stay with it. My readership keeps growing. The column keeps getting picked up by more and more newspapers."

"I know lots of people who follow you."

"The best part is they basically publish what I write. I don't have to fight over every line the way I used to do with top editors. And I can't deny it makes me a good income. Besides, I am *known* as Marian Mills. Even if I wanted to use my real name now I wouldn't be able to."

"Yeah, but everybody in Vermont and New Hampshire knows your real name." Emily referred to the considerable amount of local press I'd received.

Having changed into a pair of corduroys and a blue-jean shirt, Anthony now poked his head into his wife's study. "I'm ready," he said to me. I noticed that they hardly exhanged a glance. I told Emily good-bye as he led the way down a hall lined with portraiture of both their families: distinguished, scholarly-looking black men; and his more rough-and-tumble Scottish ancestors, the early settlers of Nova Scotia. He opened the door into a room with a large window that faced a majestic white pine tree. In contrast to the profusion of green in the rest of the house, there were no plants at all in the office. Neatly arranged with stacks of medical journals and manila files, his desk faced the door, apparently good feng shui. Two club chairs were placed equidistantly in front of it, the wall behind him paneled with bookshelves that seemed to be filled mostly with psychiatric volumes.

I looked around. "No couch."

"I do research reading here. Don't see patients out of my home."

"Well, that's good, as I'm not quite ready for patient status."

He took me seriously. "I don't mind obliging friends and acquaintances who, like you, are having trouble sleeping. If *I* couldn't sleep and thought you could help me, I'd be camped out on your doorstep."

But I'd already been distracted by something I picked out in the bookshelf, a novel called *No Name,* by Wilkie Collins, and I asked Anthony if he'd read it.

Turning around, he scanned his library until he found the eight-hundred-page nineteenth-century novel. "Oh yes," he said. "I *did* read that . . . quite a while ago. Great story, as I remember."

"His stories *are* great," I opined. "Was it recommended?"

He thought a moment. "Yes, as a matter of fact. By a colleague."

"Anyp articularr eason?"

He frowned, trying to remember. "I believe I was interested in the story of children losing their birthright because their parents weren't married when they were born. And how people suffered under that law."

"So, the psychological implications," I suggested.

"Right." He crossed his arms. "I should assume you're a fan."

I told him I'd read everything Wilkie Collins had ever published. Several times over. My dearest friend and former college roommate from Wesleyan is a Victorian scholar who spends a lot of time doing research in the UK. Theresa has managed to track down and send me all of the unavailable novels, including some obscure volumes that had seen printings of only several hundred copies. "I'm a defender of the Wilkie Collins faith," I told Anthony. "I think in his own way he's as good as Dickens."

"Tall claim, that. I don't know if I would agree."

I told him that when I taught nonfiction and magazine writing at Saint Michael's College in Burlington, I used to argue with some of the nineteenth-century people in the English department about the merits of Wilkie Collins, whom they taught mainly because of the feminist interest in *The Woman in White.* "Maybe two of his novels were on the syllabus," I told Anthony. "As part of what's called 'The Novel of Sensation.' "

He paused and then said, "You stopped teaching at Saint Mike's last year, didn't you?"

I cringed. "Involuntarily."

"They let you go?"

"In a manner of speaking."

With a gentle tone he said, "I heard from somewhere about a love affair with a student."

This was not where I wanted the conversation to head. "Former student," I said after resisting the question. "It went on for a year. Whether or not I was let go because of that relationship, Saint Mike's certainly wouldn't admit to it. They didn't have to, because I was an adjunct."

"I think I saw him once, standing at the end of your driveway as I went by. Dark hair, well built."

"Probably was Matthew." A queasy feeling came over me. I sat down in one of the club chairs. And then without even realizing it would happen, I felt the tears dripping down my cheeks. Damn, I thought.

Anthony had gone perfectly still, staring back at me with a kindly expression. And in the most gentle voice said, "Here are some tissues," handing me a box. I took them and stanched my weeping. "So you're still missing him?"

"I'm sorry, can't talk about it."

Anthony raised both his hands in a gesture of surrender. "Okay. But do you think your insomnia could have something to do with . . . him, too?"

"Probably."

"Takes a long time," Anthony said meaningfully, and I couldn't help but wonder if he was hinting at the state of his own life. "Was he just a student or was he *your* student?"

Peering out the window, distracted by the slow swaying of the pine tree, whose needles seemed to be vibrating along with my longing for him, I reluctantly divulged, "He was my student. A bit older than the others, twenty-four when we met. The affair began *after* the course was over. But before he graduated."

"But then after a year it went south?"

"Basically, yeah."

"The first teacher/student affair you'd ever had?" Anthony persisted.

I nodded.

"So how did the university twig?"

"Somebody sent anonymous letters. To the school. To his parents. And even to the school newspaper."

"Who?"

"We never found out. Could have been anybody. I had jealous colleagues, I had students who thought they were given unfair grades. And I had people who thought my being with him was . . . unseemly."

"What's the age difference?"

"Fifteen years."

"Not . . . inordinate."

"Well, depends on whom you're asking. Certainly was to his mother when she found out and to my daughter, who is only a couple years younger than he."

"So what exactly happened with the school?"

"First the administration warned me about the anonymous letters. They asked me to keep a lid on the relationship—at least until he finished school. Which I had no problem doing. But then a second round of letters were sent during the summer after he graduated. Around that time I got a pretty perfunctory phone call from Human Resources explaining they had to cut back on some adjuncts and I was one of them. There was really nothing I could do."

Anthony meditated on this for a moment. "That's awful!"

"Tell me about it."

For a moment he went reflectively silent. "So how exactly did it end?"

"Well, as I said, first all the accusatory letters. Then it got more complicated. I tried to break it off. One afternoon he got drunk and desperate and lost control and . . ." I paused. "He ended up putting his hands around my throat."

Anthony's expression froze. "Around your throat?"

I pointed to my scar.

"Did you continue seeing him after . . . that incident?"

I shook my head. "I never saw him again. Except for once. He showed up at the prison one day when I was teaching my class."

There were a few moments of troubled silence. "Obviously you've made some connection between yourself and the fact that all these women were strangled."

"Yes and no."

"Have you ever considered that . . . he might have something to do with these murders?"

"Not really. Because he moved to Thailand pretty soon after we broke up. Been there ever since. I've gotten letters from him. He told me he wanted to get as far away from me as possible. He told me he never wanted to come back."

FOUR

I OFTEN THOUGHT about the murdered ones, about where their mangled bodies had turned up: the River Road, the Wilder Dam, the train tracks just outside of Sharon, the shallows of the Connecticut River that divides Vermont and New Hampshire. I thought about where divers trolled for them, policemen roaming the marshes with search dogs, joined by concerned townspeople fearful that their idyll of rural life was changing into a killing zone. I'd scrutinized these victims, the published histories of their ordinary lives, their love lives. I'd read about them so many times it's almost as though somehow I always knew I'd end up discovering one of them up the road from my own house.

He'd been striking every six months, so this all began around seven hundred days before.

One of the murdered women was too poor to own a car, forced by the lack of good public transportation to hitchhike in order to see her boyfriend in a neighboring town. Another, the mother of three children, was jogging along a backcountry road in Meriden, New Hampshire. Another, unable to get cell service, pulled into the shadowy parking lot of a convenience store and was attacked while she was using a grimy pay phone. A mother of two was accosted at her own house and stabbed to death in the kitchen. There have been hundreds of tips and clues, fragmentary descriptions of vehicles slowing down to pick up hitchhikers: Pontiac Sunbirds, GM Saturns, Volvo station wagons, or just plain red sedans. Of course, the cars people thought they saw would be red, evil red.

Angela Parker had already left to go skiing before realizing that she'd forgotten to bring her phone. By nightfall the snow was generally all over the state and was particularly heavy in Windsor County, the temperature hovering at ten degrees. The flakes were whispery light, the wind frosted meringuelike drifts everywhere, and the snow mass was fairly easy for the plows to carve. At a few minutes after midnight, a man had notified the state police that his wife, who had driven seventy-two miles from Lyme, New Hampshire, down to Londonderry, Vermont, had not turned up at home and that when she called him earlier in the evening, at seven P.M., for some reason she hadn't said which rest area she'd stopped at. It was conjectured later on that perhaps she was hurrying the conversation along because she'd already noticed somebody. She left her ski mittens in the car; they would have prevented her from dialing the pay phone. I imagine in such a squall she might have been the only car stopped at the rest area and perhaps the killer's car swung into the parking lot while she was speaking to her husband, slowly but purposely driving toward her, headlamps stampeding the snowflakes, until he came to a stop not ten feet from where she stood. Angela Parker's last words to her husband were "Oh, I should . . . I've got to go. See you . . . love you."

The next morning, the man who plowed the parking lot of Interstate 91 apparently arrived in a jolly mood; by then the storm had blown offshore and now Nova Scotia was under siege. The weather had turned cloudless, the snow shimmered and jeweled, and there was that calm feeling of deep winter, of being far from the longest day of the year, which can be comforting to those of

Nordic mind-set. I am not one of those Nordic, winter-loving people.

So this lighthearted driver found a virgin parking lot and a mound that looked like an enormous marshmallow. He plowed toward it, used to finding broken-down vehicles in rest areas, left there due to overheated engines or flat tires or steering columns that have suddenly snapped like brittle necks. He plowed without being able to see that the car doors were ajar. He plowed without ever knowing that the snow was packed down by the pedals, a pair of ski pants with a wallet inside them lay on the passenger's side, and beads of frozen blood were sprayed on the seats. I imagined that he felt generous toward this stranded, abandoned car, because with his big yellow plowing blade he chiseled around it the shape of a heart.

Nearly all of these women were found months after they disappeared, their bodies in advanced states of decomposition that made it more difficult to find traces of foreign DNA. The only one found hours after she was murdered was Janet Tourvalon, a bosomy, fair-haired woman in her mid-thirties who lived just outside of Claremont, New Hampshire. One morning a year ago, summer, she got her children off to day camp, put on a chartreuse bikini, took her favorite sunning chaise, and sat out in her backyard facing the Connecticut River. At noon, she went inside to have her lunch, apparently noticed by several male motorists who admitted to driving by her house just to be able to have a glimpse of her scantily clad. But she never returned to her tanning spot. Hours later her sandals were found perfectly lined up outside where she'd removed them, a plastic bottle of Bain de Soleil SPF 40 lying on top of them. Her husband, an electrical contractor, had called from his job site, hoping she'd prepare a check for one of his employees; when she didn't answer the phone he came home to fetch the check himself.

He found his wife in her bathing suit, lying across the kitchen threshold, eyes wide open, smeared in her own blood, which had exsanguinated into a pool reflecting the fluorescent tube lamps overhead. The side of her head was tilted at an unnatural angle against the pocket kitchen door, her neck violet and bruised, her arms slashed so that in various places he could see the whiteness of her bones. Nothing else in the house had been disrupted; there was a freshly baked lemon pound cake cooling on a rack not five feet away from where she lay. On the kitchen table was a plate with discarded crusts of a turkey sandwich and a small creamy pile of coleslaw purchased at the corner store less than a mile away, now clustered with green flies laying fresh eggs.

For a long time Janet Tourvalon's husband was unable to articulate the feeling so familiar to me now, of entering a time warp of grief—his for the dead, mine for the living and the dead—when a block of hours in a day dislodges from one's sense of time and suddenly the fact that it's evening is a travesty. When he came through the front door and saw all that dark, viscous liquid rippling across his kitchen floor, he never cried out, but rather looked with agonized bewilderment at the mother of his children lying in a skewed position, sliced to her marrow, as still as a deep-forest kill. He somehow managed to swallow the gag that erupted in his throat, picked up the phone, and called 911 (and later on 911 would replay the tape of his conversation for the police). He sat down with his wife, held one of her cold, bloodied hands in both of his, and listened to the horrific stillness of her death. Then described how he washed his hands and felt compelled to trudge upstairs to his office and write the check that he'd come home to fetch for one of his subcontractors. This was thought suspicious by the investigators, whereas I looked upon his act as a methodical person's attempt to reaffirm his life in the midst of brutal horror. Once he'd managed to accomplish the check signing, he tried ringing the summer camp to ask that his children be kept from boarding the bus home, but found they'd already left. And so the twelve- and eight-year-old arrived home shortly after the police did, and Mr. Tourvalon was waiting for them to climb down the steep stairs of the bus. Ushering them into his car, he explained that their mother had died unexpectedly, and then, with a police escort, drove them to the house of his parents, who luckily lived nearby.

The detectives who arrived on the scene immediately suspected him. They felt his calm and disconnected affect was typical of a violent offender numbed to his gruesome act, a man able to carry on living and working and taking care of children while his wife lay mangled in their modern, up-to-date kitchen.

But when Mr. Tourvalon's employees were questioned, an airtight alibi emerged: until he left in the late afternoon to go home and fetch the check, he'd been stuck all day on his job site, his time fully accounted for. And then the medical examiner in Concord, New Hampshire, pronounced that Janet Tourvalon had died close to noon, her wounds severe enough that she expired rather quickly. Finally the investigators reluctantly abandoned the notion of Mr. Tourvalon as the madman drifting around the Upper Connecticut River Valley, searching for just the right woman to murder.

In the middle of April, two weeks after I found Angela Parker's body, Anthony called one afternoon right before I left to teach my reading and writing class at the local minimum-security prison. Apparently the warden was putting in my group a recent inductee who'd been arrested and booked just a few days before for going into a gas station mini-market at eleven-thirty at night, yanking out his sizeable erect penis, and laying it on the counter in full view of the young woman working the till. Outraged, she'd begun screaming; he in turn leaped over the counter and wedged his hand over her mouth to quiet her down. In the midst of the struggle a football player from Dartmouth College strolled into the store to buy beer, yanked the pervert off the poor woman, and then decked him. This particular inmate, Anthony informed me, was one of several locals being investigated.

The prison is located right in downtown Woodstock, ironically one of the wealthiest towns in Vermont, whose buildings and surrounding land had been conserved by twin industrial titans: Frederick Billings, the president of the Northern Pacific Railroad, who financed the western railroad systems and for whom Billings, Montana, is named; and Lawrence Rockefeller. Frederick Billings became a leader in forestry management at a time when Vermont's rolling hillsides had been deforested by the potash industries and sheep farmers. Billings planted thousands of trees on his estate, which became one of the first continuously managed forests in North America. His granddaughter Mary French, who married Lawrence Rockefeller, poured a lot of money into refurbishing this shire town's nineteenth-century brick and clapboard buildings. The result of their efforts: everything in Woodstock is almost too picture-perfect, especially the central green surrounded by grand neocolonials and Georgian mansions and Greek revivals. *The New York Times* once hailed Woodstock as the Hollywood of Vermont, suggesting that in all its beauty, it came off like a stage on a movie lot. The prison is located incongruously amongst all this prosperity in a building that was once ac ourthouse.

Most of my "students" were waiting to be transferred to the maximum-security prison down in Springfield. As this was my first day teaching since I found the body of Angela Parker, I knew that "my felons," as I affectionately called them, would ask about it. And I would tell them what I'd told the police and Anthony and everyone else, trotting out my signature description about the Coca-Cola snow and the pale, frosted face, beads of lapis draping her chest that only became visible when Marco Prozzo, wearing a pair of rubber gloves, unzipped her parka in search of corroborating wounds. I conjectured that when I told my prisoner-students my story, their faces would hardly be as shocked or concerned as those of the townspeople and the authorities, but rather greedy for further details. But who would the new guy be;

and how creepy and unnerving if he happened to be the killer—then, too, how ridiculously coincidental. And yet just as much as I might have flinched from meeting him, I actually dreaded seeing the woman with whom Anthony Waite was probably having an affair: Fiona Pierce, who also volunteers at the jail, where she teaches an art class.

A second-grade teacher at the local elementary school, Fiona Pierce happens to be one of the few people in the town of Woodstock who ever laid eyes on Matthew Blake, when, in the wake of our tumultuous breakup, he showed up at the prison and waited two hours for me in the anteroom of the warden's office.

That afternoon two years ago, Fiona and I had finished our instruction and were walking together down the long, polished cement corridor on our way out of the complex. We were brainstorming about requisitioning more art and paper supplies from the state, resolving to pick them up on our own at Staples in West Lebanon, when I saw Matthew sitting in a plastic half-moon chair and staring at us. His soft, luxuriant brown hair was parted in the center and brushed back, a throwback to an eighties hairstyle. He liked having a mane, liked having it brush against his bare broad shoulders; and it was lovely hair that added softness to a body that sometimes I'd found youthfully hard and unforgiving when we made love. It had been three months since our final incident, and all I could do was stare back at him before finally managing to blurt out, "*Why* . . . are you *here*?" Then Fiona, in a glance taking him in and saying, "I'll get going, Catherine. We can always pick up on this later."

In leaving, Fiona took an appraising glance at Matthew—and I could tell she found him attractive. And then she looked at me, competitively, I believed at the time, perhaps wondering why this man in his mid-twenties would pursue somebody fifteen years older. As I watched her heading toward the exit, I looked to make sure there were other people around: a few guards were standing in a group perhaps fifteen yards away.

I regarded Matthew again and shook my head. "You can't stay, you have to go. You promised you wouldn't come near me again."

"I know, I know I promised . . . but please talk to me," he said. "I'm in hell."

"You don't think I am?" Then I noticed the red cardboard top of a Marlboro pack sticking out of his shirt pocket. "Don't tell me you started smoking again!"

"I know I promised you I wouldn't. But I don't have you after me about it, either. So I started again and can't quit." He looked at me with beggar's eyes, and his large veined hands were shaking.

This admission pierced through my flimsy armor. I avoided staring at his face directly, a man's face on somebody so young. His pain was so much more difficult to handle than his fury.

He reached for the pack.

"You can't in here," I warned.

He said, "I know I can't. I just want it—I need something—in my hand." He took a cigarette out and held it between two shaking fingers. "I continuously feel like shit, Catherine," he said, but managed to smile again. "Seeing you . . . this is a break . . . from it."

I shut my eyes and swallowed and said, "Don't, please!"

He ran his hand tightly across the top of his head, gathering his hair in a fist and pressing it against the back of his neck. "At least you're lucky you have somewhere else to be, " he said. "Everywhere I go in Burlington reminds me of us."

"We've spent plenty of time down here at my house, too. It's not like I don't go around and find things that remind me of you, especially what you left behind."

"I guess I need to collect it."

"Better to tell me where you want me to send it."

I needed to get to my classroom and was about to inform him when he looked at me fixedly. "I'm trying to say, Catherine, that I had a life before you. All I want now is to have that life back."

"You sound quite resentful," I said. "I didn't take your life away from you."

"Well, I was happy until you came along," he said.

"And I was happy until *you* came along, " I told him.

Without another word, he got up and left the prison. He had a loping walk in which his shoulders dipped from side to side, an endearing stride that I could have spotted in a crowd; and with a terrible ache I knew I would miss it, I knew it would be a very long time until I saw him again. Shortly thereafter he fled the country for Thailand.

When I came into our little shared office in the prison, Fiona was leaning over a paper cutter, shearing large squares out of thick vanilla-colored drawing paper, the precise ripping sound that I always used to love in grade school now raking my nerves. She turned to me with a look of dolorous concern that did not belie her air of blooming happiness. Now *she* was the one in love, radiantly in love with Anthony Waite. And admittedly I was jealous, wondering what he saw in an attractive woman who I imagined was a lot less interesting than his wife.

"Catherine," she said softly, dropping her sheaf of drawing papers and moving toward me. "How are you doing with everything?"

I waved her away, something I would not have done so blatantly in the past. "I'm okay, really. Just, ya know, shook up. And therefore can't sleep. Don't," I warned, meaning don't hug me, which is something that Fiona did reflexively with many people. I could see how my defensive response offended her. "Everybody's worrying," I complained. "And while I appreciate it, I would like things to go on normally. Remember, *I* didn't know her. No sympathy should be spent on me."

"I realize that," Fiona said, "but finding a body—"

"You find people dead in your life," I made myself say. "And it's a lot worse when you actually do know them. Although in this case, unfortunately she was . . . brutalized." Fiona flinched at my choice of word. "And then lay there frozen for months. So it wasn't the ordinary finding of a body. Anyway, how are *you* doing?" I asked.

She frowned at me. "You really want to know?"

"I asked, didn't I?"

"Well, the usual: swamped at school. I have parent/teacher conferences next week."

I wouldn't say that Fiona and I have ever been what one would call "friendly." We do see each other every other Monday at the prison and sometimes have sat together at town meetings. Perhaps her greatest strength is her way of setting you at ease, as though you could confide in her and in return she'd empathize and guard your confidence. She jogs around Woodstock's stately green, stays fit, seems to have plenty of friends, mainly male friends, and there is something just a little bit disconcertingly bubbly about her. And I know I'm splitting hairs, but Fiona does have this one yellowed front tooth that I always find myself staring at, wondering why she doesn't have it attended to. That tooth drives Wade crazy. Whenever he sees Fiona he says, "I wish she'd just get that damned thing bleached!"

I put down my spiral notebook and the seven one-page assignments that I'd collected from the felons the previous session, for the most part atrociously written and which I'd gone over relentlessly with a red pen. "Did I see you drive by me the other day, Fiona?" I asked her, which of course I hadn't.

She couldn't help but glance away for a moment. "Where?"

"Up on Cloudland."

She blushed deeply. "Oh . . . I keep forgetting you live up there."

"Whom do you know up there besides me?" I asked her mildly, thinking she must realize that there were only three full-time households.

"Well, I mean, I know Anthony, but who doesn't?" she said nervously. "I . . . I actually go up there to that old Seventh-Day

Adventist cemetery back in the woods. I get rubbings from the tombstones. Distribute them to my second graders. I like to combine art and history in one project."

"Even at this time of year?" I probably sounded disingenuous.

"Snow is gone now in most spots," Fiona said, which *was* true. "I should stop by and see you the next time I go," she offered, realizing too late this was probably ill-advised.

"Yes, do drop by and see me," I said, "the next time you're up . . ." I wanted to say "doing grave rubbings" but refrained. After all, I reminded myself, who am I, who'd had an affair with one of my students, to judge? Then again, Anthony *was* still married.

The classroom has bulletproof windows, a steel door that buzzes one in and out, and a portly, pimpled twenty-year-old guard standing outside monitoring the discussion by intercom. In the five years that I've been volunteering at the prison, there have only been a few occasions when the guard—and not I—determined that the classroom was getting out of hand and burst into the room with reinforcements to restore order.

When I arrived to teach that day the guard was looking at me curiously. "Everything okay, Miz Winslow?" His question wasn't exactly unusual, but he leaned toward me when he said it so that I sensed what drove his inquiry.

"Swimmingly," I said as he buzzed me into the classroom.

"Hey, here's who's in charge," said Daryl when I walked in.

"Hello, Tattoo King," I said without missing a beat, and for a moment stood there gawking at my students. Daryl was a balding, bulky guy with Harley-Davidson flames inked up and down his arms and on his neck all the way up to his ears. He'd had a disagreement with a cousin over a lawn equipment transaction, and while they were out riding their motorcycles, he was observed running the poor fellow off the road. The cousin died and Daryl was convicted of manslaughter. Everyone else in my group was tattooed but to a lesser degree, except one-legged Jess, who, up on a rooftop in Rutland, had an altercation with a drug dealer, stuck a knife into his adversary's thigh, then was pushed off and fell five stories—luckily into shrubbery—and shattered one of his legs. When the police found him he was carrying six ounces of cocaine. He now got around either on crutches or in a wheelchair. Then there was Peter, a doughy seventeen-year-old who, in the midst of doing his biology homework, went into a fuguelike rage, grabbed his father's shotgun and, finding both his parents in bed having TV dinners, murdered them with many more rounds than was necessary. After the fact he was unable to remember his act of slaughter, and this was a source of constant torment to him.

I looked around, nodding at Raul, a quiet Latino who'd taken a piece of lead pipe and smashed in the kidneys of a man vying for the same woman. And then the new guy, who apparently liked preening his manhood in front of ladies working at convenience stores and whose name I'd learned was Jones: a corpulent fellow in his mid-thirties who could have passed for an insurance salesman out of Boston. I couldn't help looking between the legs of his orange prison pants, and saw nothing out of the ordinary. I got riled up when I thought of him trying to sexually intimidate a poor twenty-one-year-old girl. He did have a family crest sort of tattoo on one arm, definitely an old-school tattoo.

It occurred to me, not for the first time, that any of these men who took my class could possibly have it in them to murder a woman like Angela Parker.

"Only six of you today?"

"Jimmy's in lockdown," Jess said, wearing a semi-toothless smile.

"Ah . . . and Bo?"

"He volunteered for laundry," said Daryl. "Didn't think you were going to be here anyway."

"Why not?" I put down my books and papers. All throughout this exchange, I noticed that seventeen-year-old Peter was staring down at the floor, seeming almost catatonic. He looked up at me suddenly and I could see his blank eyes narrow. "Because you found a dead woman," he said with a questioning lilt to his voice.

"Trauma, you know," Jones spoke up, meeting my gaze with a devilishe xpression.

It was unusual for a newcomer to speak up so soon. Beyond this, "trauma" was a word that made me wonder if he was fairly well educated, not that educated people can't stoop to homicide. Most of my guys hadn't finished high school, but nearly all of them had areas of expertise. Daryl could take apart and put together car and two-stroke engines. Jess, who'd been in the merchant marines, knew everything about boats.

"So what was it like, finding a murdered girl?" Daryl murmured.

"You know," I said. "You're the first person who's had the nerve to ask me that."

"Hey, honey, come closer," he said with disgusting lasciviousness.

"Don't push your luck," I told him.

"So then you're okay," Jess said.

"Don't I look okay?"

"Well, just so you know," Jones said, shocking me, "none of us are that kind of guy."

The other inmates were glaring at him; his outburst struck them as impertinent.

I scrutinized this inmate, whom I found to be both flabby and slovenly. "And what kind of guy is that?" I said.

Raul cut in, preempting Jones from garnering too much spotlight. "The kind of guy who kills for no reason. Kills people he don't know."

"As opposed to people you *do* know," I said.

Jess said, "If somebody fucks with you and then you kill them, man, that's different." He glanced around at his fellow inmates.

It always fascinates me how they differentiate the severity of their offense from those committed by their fellow inmates, as though to calibrate what kind of crime is truly reprehensible.

"I don't think he knew her."

"Probably didn't know her if he's a serial killer," Jess went on, doing a push-up on the arms of his wheelchair. "Serials do their thing. They have a plan and they stick to it. So whoever drives into the rest area at seven P.M. . . . . boom."

Normally I might have let them carry on conjecturing, but today I just didn't feel up to hearing any more of the sort of discussion that I'd already been having with myself, with Anthony, and others. And so I said, "Let's table this for now. Thanks for your concern. Did you all finish the reading I passed out?" I'd given them the short story "The Captain's Daughter" by Alexander Pushkin.

They all nodded, except Travis, a young, skinny black guy wearing a do-rag. He'd said nothing thus far and looked angry and bored.

"Okay, so . . ."

Jones surprised me yet again by having managed to get a copy of the story from one of the other inmates and reading it. He began the discussion. "Tell you one thing. It snows a fucking lot in Russia."

"Yeah, even more than here," Peter spoke up.

"Got to be way north of here," said Jess.

"I love the bad guy in the story," Daryl said. "The fake czar."

"How so?"

"He was all dressed in black and shit and the way he just turned up in the middle of that snowstorm. Boy, he turned out to be one no-nonsense dude."

"Riding his horse all over the place, taking out towns, cutting off heads. Not bad for a badass life," said Raul.

"Well, until you're caught and executed," I pointed out.

"I hated that servant," Peter spoke up. "I wanted the fake czar to kill him."

"And why did you hate him?"

"He was always interfering."

"The captain's daughter . . . she was kind of like an olden-days version of a bimbo, wasn't she?" Jones said, and everybody laughed.

His manner was a bit too flippant for my liking, much less to be harboring the secret of having stalked and killed several women within a short period of time. But then again, the brand of insanity that might drive such a serial murderer was probably something I could hardly fathom. I supposed I had to reserve judgment on Jones.

When the class was over, Peter waited behind as he often did. He'd been writing journal entries, scribbling dispatches about his life up until the school night when he committed an act of such extreme violence, claimed by his teachers and friends to be a dumbfounding contradiction to his quiet and self-contained nature. Then again, wasn't it always the quiet types, the intro-verts, the dreamers who ended up surprising us with unforeseen malice? Peter seemed genuinely bereft and agonized to be held responsible for his parents' murder. He'd been put on a potent psychotropic medication that, he confided to me, only made him feel fogged in. Despite my revulsion at what he'd done, I managed somehow to feel motherly toward him.

"They say you actually knew her," he spoke up. "The woman who was killed."

I told him she drew my blood at the hospital, and that even though plenty of photos of her had been published in the local newspaper, when I found her I didn't recognize her, but quickly assumed who she was.

Peter's face wrinkled up. "My mother used to follow them, the stories of these murders. She used to worry about them." He hes-itated again. "She even got scared whenever she was alone."

I pictured him grabbing a shotgun, slowly and purposefully climbing the stairs to his parents' bedroom, hearing their mur-

muring voices, the look of terrified disbelief on their faces when he aimed at them, the concussion of firing, the impact of hailing lead, the splattering of their blood everywhere, even on him, and the smell of gunpowder in the mortal quiet that followed.

FIVE

IN THE MIDDLE OF MAY I received a letter from one of my readers in Birmingham, who claimed the best way to unclog a drain was dumping in baking soda and chasing it with white vinegar. Down in the shallow cavern of my two-hundred-year-old cellar was an old clothes-scrubbing sink whose drain had been clogging and backing up for years, resisting conventional cleansers, and the diligent efforts of plumbers. Watching the bubbling mixture with the same fascination I had when I combined vinegar and baking soda in elementary school, I felt torn. For someone who'd begun a career as a college intern at *The New York Times,* approaching journalism with the loftiest ideals of exposing fraud, corruption, of developing the instinct to recognize the glimmering, elusive fact that might illuminate the dark soul of an interviewee, here I was watching a practical alchemy that might or might not unblock a drain. It could be argued that I was helping the world of domesticity like the clean-it-fix-it-find-it equivalent of Martha Stewart; however, as popular as my column had become, I sometimes felt a pang of having abandoned my true calling. This despair was obvious to people who were close to me. Matthew used to ask me why I just didn't take up investigative journalism again. And my answer to him was my answer to myself. I didn't have the mettle to keep battling egos for the integrity of turns of phrase. I was tired of my prose being re-written, hacked into more pedestrian form. Once I stepped out of the ring, I just didn't have the heart, or the drive, to throw myself back in with the big-timers. I guess I discovered that I wasn't as ambitious as I thought I was.

Instead, I was helping housewives wow their husbands with Moroccan tagines made with lemons that marinated for months in earthenware jars, spreading the word of where to find shoes for tiny feet, or feeding brewer's yeast powder to dogs to help rid them of fleas—there was something quietly satisfying about this pursuit. With that thought, the cordless phone rang in the pocket of my baggy Carhartt jeans. I wiped my hands with a towel, checked the incoming number and, seeing it was Anthony, trot-ted up the steep wooden stairs and answered.

"You sound all breathless," he said to me flirtatiously. "Any-body I know?"

"Dream on," I said, and then explained where I'd been and the procedure I was testing.

"Let me know if it flies."

"Read the column, save me the trouble."

"Catherine, do you really care if I read your column?"

"Of course I care!"

"Whenever you speak about it, you're always so disparaging."

"Self-protection of a battered ego," I explained, heading into my study with the phone cradled between my shoulder and my ear. There was a short lull. "Something tells me this is not a social call."

"It's an update call," he said. First he told me that Roderick Jones, the new guy in my prison writing class who'd exposed him-self and forcefully fondled a cashier, had been cleared of suspicion in regard to the River Valley murders. Jones had been able to sub-stantiate he was in Massachusetts the night of Angela Parker's ab-duction. "He's one of those guys who sits on every receipt. And he's got one from a liquor store in Acton right outside of Boston that we were able to verify. Says 9:07 P.M. So that fairly rules him out. It was a mother of a storm and the roads all over the northeast that night were a complete mess."

"Good," I said. "I didn't relish the idea of instructing the man who dumped a body in our orchard."

Anthony went on to say that, believing that the Seventh-Day Adventist pamphlets shoved into the pockets of Angela Parker and Marjorie Poole might bring a more significant clue to the murderer's identity, he had immersed himself in the Church's literature, focusing in particular on the religion's view on health and medical care and dying. He'd discovered a belief in vegetarianism, general respect and reverence for plant and animal life, the sacredness of trees, which many believers felt had an animus.

The last fact had special significance. Anthony went on to confide that (being kept from the public record), three out of the five bodies of the dead women had been discovered near a downed tree. "Janet Tourvalon was murdered in her house, so she wouldn't be part of the statistic."

"What about Angela? I don't remember seeing a tree down."

"Oh yeah, it was right near her. A big one. It was still covered with snow when you found her."

And then I remembered that when Leslie Fullerton and I first went to find the body, the Statie had tripped over a tree trunk and tumbled into the snow. I mentioned this to Anthony.

"Noted. Anyway, the more I read about this particular religion the more I'm not sure whether or not the killer is a member of the tribe or just borrowing their philosophy merely to cast suspicion in another direction."

"Or just one of those Adventists whose wheels have come off," I said.

"Precisely."

"Just don't assume that this religious sect is as peace-loving as they proclaim."

"What do *you* know about them?"

"I've known a lot of them over the years. When I was growing up and went to a youth camp down in Putney there were some Seventh-Day Adventist kids who lived on the lake we occupied and who always bullied the campers. One girl even beat me up."

"Yeah, but you can't indict a whole culture due to a couple of miscreants."

"True. I just want you to see there might be a flip side to all this vegetarianism and pacifism."

"I hear that."

Then something struck me and I momentarily let my thread of the conversation drop. "Are you with me, Catherine? Are you there?"

"Yeah," I said foggily. "I was just thinking. There is something familiar about dead women being found by downed trees with religious literature shoved into their pockets. I could swear I read about it somewhere."

"Where is somewhere?"

"Good question."

The conversation lagged for a moment or two and then Anthony said, "Maybe a newspaper story?"

"Don't think so."

"Online?"

"I think it's probably a book," I said, staring across the room at a suite of built-in bookshelves, chockablock with volumes. When Saint Mike's let me go I had to clear out my office, and two years on had yet to incorporate my two book collections: towering piles on each of the stairs up to my second-floor bedroom, and at least twenty novels stacked on my nightstand. I desperately needed to thin out my collection, but as yet had been unable to do so—like getting rid of a beloved dead person's effects, in this case my five-year stint as an adjunct professor of journalism and nonfiction. Then again, it was difficult for me to get rid of books in general. Among the one hundred or so I read every year, I find myself sloughing off few of them, even the ones that I dislike and abandon after a few chapters. "It'll probably drive me crazy until I figure it out. All the more reason to get back to my drainage. How 'bout I call you when I remember."

Fact of the matter: I was on deadline for my column, which meant returning to the dirty basement and monitoring the problematic pipe. Just as I was watching the foaming clot blocking my drain miraculously get sucked down into the depths, saying to myself, "Kudos to the reader from Birmingham," it occurred to me that the book I was trying to place was probably a nineteenth-century novel.

That old hankering to track down a lead. I climbed the steep stairs, crossed my study, and stood before a built-in bookshelf overflowing with volumes by Dickens and Mrs. Gaskill, George Eliot and the like. I ran my finger over the literary landscape of the nineteenth century, feeling like a needle on a Ouija board trying to get a stronger sense of which author it might be. And then it came to me: the Gothic nature of the subject matter made it likely to be Wilkie Collins, plus the fact that I'd read his novels many times over. I shifted to the part of my bookshelf that contains the majority of his work and started flipping through the obvious ones: *The Woman in White, No Name, The Law and the Lady, No Thoroughfare,* and *The Moonstone,* whose last lines I find to be among the most elegiac in all of English literature. As I was drawn into reading them once again, I was suddenly struck by the name of a book of his called *The Widower's Branch,* a flash of recollection that it dealt with the serial murders of mostly married women whose dead bodies were found near . . . fallen trees! I was relieved and even proud that I'd figured it all out relatively easily.

Curiously, *The Widower's Branch* is actually the very last novel Wilkie Collins ever wrote. Theresa, my Victorian scholar/former college roommate, claims it was written after *Blind Love,* which many scholars advance as the author's last work, whose completion was interrupted by his death. Knowing he wouldn't finish *Blind Love,* Collins arranged for another writer named Walter Besant to finish the work from detailed notes. *The Widower's Branch,* on the other hand, was never tampered with by anybody; it was left by his literary executors as a fragment, a mere eighty pages with a detailed outline published posthumously in an extremely limited edition, a copy of which Theresa managed to procure for me.

I kept my Wilkie Collins in chronological order and meandered along the bookshelf, looking at the various spines of his novels until I came to *Blind Love.* There was a slender space between it and the flank of the bookshelf; *The Widower's Branch* was gone.

I stood there blinking, realizing that it had vanished. It was as though my mind were playing a trick on me. I was confused. The first thing I did was go backwards through the other volumes to see if any more were missing. The only other one I couldn't find was *Armadale,* but I happened to know it was upstairs on a bookshelf outside my bedroom. I keep close tabs on the books and authors that mean a lot to me. I began to worry that I'd somehow lent it out and completely forgotten to whom. Perhaps my memory wasn't so good after all.

Then a comber of panic slammed me, as unnerving as losing sight of a neighbor's child at the beach. I tried to think clearly, to remember where it could be. The phone rang again and it was Anthony.

I was so riled up I almost didn't pick up. "Now what?" I said to him.

"You still circling that drain?"

"Why and what's it to you?" I said a bit sharply, still unnerved.

"Marco Prozzo just stopped in to see me. He's here for a reason that . . . well, I haven't discussed it with you. Having to do with a suspect, one of the people we're investigating."

"Somebody *I* know?"

"Yeah. This is his idea: he wants to ask you a few questions. He thinks you might be able to help."

That's curious, I thought. "When would this be?"

"How's about ten minutes?"

I glanced at my watch: I didn't have time for much of anything—my deadline was looming. "It's not the most convenient moment."

"I'm sorry, I didn't think—"

My curiosity took control. "All right, come on over. I do have one other thing in the works besides the drain: dog biscuits."

Anthony laughed. "Just as long as you don't pawn them off on us."

Right after I ended the call with Anthony, my editor at the newspaper syndicate rang to chitchat. The man, a hard-bitten, inveterate flirt, was not one to read subtleties. Itching to get back to work and spare a few minutes to continue searching for the Wilkie Collins, I was nevertheless unable to untangle myself from the hand that fed me until I heard the knock on the sliding glass door that led into my sunroom. "The dogs are barking because the cops are here," I announced. "Sorry, but I got to go," and was finally released from my editor's burbling bondage.

When I met Anthony and the short, squat detective at the door, I noticed Prozzo wore the same sharkskin suit he was wearing when he came to my house six weeks before in the company of the other Staties. "I've been on the phone with my editor in New York," I told them. "Go on into the kitchen and give me five minutes. I've got basement crud all over me," I added, patting the dogs to calm them down.

I rushed upstairs to wash and change into a button-down shirt and a pair of tan slacks. I did a quick scan of the floor-to-ceiling bookshelf in my bedroom for the missing Wilkie Collins and once again came up empty-handed. I gathered my thoughts and returned to find both men sitting at the kitchen table, Prozzo patting the big head of Mrs. Billy, my bullmastiff. Anthony was also dressed in a suit, but his was a loosely cut lightweight gabardine. I wasn't used to seeing him so spiffy and couldn't help wondering if it had something to do with Fiona. During the last six weeks since Wade told me about the affair, I'd been keeping an eye out but hadn't spied her VW Beetle tootling up Cloudland.

"What's baking?" Prozzo said. "Smells heavenly."

"Canine heaven," Anthony told him. "Dog biscuits."

I said, "They'll be out of the oven in ten minutes. You're welcome to try one. They're actually not bad. Just a bit bland. Salt isn't especially good for dogs."

"So you try out all the recipes and remedies?" Prozzo asked, crossing his legs at the ankle.

"Have to. At least the ones that I can. One of my most popular prescriptions turns out to be what to do when your dog gets skunked. You squirt your pet with Massengill vinegar disposable douche. I didn't have the opportunity to test it before it was published, but my readers say it does an amazing job reducing the odor."

"No kidding," Prozzo said, laughing. "That's good to know."

"And get this, a guy sent me the formula. I wrote back to him and asked, 'How did you stumble upon that little miracle?'"

Both men laughed.

"But then I have readers who have nothing better to do than find something wrong with my concoctions. They send complaints to the newspaper syndicate, who, when they believe I'm mistaken, feel obliged to publish my errors."

"Even if you've already tried it yourself and it works?" Prozzo wondered.

"Then I tell my editor; more often than not he backs me up. But I *have* been wrong a few times. And it isn't fun to have four hundred newspapers print your failure."

"My wife and my daughter read your column," Prozzo told me. "They love it. Especially those great cake recipes."

"Believe it or not, most of those recipes come from far-flung readers. Not some San Francisco gourmet. Sorry that I don't have a cake on hand to offer you. Something to drink, though, either of you guys?"

Prozzo waved his hand to say he was fine. Anthony said, "What do you have?"

"I was about to make some hibiscus tea."

"Sounds great," he said.

"Good for cognitive brain function, apparently," I said, again dogged by thoughts of the missing book.

"No kidding . . . speaking of which," Anthony went on. "As I was saying on the phone, Marco would like to ask you a few questions."

I reached for a cornflower-blue ceramic teapot, poured in water that I'd heated in an electric kettle. Facing them again, I said, "I'm dying to know whom you're investigating."

Anthony and Prozzo exchanged a glance. Anthony said, "It won't make you happy."

"It's okay. My day is already getting punky."

Prozzo said, "We're getting some heat on the guy who carts away dead animals."

"Hiram Osmond, the knacker man," Anthony said.

"Oh, no!"

There was a cylindrical vase of daffodils in the middle of my oblong dining table and Prozzo began batting it back and forth between his large, meaty hands. Terribly dismayed, I resumed, "I mean, we're talking about a gentle guy whose wife left him and then he lost custody of his daughter."

The detective looked up at me and said quietly, "These are just the sorts of people—"

"It takes all kinds," Anthony interrupted. Echoing my thoughts he said, "Sometimes the quietest, most mild-mannered end up being the most brutal and remorseless killers."

"I'm aware of that," I managed to say, in a state of disbelief. I'd known Hiram from summers I'd spent in Woodstock as a teen-ager. I'd known him to be kind and hardworking. "I guess I never thought the murderer might turn out to be somebody I'm actu-ally acquainted with."

"Anyway, hear us out," Prozzo said.

"What choice do I have?"

As more motorists driving in the blizzard of January 17 were interviewed, a profile arose of someone trudging along Route 12 in a long green military coat and a Russian fur hat that matched the description of Hiram Osmond's signature winter gear. Osmond already admitted to having been out on the road that night, hoof-ing it homeward because his truck had gotten stuck in a driveway.

He claimed to have received a call from an elderly woman who informed him that one of the two dairy cows she kept had dropped dead. A mild spell of January weather during the week leading up to the blizzard indicated that a dead animal lying in deep snow would already have begun to ooze fluids, which would, when the mercury dropped, freeze and make the carcass difficult to prize away from the ground. Hiram always listened to a twenty-four-hour weather drone on his shortwave radio and had heard that the temperature would edge up to forty degrees for two days before the major storm ascended from the Carolinas. He decided to wait until it got just a bit warmer before driving to the old lady's house to hack the beast's head off and winch the two-thousand-pound carcass up into the back of his pickup truck.

But the meteorologists at the Fairbanks Museum in St. Johns-bury (who, in my opinion, spend too much time citing the warm-ing and cooling trends in faraway North American places like Hudson Bay and Saskatoon) predicted that the snow would begin a lot later than it actually did. And at one point during the early afternoon of the day that Angela Parker disappeared, Hiram Os-mond told the police that he found himself standing near his barn with his measuring stick, calculating that within a few hours, twelve inches had already fallen. The temperature was hovering at thirty-five degrees. Knowing that it was now or never in terms of the dead cow, he headed to the farm but skidded into a ditch on the old lady's long, icy driveway. He bushwhacked three miles home, got another truck, drove back, hauled the first one out and towed it home. He gave up at that point. Two more feet of snow fell before the storm diminished, obscuring the place where he'd gotten stuck. The woman whose house he'd been driving to apparently never heard the rumor of an incapacitated vehicle, the sounds of tires whipping around and caterwauling, digging themselves into the hard ground, spraying up fine frozen grit. All she cared about was that her cow had never been removed and would continue to lie inhumed in several feet of snow and, like Angela Parker, remain frozen until spring.

Producing a pocket-sized notebook and pen, Prozzo said, "Have you been out to the Osmond farm?"

"Not since I was a kid."

He noted that. "Do you remember it?"

"Vividly."

I remembered dead fauna in various stages of rendering, a repository of sharpened instruments: long, scabrous knives, ponderous yet shiny cleavers for skinning and hacking limbs into small enough pieces so that they'd fit into the metal vats under which the Osmonds built wood fires. I remembered bones scattered all over the property, hides of various mammals hanging out to cure before being sold to tanneries. Somebody recently told me that Hiram had struck a lucrative deal with a high-end company in Arizona that purveyed animal skulls to rich ranchers who used them for décor.

The timer for the dog biscuits sounded and, taking a quilted mitt, I opened the oven and pulled out the tray. Even though I had a cutter that could have sliced dough into bone shapes, I'd chosen to make the canine cookies round. They had browned perfectly.

"Do you know much about his marriage breaking up?" Anthony asked.

Setting the hot tray on top of the stove burners, I said, "Oh yeah. I ran into him a while ago at Billings General Store. He told me that Celia had finally left him."

Prozzo said, "He mentioned they were married ten years."

"That's about right," I said, remembering how the day I encountered him, Hiram had complained to me that Celia no longer could abide his lifestyle; staring at his blood-tainted hands, at the reddish stubble he never seemed to shave, I'd imagined her living with the smell of rotting flesh and his devotion to rendering dead carcasses. I told Anthony and Prozzo, "Stupidly Hiram showed up in divorce court without a lawyer, and a sawtooth knife in the pocket of his pants. It rang the chimes of the metal detector. Celia jumped on it. She lied to the judge, said he was dangerous and violent, and he lost his bid for joint custody of their ten-year-old daughter. And get this, that judge granted Celia the right to go and live all the way down in Georgia. Now he only gets to see his child a couple times a year."

"I couldn't live with that," Prozzo said. "Not being able to see my daughter."

"Neither could I," I agreed with him. "Is she your only?"

The detective nodded and looked troubled.

"So is mine."

"Well," Anthony said, "sometimes children actually find it easier to live with one parent rather than to go back and forth."

"Maybe so," I said, "but for Hiram this was tragic."

Prozzo went on, "Unfortunately, there are a bunch of complaints against Osmond on record at the family court in White River Junction. Photographs of Mrs. Osmond with bruises and lacerations. There was a relief-from-abuse order filed."

I was flummoxed. "I have to say that really surprises me. Any way her accusations could have been trumped up?"

"Oh, sure," Prozzo said. "Happens all the time. But how well do you know this guy?"

"How well do you know anybody?" I said to them. "The

Osmonds were all no-nonsense hardworking people. Osmond père would come over and fix stuff. Hiram we hired to do yard chores. Always really sweet and dedicated. Always seemed incredibly gentle."

"He's not in what you'd call a gentle profession," Anthony pointed out.

"Well, no, but he inherited that job and the farm. He had no choice. Couldn't go to college. Wasn't allowed to because he had to help out."

And then I thought of Wade, who, with his horrible upbringing, his violent desecration of Paul's house, would make for a much more compelling suspect.

"And what about her, about Celia?" Prozzo asked.

"She's five years younger than Hiram and me. Didn't know her as well."

"Any impression?" Anthony wondered.

"Like I said, the Osmonds were industrious, lower-income people, whereas she, as far as I knew, was . . . no other way to say it, white trash. Parents had the family on welfare and were known to be druggies. Her father had a garden equipment repair shop that didn't seem to do much business and was suspected by the locals as a front for a drug-selling operation."

"Kind of like our waitress, Sheila," Anthony said.

"Ish . . . maybe I'm jumping to conclusions, but I *have* heard Celia is a notorious liar."

Prozzo said, "He was already living alone two years ago when the first murder occurred."

"That woman who was hitchhiking out of Weathersfield."

"Right," Prozzo said.

I grabbed the teapot and poured steaming red liquid into three mugs, pushing one at Prozzo. "I know you didn't ask for some but I want you to try it anyway."

"Be glad to," he said, accepting my offering.

Then I said, "Look, obviously I know where you're going with this."

"Past history is everything," Anthony pointed out. "His early life, his relationship with his parents."

Looking back and forth between the two men, I said, "I guess up until now I never imagined that Hiram could harm anything that wasn't already dead."

Prozzo nodded his head respectfully. Then resumed, "Didn't the Osmonds for a time make an additional living selling pigs?"

"Until the pigs were found to harbor trichinosis. The health department shut them down."

Both men stiffened. Anthony finished his cup of hibiscus tea and complimented it. Glad to be stepping away from the subject of Hiram Osmond, I said, "It's great on a winter night when you've already had too much caffeine."

"Speaking of winter," Prozzo said, "might we go back to the night of the snowstorm . . . what you saw and heard?"

Six weeks ago, when the body was found, I'd ended up being questioned by Woodstock police chief O'Reilly, and not by Prozzo, who'd merely read my testimony.

"Sure, if we have to."

"If you don't mind."

I once again recounted how I'd been preparing my column, transcribing a list of nineteenth-century medicinal preparations largely unavailable in most of the country but sold by mail order at a pharmacy in Nebraska, the price lists of sassafras oil, witch hazel gel, spring tonic, coal tar ointment, when I heard the plow plundering the road.

"And where were you sitting?"

I pointed to the green leather love seat in my television room, which was visible from where we were clustered at the kitchen table and where Mrs. Billy was sprawled and snoring with some of the teeth showing from her black boxer's mask of a face. Almost as though she knew I was looking at her, she picked up her head and looked at me groggily.

"And from there you hear things pretty well out on the road?"

"Well, it depends on the barometer. I tend to hear things a lot better when the pressure is low."

"So during a storm?"

"Usually before or after a storm I can hear the Great Northern freight train crawling through White River Junction. But during a storm there is too much wind and precipitation to hear anything coming from afar. The night of the blizzard, for example, the wind was crazy, the snow was pitting itself against the windows. I listened to it, shivering and huddling under a blanket. The lights went out at some point. I remember holding the medicinal vials up to the woodstove's light."

"But you *did* hear the plow?"

"Yeah, I heard it scraping and rumbling past."

Prozzo wrote a few sentences and then looked up at me. "And can you remember anything else?" His voice momentarily went hoarse.

His asking the proper questions was making a difference; something in my memory became dislodged and, like a weightless flake, funneled up to the surface of my reasoning. Perhaps a half hour before I'd heard the plow, the dogs began barking: Mrs. Billy exploding into a deep-throated yipping, stopping to growl and then letting loose again; Virgil, my old Labrador, throwing his head back and slowly woofing like a bass beat to Mrs. Billy's wailing; and Henrietta, riled up by both of them, scurrying around, trotters clattering over the hardwood floors. I now wondered aloud: had another car passed in the storm just before the plow; had all my animals been able to detect a dying woman being driven through a blizzard?

Detective Prozzo looked confused when I described having a potbellied pig. "Where is this . . . where is *she* now?" he asked.

I pointed to the far end of the table under which my darling was sleeping on her side, her back hooves twitching from a dream in which she was probably feasting on scrumptious apple parings and vegetable scraps.

The detective glanced at the floor and when he noticed sleeping Henrietta said, "Holy moly. I thought I'd smelled something funny in here."

"Still a city boy after all this time," I teased him.

Staring intently at Henrietta, he said, "Is she friendly?"

"Until you cross her."

He looked up at me. "Protective?"

I found myself wondering yet again what Henrietta, snoring under the table, was truly capable of. "I hope so."

"Anyway, back to my question. Your animals were reacting to a vehicle going by?"

"Something was definitely bothering them. It took me a while to calm them down."

I knew from my reporting experience that some serial murderers, determined to avoid capture, cut a wide enough swath in order to be elusive, while others stick to the turf they know, aspiring to a seamless execution of premeditated violence and perversely risking being caught.

I turned to Prozzo. "Anthony says you all think it's somebody who knows the area."

"Yeah, a local. Somebody who'd know the roads down Springfield/Claremont way as well as around here. Hiram Osmond fits that description."

"And the only person seen anywhere near where her body was left," Anthony added.

"But he was just walking down the road," I pointed out.

Prozzo answered, "Like I said, claims his truck broke down. That may have happened and he's just refashioning the rest of his alibi. Anyway, he's agreed to take a lie detector test. So we'll see where that lands us."

71

The detective's last words coincided with a clattering commotion under the table: Henrietta preparing to put in an appearance. A moment later she'd trundled out from one end and was staring at us, her mottled snout quivering. I began scratching her flank and she moaned in pleasure. "Jesus, Mary, and Joseph," muttered Prozzo.

"Honey girl," I said to Henrietta, "go on in the other room and find the missus. Go on." At the sound of my voice, Virgil appeared with his gray beard on his black face, his tail thumping against the door that led between the kitchen and the television room. "You stay there," I ordered him. "March, Henrietta!" I pointed. She glared at me, bobbed her head once, and then slowly began trotting toward the television room. I scratched her rump as she wriggled by and she grunted. She stopped and took a long leak down through the grate that used to allow forced hot air up from the basement before I switched the house over to baseboard. Watching her urinate, Prozzo said, "Will you look at that!"

"That's her P-spot. I have a big rubber tub down below to catch her stream."

"Yuck," the detective said. "Where does she poop?"

"Outside, with the dogs."

"Smart little bugger, isn't she?" said Anthony.

"My daughter always wanted a house pig," Prozzo said, fidgeting in his chair.

"How old is she?"

He looked at me squarely and something about him seemed melancholy. "She's twenty-seven. And yours?"

"Twenty-two. She live near you?"

"Well . . . yes, as a matter of fact . . . yours?"

"Down in New Jersey."

"My home state. Where?"

"Morristown."

"Nice little upscale place," he said with a bit of an edge. "Where

I'm from in Perth Amboy, we called Morristown the other side of the tracks."

"I wouldn't know. I have yet to visit."

"What are you waiting for?"

I chuckled and then I said, "Trust me, you don't have time."

Glancing at his gaudy, gold-plated watch, Prozzo said, "You're right. But sometime I might." He stood up and said he had another appointment, flicking his head at Anthony, as though expecting him to follow.

"Why don't you go along," Anthony said. "Catherine and I have a few other things to discuss."

The detective looked disappointed.

I caught his eye. "Sorry I couldn't be more helpful about Hiram."

He made a dismissive gesture. "Oh no, you were helpful. You were great." He shook my hand and then something seemed to occur to him. "Oh, there's the other thing." He tilted his head toward Anthony. "You think you know of a place." He hesitated. "A book maybe where similar murders occur: women found dead near fallen trees with religious tracts in the pockets."

"I do. I now think I know which one. Just been trying to find it. To make sure."

"So what is it? What's it called?"

"*The Widower's Branch.* By Wilkie Collins."

Prozzo said to Anthony, "You'll let me know if she finds it." And then to me, "And if not we can always get a copy."

"Not so easy," I said. "It's really quite obscure."

"We have our sources." Prozzo winked at me and told us good-bye.

SIX

I WAITED UNTIL I HEARD the detective's car starting. And then said, "He's an interesting customer. Very professional, but there's a sadness there, wistfulness. Don't you think?"

"Yeah, I noticed it when he was talking about his daughter. He mentioned to me she's had a rough time with depression."

"So has Breck . . . as you know."

"I got the sense that his daughter has been living at home. And isn't working."

"He actually reminds me of a guy Daddy used to do business with. A larger-than-life toughie with a big heart who owned a bowling alley on the Lower East Side."

Anthony looked puzzled. "Didn't you tell me at one time your father was some kind of blue-blooded loan shark?"

"I would never say such a thing."

"I could have sworn you did."

"Must've been babbling drunk."

My father, who was a collector of rare books and manuscripts, seemed to have business dealings with certain people outside his esoteric world, associations that made no sense. Before she divorced him, my mother alluded to illegal money lending.

Anthony was staring at me, unsmiling. One of his eyelids was twitching, and when I studied him more closely, I saw that his eyes themselves were slightly bloodshot.

"Would you mind taking a walk with me up to the orchard to check it out again?" he asked. I hesitated. "Would it make you feel too uncomfortable?"

I considered the idea for a moment. "I guess not if I had your company."

We went outside and began strolling down the driveway. The mid-May sun was out and New England was weakly warm, a breeze stirring the tall, lanky grasses, the blooming larkspur farther off in the meadows. Spring cranks itself out in fits and starts in Vermont, and the desolate brown arduously trades itself in for greening weeks after New York and Boston and even Portland, Maine. That day, on the surrounding hillsides, the trees were mostly budded, but the leaves were still that light electric green that set the darker, coniferous trees in relief. My lilacs were just barely blooming, the apple trees decked out in luxurious boas of white and pink flowers, beset by loops of honeybees, the air graced with the sweet smell of pollen. Depending upon my mood, the land either seems to breathe and expand or close in around me. The good thing about living in a rural place is that the cycles of nature, ever-changing, help give a broader perspective, particularly when you're down in the dumps.

Just a few hours earlier, the road graders had come out for their springtime siege. The dirt on Cloudland Road was freshly raked; at least we didn't have to hopscotch over potholes and ruts. The thoroughfare was now a smooth tabula rasa that allowed us to walk easily up a long hill to the orchard. Fields stretched out on either side, and we could hear the orchestral trilling of the bobolinks nesting right smack in the field grasses. Every year these birds seemed to arrive later and later from their migration to South America, and more were perishing in a massacre of metal blades when the threshers commenced the first haying of the meadows. I'd lobbied everyone on Cloudland—Paul and Wade and Anthony and even the biotech CEO from Boston—to delay their first haying by several weeks, to insure that these birds and their nests wouldn't be churned under.

When Anthony and I finally reached the orchard, I saw that it was still cordoned off with yellow police tape. There, in the middle of everything, was the downed tree. Pointing it out to Anthony, I said, "How close was it to the one she was leaning against?"

"Five yards."

Even though the orchard had morphed into a whole different landscape, ferns unfurling and dandelions sprouting, my mind was wandering back to the bleakness of January, of perished plant life and animals long dead in the cold. Looking around again, reminding myself that it was warm now and Angela Parker's body gone, I told Anthony I thought it looked like a crime scene right out of *Law & Order.*

"Just what Emily says," he agreed. "That this orchard looks condemned."

Remembering how heaps of snow had been transported to the labs in a refrigerated compartment, I believed I could detect the indentation in the dampened ground exactly where Angela Parker had lain for seventy days against an apple tree. "Can you see where she was?" I asked Anthony. "That concave bit?" I pointed to it.

He squinted. "Not really."

I broke from his side and went to the depression. Anthony followed, knelt down, and scanned the area with his hands. "I do see what you mean, but I think this just might be from all the officials and policemen and detectives taking samples—"

"She was a hundred and forty pounds," I found myself saying. "Probably closer to one fifty with all her ski clothes."

"They were soaked when she thawed."

Neither of us spoke for a while and then Anthony said, "I went over the data from the autopsy." He cleared his throat before continuing, "The coroner first concluded that she died in the parking lot. But when we spoke recently he told me he changed his mind."

"How so?"

Anthony shielded his eyes with his hand and looked toward the dense sea of trees beginning at the edge of the orchard. "They found too much blood here on the site. She was still alive and bleeding and probably fell asleep due to the exposure."

I quailed with a sudden chill and told him I wanted to go home. And so we walked back, each of us inwardly revisiting our conversation, spooked by the orchard's eeriness. Just as we reached my long driveway and I noticed that one of the split rails that lined it had collapsed, Anthony said, "Something I've been meaning to discuss with you."

I turned away from him, approached the dislodged rail, and began lifting it. He rushed over to help and together we jammed it back into its groove. When we finished I could see that he looked terribly perturbed.

"Emily is going to be leaving," he said in a quavering voice.

Shaking my head, I said, "Oh?" and continued walking toward the house, trying to conjure up how to respond, realizing my somewhat muted reaction was probably an inkling that the news hardly came as a shock. But also I was remembering what Granny had once inferred about Anthony, that he might be capable of some sort of meanness or cruelty, so naturally I was wondering if Emily had found out about Fiona or if he'd paraded his affair in front of his wife. And I was also wondering if Emily had volunteered to leave because, as she'd casually mentioned to me several times over the past three years, she'd wanted to move closer to her family in North Carolina. Looking over at Anthony, I made myself say, "You mean you're separating?" He nodded.

"What about the girls?"

"They'll be going with her."

No wonder he'd reacted as he had during our earlier discussion about child custody. I assumed that his affair with Fiona was the unfortunate trade-off.

"Is this a mutual decision, or is it more one-sided?"

"Mutual. You'll probably find this hard to believe, but it's been coming on for a long time."

What did I know? The depths of other people's relationships were always inaccessible. The news of any breakup always made me sad. It provoked thoughts of my husband and my inability to forgive him, the loss of Matthew and the fact that he'd had to go all the way to Thailand to feel sufficiently cut off from me.

As soon as Anthony left, with renewed vigor I went back to looking for the Wilkie Collins novel. I spent a frantic hour combing through my piles and my shelves and then suddenly remembered that Breck had asked to read it and I'd lent it to her.

I looked at my watch. It was three-thirty in the afternoon. I knew the best way to reach my twenty-two-year-old was sending a text, a method of communication that all my friends, including my college roommate, Theresa, used but which I reviled partly due to the fact that my cellular phone was more than five years old, equipped with a number pad rather than a keyboard. I grabbed the digital fossil out of my night table, turned it on, and seeing that it barely had a charge, plugged it in and sent my message: *Didn't I lend you a novel called* The Widower's Branch, *a Wilkie Collins?*

The message was returned almost instantaneously.

Yup. Hey from Short Hills Mall. Why?

I'd like you to overnight it to me.

Done. Now, can I call you?

The house phone rang a moment later. "How long have you had it?" I began.

"Like a year and a half."

"But of all his novels, why did you want to read something unfinished?"

"For just that reason. I found that bit intriguing. It also looked interesting and kind of creepy. I thought it might be a fun, quick read."

"With no resolution."

"No, but an outline."

"Well, I got nervous because I couldn't remember what I did with it. What did you think of it?"

"I actually didn't get a chance to read it. Vi snapped it up and read it and then I forgot about it. But I know exactly where it is. It'll be no problem to get it to you. Here in *New Jersey,* the overnight shipping companies actually pick up from your house."

"Certainly a great reason to live there!" I quipped.

"You can't be sarcastic about it since you've never been to visit."

"Yes I can. I know New Jersey. I grew up in New York City . . . hello! And I *will* visit."

"Not holding my breath for that one. Anyway, I'll package the book up as soon as I get home."

Once we got off the phone I decided to be whimsically out of character and send her another text. *Thank you, darling lamb.*

NP, was her response.

She knew I hated it when she made words into acronyms.

I had Breck when I was twenty. During her childhood she would accuse me of naming her after the popular shampoo that disappeared from the market when she was around five years old. I actually intended to name her after Hemingway's Brett Ashley; however, when the hospital misspelled her name on the birth certificate, her father and I decided we liked "Breck" better.

Our relationship became strained when Breck was thirteen and I discovered that her father was having a long-term love affair. Rather than agreeing to end it immediately, he asked for a "timetable" that would allow him a chance to wean himself away from the woman, as though she were a drug that would cause him acute withdrawal if he cut off his reliance too quickly. Outraged, I immediately filed for divorce. At the time I foolishly tried to explain the dynamics of the situation to Breck, who, Daddy's girl that she was, futilely begged me to give her father the second chance he'd requested.

However, as soon as I began divorce proceedings, my husband promptly ended his affair and begged for a reconciliation. But how could I reconcile? I was afraid of forgiving him, afraid that if I gave in he'd just eventually find somebody else and hurt me again. Little did I know that this fear was going to tamper with the rest of my life. I became so opposed to caving in and accepting my husband again that I even managed to find a temporary distraction of my own, a man whose welcoming face and deep blue eyes decisively numbed me to my husband's entreaties.

Six months to the day after signing the final divorce papers, my ex-husband was diagnosed with incurable throat cancer. He was by then unattached and living alone. Breck asked that I allow him to move back into our New York apartment—this was still two years before I moved full time to Vermont. I agreed, he came home again, and together Breck and I nursed him until he died. And in those last days of his life I came to deeply regret my decision not to forgive him. I even guiltily wondered if my refusal might have played some part in his fatal illness. Worse still, Breck has always blamed me for not having it within myself to reconcile with her father once he'd terminated his affair. And after he passed away, she confessed to me that even though we all managed to be together again during his last days, her sense of family had been irrevocably shattered.

And probably even more painful to her were a few men who in the coming years came to live with us temporarily—each of them no longer than six or eight months—but ultimately never enchanting me as much as my ex-husband. Breck naturally hated all these "pretenders," comparing them unfavorably to her father and resenting me because I so easily allowed them to move in after having refused her father's attempt to mend the marriage.

Then at the age of seventeen, and right after I began teaching at Saint Mike's, Breck began to lose interest in eating. She got morbidly thin. I remember standing with her on my bowed, nineteenth-century bedroom floor, pointing at the full-length mirror, trying to show her how much bigger I was than she—my wrists, my arms, my trifling breasts (she was virtually flat-chested). And I've always been considered a slender, leggy woman. "How can you not see this?" I pleaded as we stood there.

"I can't, *Mom,* I can't. To me, I look huge."

"But do I look huge?"

"No, Mom, you look just *fine.*"

"But you're way thinner than I am."

"No, Mom, we're different body types."

"We're not. We have exactly the same build."

"Not true. I'm built like Granny," she insisted, which was understandable and yet delusional. "And anyway, you're older. Pushing forty. Standards are different for you."

I argued no further.

That summer Breck ate so little and grew so thin she stopped menstruating. Her face grew positively skeletal, as did her arms, her stomach stretched tight and concave, and her doctor strongly advised me to commit her to an inpatient eating-disorder clinic. But before I gave in, I nurtured a hope that if we made a trip up to Granny's house (which by then I'd inherited) on Grand Manan and spent a few weeks by the sea, walking low tide, picking wild blueberries, buying fresh lobsters, and just being alone with the boom of the breakers, that Breck would get a perspective on what she was doing to her body, to her psyche, and start nourishing herself again. And so we drove eight hours up through central Maine with its lake regions, its wildly verdant and rocky mountains, and crossed into barren New Brunswick. Leaving our car on the mainland, we made our ferry crossing.

Perched on a cliff high above the Bay of Fundy, the houses have shingled sidings, many of them old and buckling and a tarnished natural sea gray color after withstanding decades of salt air. Breck always loved driving up there, and on every visit she hounded me for stories about indomitable "Granny," the dowager empress of the island, and the summers I'd spent on Grand Manan.

Upon arrival during that time of her illness, Breck and I enacted our usual ritual: cleaning windows grimed with salty spray. We grabbed squeegees and old plastic buckets and filled them with water and vinegar and carved ourselves out a clear view of the cold ocean visible in a great molten welter from our cliffside promontory. It was fun, chattering work and Breck's mood seemed to elevate. I'd already convinced her to read *Anna Karenina*, and the first night we were there she stayed up late laughing and crying over it. I lay in my bed in the room adjacent, worrying about her, deluding myself with the idea that literature is always a balm—Tolstoy, with your great baggy novel, you'll help her get a handle on this self-destructive phase, won't you? But soon I realized that grand narrative sweep had done little to break my daughter's compulsion to starve herself, that the fresh lobsters we bought in the harbor repulsed her (she said their meat reminded her of dried red cottage cheese), that the wild blueberries we picked right off the bushes resembled blood clots, that rice tasted like pebbles. The only thing she could eat was egg whites cooked until they were crisped and which she laced with ketchup. However, some days she found it impossible to get anything down at all, even lozenges of milk chocolate, which as a last resort I tried to press on her just to provide some calories.

Shortly after we returned to Vermont, Breck allowed me to place her in a psychiatric facility down in Brattleboro. The medical staff forbade me to see her for two weeks, making me feel that I was the cause of her illness. Wasted from her self-inflicted starvation, her organs were functioning weakly. She had to be put on intravenous sustenance and the hospital feared that her heart might give out. When they told me this bit of news, I remember looking through the antique rolled-glass windows of my study at my red barn with its sagging, rusted metal roof, to my exuberant garden of tiger lilies, Cherokee sunsets, and golden jubilee. The heads of the flowers bowed over, looking dried and sapped of life as though a fierce spell of winter had suddenly invaded July. I knew Breck's life was in peril and, having already lost my husband, I didn't know how I would go on if my daughter died.

I lived from day to day in a stupor of anxiety, hardly eating anything myself, waiting for bulletins that were never very promising. "She's the same today. Not eating. She sleeps mostly, even without medication. She's too weak to walk very far. She's dizzy." What they didn't tell me, couldn't tell me, wouldn't dare to tell me was "She wants to kill herself."

And it was just when things were looking particularly dire that Breck responded to the idea of having some white toast with butter and maple syrup spread on it. It was the first good-news phone call, and the flood of relief allowed me to sleep for several hours, the first substantial bout of sleep I'd had in days. The small meals increased over the next ten days and slowly Breck found her way back into the rhythm of regular eating. After a few more weeks of gradually expanding food intake and intensive therapy, she was released from the hospital.

But the problem persisted, particularly whenever she felt depressed or overly anxious. She left for college that autumn, ironically in Maine, and while most women report gaining weight during the first semester, Breck returned home five pounds lighter. The doctors had already explained to me: now she'd come so close to dying she'd be more susceptible to bouts of anorexia—I suppose the way fingers and toes, once frostbitten, are forever prone to it.

The day after Breck and I conducted our exchange of text messages, I returned home late in the afternoon to find that UPS had left leaning against my back door a small package with her return address in Morristown. I tore off the wrapping to find a book whose antique vellum dust jacket was inscribed with an etching of a huge willow tree overhanging a river, with the words *The Widower's Branch* superimposed over the image, and below it *Wilkie Collins' final work.* I was relieved to have my rare book in my hands again. On a yellow Post-it in her characteristic up-and-down flourish, Breck had written, *Ma, sorry I sat on this one for so long. Love B.*

I thought of Gogol dying in the midst of writing *Dead Souls,* a great work in comparison to this very slim volume, whose text, not even one hundred pages, opens with a description of the River Nene in the East British Midlands, a place that I remember visiting once with Theresa and a bunch of loopy American tourists. Somehow, in the last bit of prose he ever wrote, Collins is able to rise to a fairly considerable height of descriptive powers: bogs and camphor trees draped in misty eeriness and situated on a river (whose current is even more powerful than the Connecticut) that requires a boat full of oarsmen to navigate upstream.

One morning shortly before dawn, a young clerk wandering along the river shore trips over a shriveled, blackened foot sticking out of the mud. Despite the strong pithy odor of rotting flesh, he feels compelled to reach for the dead limb, which separates from the buried body like a piece of tenderized meat. The narrative ends abruptly; the last phrase of fiction that Collins may have ever written was: "the man to whom she was soon to be married," describing his young protagonist yearning for the woman he loved, who had recently announced to him that she was engaged to somebody else—the reason why he'd been wandering the riverbank all night long, nearly out of his mind with wretchedness.

According to Theresa, Collins never made any arrangement for the book to be completed. What follows the text is the author's twenty-page outline of the plot, which proposes that other dead bodies, including the body of the main character's beloved, will be similarly found "next to large, tumbled-down trees" and that "scrambled religious writings of a fanatical nature would be discovered in the pockets of their soiled clothing."

So here it was, a ghostly antecedent to the murders unfolding in the Connecticut River Valley. I held my breath for a moment.

But then I began to reason. This, after all, was a general reference in a book that was quite obscure; I couldn't imagine there being very many copies in the United States of an unfinished piece of fiction privately printed in Britain. Beyond this, in rural areas such as ours, plenty of dead bodies must be found near fallen trees; and at least one of the women murdered in the Upper Valley was not found this way. So really, were the religious writings the hard-and-fast link to the River Valley murders? How significant was this coincidence?

As far as somebody in the area being able to get their hands on the book and copy the plot, I was familiar with Dartmouth College's collection of Wilkie Collins and knew definitively that its Baker Library had neither acquired this novel nor *Blind Love*. There was no other library within a hundred miles whose collection of Wilkie Collins would be nearly as extensive as Dartmouth's.

Then I thought: Let's just see how available this book actually is. I booted up my computer and typed my way to the Wilkie Collins Web site, where most of his novels (now in the public domain) have been digitized. As I suspected, *The Widower's Branch* is given an entry with no available online text. Next I did a general library search and found four hard copies: UCLA; the University of Wisconsin, Madison; the University of Delaware, Newark; and Yale University; the last of which was nearly two hundred miles away.

There were other considerations. For example, I knew that writers such as Charles Dickens and Wilkie Collins and Edgar Allan Poe were galvanized by grisly crimes, avidly following the progress of murders or abductions reported in the newspapers, which in the nineteenth century were more opinionated and often rendered judgment—unthinkable nowadays—on whom they felt the murderer might be, as well as commentary on how investigators were proceeding. Murder trials themselves tended to attract gargantuan crowds. Collins and Dickens often exchanged theories about these felonies and their outcomes. Both of them, for example, had been electrified by (and had written about) the Road Hill Murder of 1860 in which a three-year-old boy had his throat slit by a jealous older half sister who then threw his body down into the servants' privy. This sort of crime seemed to have its heyday in Victorian England when the queen went into perpetual mourning over her husband's death, casting a general pall of dreariness over the entire realm. Might there have been a famous murderer during the Victorian era where female victims were left by fallen trees with religious matter stuffed in their pockets? Theresa probably would be able to answer that question fairly easily. I sat down immediately and wrote her an e-mail.

Afterward I called Anthony and told him what I'd learned; intrigued, he promised to run the information by Prozzo and get his reaction.

SEVEN

TWO WEEKS LATER, on June 1, I turned forty-two. After a fitful night's sleep, punctuated with my third rereading of *Bleak House,* a novel that I cherish despite the fact that its treacly heroine, Esther Summerson, annoys me, I woke up with the tome splayed across my chest. More often than not, the first thing that struck me when I awoke every morning was a feeling of dread, of being alone with no one in bed with me. I'd think of Matthew, who, in a better world, might still be next to me, his slumbering body softly stirring, the impish smile radiant on his face when he'd wake and realize that I was there. Instead, I felt the black muzzle of Mrs. Billy, which was soon replaced by a fierce tongue bath from Virgil. Almost as though they knew it was my birthday, both dogs had left their usual sleeping habitat downstairs and had come during the night to curl up with me. I lay there looking groggily at their big sleepy heads, listening to them breathing and snorting, and kept thinking: My lovelies, my children. The sunlight was streaming through an eastern window and illuminating a spray of white iris with yellow throats that I'd filched from my garden and submerged in an azure bottle of Venetian glass. There was a marble on my nightstand. I closed my book, stacked it on the night table, and in a moment of whimsy tossed the marble and watched it roll with the slant of my nineteenth-century floor. The dogs perked up their heads at the sound.

I took a shower, wrapped myself in a terry-cloth bathrobe, remarking that the ache for Matthew was at a manageable distance now. I could get on with my day.

I studied myself in the mirror. When I kept my chin up my skin looked pretty tight and my high cheekbones were still prominent. Comma lines were just beginning to form on the right side of my face, and when I smiled there were faint crow's-feet around my eyes.

As I transited my thirties and edged past forty I began to find to a far greater degree that anytime I mirror-gaze I see my mother, who everyone says I resemble greatly but whose resemblance I refused to acknowledge until after she died of an aneurysm ten years ago. She was Ukrainian, the bloodlines visible most acutely in the exotic slant of her eyes and in her high cheekbones. As a child I bore no likeness to my blue-blooded father, a fact that some of my paternal relatives found troubling. It was commonly known that early on in their marriage both my parents had had affairs; my father's sisters subtly let me know they thought that I was illegitimate, and treated me in kind. This sense of dubious identity was incredibly difficult for me growing up; I was so afraid it might be true. Luckily, by the time I turned sixteen, I'd grown a good deal taller and lankier and it was hard for anybody to deny that my limbs and my gait were just like Daddy's.

I deliberately took out a pair of blue jeans I hadn't worn in perhaps fifteen years, delighted that they still fit me. I made myself a little pot of espresso on my stovetop, then took Virgil and Mrs. Billy and went for a five-mile hike along the Appalachian Trail.

The forest had a sharp aroma of spring earth, and wildflowers were burgeoning—purple wood violets, Dutchman's breeches, trillium and hepaticas, and long unfurling tongs of new ferns. I pushed myself hard up the inclines, hugging the hillside when the trail narrowed and partly etched into a steep face of rock.

Luck led me to three morel mushrooms that I brought home and made into delicious pasta with butter and Parmesan cheese for an impromptu birthday lunch. I felt okay, perhaps just a tad melancholy. But I couldn't dwell on this too much because I was once again on deadline.

A Houma, Louisiana, homemaker claimed that soaking white clothes in a solution that was one-third dishwashing powder, one-third nonchlorine bleach, and one-third water would have a remarkably rejuvenating effect far beyond that of plain chlorinated bleach or even Mrs. Stewart's Bluing solution. I owned several dun-white Oxford shirts that I'd saturated in a blue plastic pail. I'd picked up one of them by the collar and was noticing a marked improvement when I heard a car pull up: Wade's Ford Ranger. Through the antique-glass dreamer's windows in my study I watched him climb out and approach the house holding before him something in a small white box. I met him at the door. "What brings *you* here?" I said. Even in these rural parts it's still uncommon for neighbors to drop by without notice.

"I would have called but didn't want to spoil the surprise. Happy birthday." He folded back the top of the box and showed me a tall, beautifully iced white cake. "It's carrot," he said. "Your favorite. You tied up?"

I looked at my watch. "Kind of. But I can spare a few minutes. Are you on the way in or out?"

"Out. I went home and had a BLT with Paul."

Taking possession of the cake and leading the way toward the kitchen, I asked Wade if he'd like a piece.

"I'm good for now," Wade said, and then informed me that Paul had a gift for me as well and would be dropping by at some point.

I set the cake down on my oblong cherry dining table and then put on my electric teakettle. "Tea?"

"You still have that Lapsang?"

Definitely detecting something troubled in his manner, I told him a new batch had just arrived by mail. I half filled the kettle and, switching it on, said, "I might have a piece of that cake now." Turning back toward him, "Sure you don't want one?"

He caught me appraising his emaciated frame. Nervously combing his wispy mustache with his thumb and forefinger, he said, "I know what you're thinking, but don't say it."

"What am I thinking?" I challenged him.

"That I could use the calories."

"Well, you could."

"You just worry every skinny person is suffering from anorexia." He reminded me in his case, conversely, he'd been trying to put weight on, taking high-caloric food supplements, and consuming heavier meals and lots of red meat. He looked down at himself. "But nothing seems to help. Speaking of anorexic, heard from Breck?"

I pointed to a gorgeously arranged bouquet of gerbera daisies, ranunculus, and peonies. "Those arrived. And she sent me these earrings," I said, pointing to the retro mod sixties white hoops in my ears. "I haven't heard from her today yet, but I will."

"Very fetching," Wade approved as I saw his face furrow and darken. I was thinking that we were not having our usual spirited repartee when he said, "Look, I need to talk to you."

"I'm all yours. You know that, Wade."

He sounded nervous. "Where do I begin? Yesterday I spent an hour with this guy Marco Prozzo."

I inwardly groaned. Having imagined that Wade would make a better suspect than Hiram, I'd obviously put my finger on the pulse of something. "Oh, *him*!" I forced myself to say.

"Do you *know* him?"

I mentioned that the detective had visited me recently in the company of Anthony. "So why is he sniffing around you?"

"He questioned me to the nth degree. Not exactly as though I have a clean slate."

Although I agreed, I thought I should try and console him. "He's probably questioning all former juvenile delinquents."

This managed to make Wade chuckle. "Great," he snorted, but then his face soured again. I poured us mugs of tea and set his down in front of him with a loud knock. He went on, "Look, I can't account for myself the night Angela Parker was abducted. And Paul, whose memory is for shit, can't either."

I was momentarily perplexed. "What do you mean, Wade? It was the major snowstorm of the winter. How could you *not* account for yourself?"

"I can remember the snowstorm, you dingbat. But I spent the night in my office. Paul doesn't remember where I was. He looks at me with those huge infantile eyes of his and says, 'Gosh, weren't you home?' "

"So why did you spend the night in the office?"

"Catherine, come on. I couldn't get up the fucking hill, for fuck's sake."

"But you have a pickup truck."

"Even so, the snow got too high."

"But the plow."

"*I* didn't know when the plow was coming."

"Paul easily could've called you when it came through."

He glared at me. "You're suspicious, too."

"Who wouldn't be—"

"Look, *I* decided I was going to spend the night in the office. No big deal. It's not like I haven't done it before."

I reflected on this for a bit and my instinct was that he just didn't sound convincing. "Does Detective Prozzo take into account that you weigh one hundred and twenty-five pounds and that some of these women arguably were heavier than you?"

"When somebody goes postal they're capable of more than you'd imagine."

"Some hidden meaning there?"

"No," he said innocently, and I decided to let him slide. "So why did the detective come to see *you*?"

"Because they're looking at a suspect they've sworn me to secrecy on."

Wade looked perturbed. "And . . . that would be me?"

"No!"

Wade was nervously sucking one end of his wispy mustache. "Do you promise?"

"I swear on everything that is sacred. My dogs, my pig, my daughter. What else is there to swear on?"

"How about your ex-lover?"

I winced. "Him too."

Wade crossed his arms over his chest. "Come on, Catherine. You can tell me."

"Wade, I can't!"

"Since when did your big mouth shrink to a pucker?"

"Since I turned forty-two at three o'clock this morning."

"An inconvenient time to be born, if I must say."

"So said my mother my whole life."

"Nasty bitch that she probably was." Then he looked at me forlornly. "A hint?"

"Yes, a hint, you don't know this person."

"Have I heard of them . . . *him,* I guess I should say?"

"Yes, but that's as far as I'll go. And from henceforth I am mum. Now, come on," I cajoled, "snap out of it and have a piece of your carrot cake."

"No thanks."

There was a strange tension in the room. At last I said, "If you're innocent, Wade, why so worried?"

"Come on! How many innocent people have gotten convicted of crimes, especially before DNA testing?"

"Yes, but there is something called evidence."

"And it begins with whereabouts. Which I cannot establish," he said crossly.

"Suspicion and arrest require a lot more than that."

He stared at me for a moment and then said, "I've got to get back to work."

We hugged tentatively, I thanked him for the carrot cake, and then he left without a further word. He seemed unusually jittery for someone who theoretically had nothing to worry about. And yet I knew that if I were Prozzo I'd be questioning him, too.

Breck called me just as I was washing the cake crumbs off my plate and asked if I'd seen today's *Times*. I hadn't. "Well, I guess they wanted to give you a birthday present." She went on to inform me that there was a long article on various unsolved serial murders in New England, including the ones in the River Valley, and that the most recent body had been found by Catherine Winslow, "an esteemed journalist, a *Times* contributor, and former editor" at the various magazines with which I was once affiliated.

"Esteemed journalist who now makes a living hovering over clogged drains."

"What*ever*!"

"I wonder why the *Times* didn't even contact me. I could've given them some good copy."

"If you check out the article then you'll see it makes sense they're not calling you. It's more of a roundup. Your commentary probably would have made your mention a bit top-heavy."

"Listen to you."

"Well, I *am* the journalist's daughter. Happy birthday, by the way."

"Oh yeah, there's that. And since it's my birthday and we're on the subject of *The New York Times*—"

"Oh God, do I know what's coming."

"Then need I remind you of my one and only death request?" I laughed.

"Ma, you just turned forty-two. Don't go all doom and gloom on me yet."

"Excuse me. A serial killer just happened to drop by my rural outpost where only three families live full time."

"I assume that lightning won't strike twice in the same place. But okay, your point landed . . . you want to make sure the *Times* mentions that Aunt Eleanor Roosevelt was your second cousin twice removed."

"Now don't be flip. She was hardly that distantly related."

"Mom, you've got more going for you than your pedigree."

"Hey, I'm a burnout. You have to stress what you can."

"I can't believe we're talking about this . . . you're still going strong. An established journalist. And now a nationally syndicated columnist."

"I'm only half serious," I told her. "Anyway, I'm a household hints columnist. The *Times* really has high regard for that!"

"I disagree. Your accomplishments would make for good enough copy to get your own article. Not to mention related to Eleanor *and* several presidents of the United States. Anyway, why are you so hung up on what The *Times* thinks and does?"

"Because I used to write for them until The Sophisticated Traveler killed my piece on Venice. When some famous novelist decided *he* wanted to write about it."

"There are other sections to write for."

"I guess my pride has gotten in the way."

Hesitating for a moment, Breck said, "Look, I really hate getting into this . . . but I actually asked somebody I know who works at The *Times*. You remember Sarah, my college field hockey friend? She did a stint in Obits. I mentioned your crazy concern about your morbidity and she said somebody like you would definitely be, in her words, 'on ice at *The New York Times*.'"

"Ah, that's birthday music for my ears!"

"I'm glad *that* makes you happy."

"By the way, thanks for sending the book back so promptly. I didn't mention it to you but I needed it back for a reason."

I told her I'd reread it and then detailed the curious coincidences between the plot of *The Widower's Branch* and the River Valley murders.

"So you think the book has something to do with it?" Breck sounded doubtful.

"I have no idea."

There was a distinct silence on the other end of the line. And then Breck began again. "I meant to tell you I noticed a slip of paper in the book when I was getting ready to send it. With some writing on it. Wasn't anything remarkable, so I threw it out."

"What kind of writing?"

"It was barely anything. It had like three words: 'you and her,' something of that order. Didn't resemble your handwriting."

"Maybe Vi's?"

"Nope, not her handwriting, either. It was kind of scrawled. Vi grew up in the era of penmanship."

"How odd," I said, and then let it go.

"But I mean how *is* the investigation going? Do you think they're even on the right track?"

"Hard to know. They think it's probably somebody local who knows the back roads and isolated areas. Believe it or not, they've just questioned Wade."

"Now, *that* nutjob makes total sense."

"Breck! Don't be unkind."

"I'll be honest with you, Mom. I've had the weirdest, creepiest feeling all along that we might know the person who has done all of this. Somebody who goes off on a rampage and then quiets down and lives normal. Then the cycle begins all over again. Somebody like Wade, with a fucked-up early life."

"Some would say *you* had a fucked-up early life. And you're not going around killing people."

"No, but look how angry *I* was."

Still are, I thought but didn't say.

Breck continued, "In my case I turned it inward on myself. I easily could've become . . . an aggressive delinquent."

"I don't think so. Not in your nature."

"Come on, don't be so naive."

"Says she who took Psych One in college."

"Anyway, whenever I see him, Wade always seems wound so tight."

"He is, but that doesn't mean when he uncoils he's going around systematically killing people. Remember, he committed one act of violence at the age of fourteen."

"It has been proven that violence toward objects can easily become violence toward living things."

I thought of changing the subject by confiding Anthony's suspicion of Hiram Osmond but then decided not to.

"Who's running this investigation, anyway?" Breck asked after a pause.

I mentioned Marco Prozzo and Breck thought his surname sounded blunt. I told her he'd loved my hibiscus tea.

"Ah," Breck said. "That reminds me. I knew I wanted to ask you something. Vis-à-vis tea."

"Is this going to be painful?"

"Doesn't have to be. I guess it all depends on how attached you are to a certain heirloom."

"I knew it, I knew it! What do you want *now*?"

"The tea tin we brought back from Grand Manan, the one that belonged to Granny. It has that delicate design of yellow roses."

"I used it yesterday."

"Ah, so . . . it's in circulation?"

"You always do this to me!"

"I was fantasizing about how it would look in our kitchen— and wasn't sure if it was . . ." She didn't finish her sentence.

Our kitchen. Even though I felt possessive over this relic of my childhood, I forced myself to be generous. "Well, it *is,* but you're welcome to it. I've got tea tins up the ying yang. Just do me one small favor. If anything happens . . . between the two of you, just make sure that you don't lose it."

There was a disagreeable pause and I was about to broach it when Breck said, "You never even ask how she is."

"I'm sorry, Breck," I said. "You're right. How *is* Violet?"

"Violet is actually fine. She's wondering when you're coming to pay us a visit. We were going to invite you for the Fourth of July."

Here was precisely where, to my great mortification, I had further failed my daughter, having had difficulty accepting the fact that she was in love with another woman.

Since Anthony and I had been more in touch of late, I'd recently spoken of this to him. His opinion was that women can be more fluid in their relationships, that a fair percentage float back and forth between male and female partners, that I shouldn't assume that Breck (at the age of twenty-two) had settled down with a woman for the rest of her life. "Maybe she's trying to find the love that she thinks she didn't get from *you,*" he actually said to me. "Work it through with another female . . . an older female," he added.

"Oh please, that is so trifling and simplistic," I berated him. "How can you even call yourself a shrink, slinging that hash around?"

Somehow he'd maintained his patience. "Okay, Granny," he retorted, but then pointed out something that actually *did* sink in: I had better be very careful, because any ambivalence, any disapproval of my daughter's romantic life could do even more damage to our already tenuous relationship. For how could I, having had an affair with a man close in age to my own daughter, not support any serious relationship Breck was having, no matter with whom? Quite right.

"Honey," I resumed to Breck, "you know how little I've traveled in the last few years. The dogs, Henrietta. It's hard when you have critters."

"You'll bring the dogs. And I thought you had that young vet student who likes to come and look after Madame." Her nickname for our beloved pig.

"As long as I can get him. That's a popular weekend and I'm not the only person he pet-sits for who has an exotic animal."

"Your *only* child has been living in New Jersey for over a year," Breck reminded me. "A five-hour drive. If it comes down to it, we'll send a car for you." Violet made a pile working for the World Bank.

"Don't waste that kind of money. I can drive myself. If you have so much dough lying around, for God's sake give it to a charity."

"Granny used to send cars for you."

"I was a child. What choice did I have? Even then I thought it was needlessly extravagant."

There was a lull in the conversation and then Breck said, "What about dear Aunt Laura? You go and visit her and her partner."

"That's the previous generation. I visit out of respect."

"And devotion. You love them both."

"I do love them, that's true."

There was a thoughtful lull and then Breck spoke to me in a wobbly voice, "Well . . . if you got to know Violet . . . maybe you could love *her* too."

EIGHT

A FTER SPEAKING TO BRECK, I drove down to the Billings
General Store to get my mail from the smart-ass postmaster
who was always reluctant to hand anything over whenever I neglected to bring my mailbox key. Once I misplaced my key for
almost a year, and even though the man claimed to have ordered
one, it never seemed to arrive, which forced me to request my
mail every time I went in, giving him a chance to harangue me.
I'd neglected to get my mail for several days now and a pile of it
was wedged into the postbox and needed to be yanked out. "How
about those yellow slips you got for those packages last week?"
the silver-haired fortyish man said to me.

"They're at home."

"Not where they should be," he said with a smirking sort of
glower. "Make sure you bring 'em in next time you come."

"I'll try to remember."

He shook his head. "Don't try. Remember! If I don't get them
back here, I'm not giving you your mail the next time you forget
your key," he said.

"You're so wonderfully kind."

"I'm being more than kind!"

Billings is a nuts-and-bolts general store, selling milk and basic staples: solid, unaffectedly prepared food, unlike the surrounding general stores that offer an array of Vermont food products and fancy sandwiches made with such garnishes as mango chutney. Billings attracts a cluster of die-hard locals who gravitate to the back of the store and gather around a butcher-block table and a coffee machine—some of them gossip-mongers. I was standing near a group of them, sifting through my wedge of mail, when I felt a tap on the shoulder. Dressed in a cut-off T-shirt and baggy shorts, Anthony was standing behind me, holding a cardboard soup container. He was wearing a bicycle helmet.

"Happy Birthday," he said. "Emily reminded me."

"That my present?" I asked.

"No, it's my lunch. Corn chowder."

"Ah, they do make the best here." I turned to see a line of people waiting to pay, holding containers of soup and half gallons of milk and cans of soda. "You've been scarce the last few days," I remarked.

"Been around the house a lot." He glanced away. "Emily is getting all packed up and ready to leave. I've been helping her."

Then I realized Emily had left me a phone message a few days ago and I had yet to return it. I mentioned this to Anthony and said, "Please apologize for me. I hope she doesn't think I'm avoiding her."

"I will. Don't worry. She's been really busy." He managed to grin.

Intent upon avoiding being overheard, I motioned Anthony to step outside, and once we went through the door, I said, "Wade came to see me. Is Prozzo now changing course?"

"No, just widening his lens. He's obligated to check out certain offenders with records."

"But Wade is physically not very strong. It's hard to imagine him overpowering women in a car, strangling and stabbing them."

"I get your point. But nothing can be ruled out until all the i's are dotted and all the t's are crossed."

"But would he dump a body in his own neighborhood?"

"If it turns out to be somebody down Claremont/Springfield way, they'd be dumping bodies in *their* backyard."

"True. But Angela Parker weighed more than Wade."

"Doesn't matter."

"Seems like I know all the suspects."

"People give themselves away. You'd be surprised."

"I don't think anything would surprise me," I said. "Except if the killer were you."

"I have a wife and children who can vouch for my where-abouts on January seventeenth." He winked at me. "Who out there can vouch for you?"

"My pig."

"That should fly."

"Anyway, your kids are too young to be credible witnesses." I winked back at him. "Maybe the real reason why Emily is leaving is she can't bear to lie for you any longer."

Anthony suddenly looked incredibly sad. "I know you're joking, but I guess I don't have a sense of humor today."

Realizing I'd pushed him too far, I apologized.

"It's all right, for obvious reasons it's just not a great day." He glanced at his watch. "And now I have to go meet Marco to discuss a finding at Angela Parker's crime site that somehow got overlooked."

"Can you tell me about it?" I asked tentatively.

"As a matter of fact I was encouraged to tell you about it . . . by Marco. He seems to want to keep you in the loop. He agrees that you're a good sounding board. Must say, it's unusual for a seasoned investigator to want help from a civilian."

"I guess I charmed him with dog biscuits and my homemade hibiscus tea."

Anthony laughed. "So anyway, here's what we have."

On the verge of Cloudland Road, next to the orchard and right below the snowbank that was made by the plow, the Staties had found a pair of frozen tire tracks in the mud. "Those tracks were half thawed out the day you found Angela Parker," he said.

Assuming where he was headed, I said, "But they could have been any pair of tire marks."

"True. But remember, the snow was pretty scant up until the night of that blizzard. And the location of tire marks are off the road, meaning the driver pulled over. And then there was all that snow . . . to petrify them."

"What make?"

"Bridgestone. SUVs and pickup trucks."

"That's a wide category."

"It's a certain popular issue of the tire that hardly allows us to narrow it down much except to suggest the vehicle in question had to be an SUV. The irony is that two of the models they come standard on are Wade's and Hiram's and my pickup truck." I probably looked at him malevolently because he raised both hands. "Just saying."

Then I saw some humor. "That contradicts the claim of all those folks who swear they saw some of the murdered women climbing into smaller cars. Red Ford Focus and Saturns and the like."

"Pinch of salt with eyewitness accounts," Anthony said. "You and I always said that only a vehicle with substantial clearance could have traveled that far up Cloudland Road, even in the beginning of the storm." He tilted his head in the direction of the store entrance. "I have to go back in and pay for my soup. I'll check in with you later."

When I arrived home and began sorting through the mail, I noticed a blue aerogram that made my breath catch: the hand stamp of Matthew Blake. This was the first I'd heard from him in nearly two years. The letter showed domestic postage and the mailing mark was Cambridge, Massachusetts. I needed to steel myself before opening it. I sat down at my desk, shoving aside correspondence from readers and displacing my towering stacks of paperbacks.

Inside the envelope was a photograph of me that Matthew had taken and a printed letter—very unlike him, who always preferred to write by hand.

Dear Catherine,

I am hoping that this reaches you by your birthday. I came back to the States in early April and just happened to read about your finding the nurse's body in *The Boston Globe*. When I first read it, I couldn't imagine the shock of finding somebody murdered. I wanted to write to you then, but I was afraid you wouldn't respond. Since I've come home I've just been trying to carry on and not think about you. But I have to admit it has been really difficult.

I don't know if you remember when I took this photo, but it was toward the end. I can't imagine that you look much different on your 42nd. Still beautiful, of that I am certain.

Love,
Matthew

The photograph he enclosed was taken in my apartment in Burlington in front of a cupboard where I'd displayed some of the old china that I inherited from my father's side of the family. My dark hair was longer then, clasped behind my head in a braid that had come partially undone; and I remember we'd just finished making love. My gray eyes are lighted well, I am slightly disheveled, my cheeks rosy. And I remember thinking at the time that in the picture he'd caught me at an angle where I looked more attractive than I actually felt I was. This was flattering, obviously, but oddly painful.

Matthew had wanted to frame the photo but I had discouraged him because I felt it was an unfair representation of what I looked like. I feared finding it in years to come (after the affair was long over) and then having to witness what would strike me to be some kind of momentary (and even artificial) radiance. But now I realized with a pang this is exactly how he saw me, and, more important, perhaps how I actually appeared. And I realized that grief over this love was unalloyed with such things as survivor's guilt, and that it probably would last the rest of my life as a series of pictures and painful memories.

I went upstairs to fetch the cardboard box where I'd stored all his letters, arranged in translucent plastic folders. I reached in and randomly selected one of two blue aerograms he sent me from Asia before he abruptly stopped communicating, my name and address penned in fountain ink, foreign stamps in oriental filigree.

"I've been reading Maugham," he wrote to me. "Seems like the sort of thing you should read if you're in Bangkok. The bookstores here have British editions and he seems to be very popular. Luckily I am living in a guest quarters that has a pretty good library. I think about you a lot and lately I've been doing some of the writing exercises you had us do in class. . . ."

I had a hard-and-fast rule that I advanced to all the students in my seminars. Avoid writing about animals, especially dogs. When you write about animals, you engage sympathy without necessarily earning it, and then the reader can quite easily feel manipulated, something you want to avoid at all costs. A student turned in a piece about his German shepherd being hit by a car that crushed its leg and how the animal bled to death on the way to the veterinary hospital. As soon as I finished reading it, I scanned the list of student e-mails and fired one off, asking the fellow to come and see me during my office hours.

Matthew had taken some time off and, at twenty-four, was several years older than most of the other students. He arrived and left class with a bit of a swagger, with an arrogant grace, but also gave off a kind of troubled air. During the most recent class, in which he wrote about his dog, I remembered that he'd been one of the early finishers of the assignment. He'd worn a football jersey that draped barely past his belt buckle so that when he leaned back in his chair to stretch, the shirt hiked halfway up his taut belly, showing a mature line of hair weaving its way down to his beltline. I swallowed and said nothing. I'd had plenty of other male students who'd done similar things, wore their pants inappropriately tight, showed up to class in cut-off muscle T-shirts or with jeans worn low like prison garb, showing the crack of their ass, and I knew they did this out of some kind of insecurity. A remark like "This is a classroom, not an athletic field" was usually strong enough to beat the boldest boy into abeyance. But when Matthew Blake leaned back I said nothing to correct his posture, and failing to do this made me worry about the effect he had on me. I resolved then and there to make him transfer to another writing section or drop the class. The dog piece had now presented me with an opportunity.

For sometimes there are students, sexually provocative students, who question you at every turn—an unnerving mix. They know their power, they presume that you're attracted to them. I'd been at Saint Mike's for five years and I could spot this sort of narcissistic student pretty easily.

When he came to our first meeting my door was closed. There was a knock, Matthew opened it and poked his head in without waiting for an answer. I saw dark hair tumbling over a pale forehead, reddish brown eyes, a faint dusting of acne over his broad cheeks. "Did you hear me say come in?" I challenged him.

"No," he admitted.

"Well, but here you are *inside* my office." I spoke sharply, expecting an apology.

There was none; instead he remained unruffled and said, "Should I go out and start again?"

"No, but next time wait until you're invited."

He breezed in and immediately coasted into a chair. He looked around the office and noticed the inverted map of the world that I'd pinned up on the wall, with the continents of Australia and Africa and South America upended. "Wow," he said. "That's fantastic." He asked where I got the map and I told him obviously in the southern hemisphere. He said, "Maybe the world *is* like that. And it's just a question of perception." I was secretly pleased by this remark.

"Well, let's talk about that . . . perception," I said. "I just want to make sure you're aware why I asked you to come in."

"Because I'm not to write about animals getting hurt or killed."

"I told the class 'avoid.' I suppose that's not quite as strong as 'don't.' "

He grimaced. "I just couldn't think of anything else."

I reminded him that he'd finished the in-class assignment early. And perhaps he didn't ruminate long enough on what might be an appropriate subject to write about. "There must be other harrowing things."

"There are, I just don't want to write about them."

"But that's the whole point. You want to dip your pen into that well of discomfort. That's where the good stuff lives. I mean, what are some of the things that frighten you?"

He wavered. "I don't know. Relationships, I guess."

"Are you in one now? If so, maybe that might be a worthy subject."

He frowned and said, "Not really. Just . . . dating different people."

"Is there anything that frightens you when it comes to dating?" I didn't want to say "women," not wanting to assume what his sexuality might be.

"The out-of-control part. The possibility of great pain."

"That's a good subject."

This seemed to frustrate him. "So was my assignment any good at all?"

"Not particularly." He looked crestfallen. "You clearly rushed it. You dryly state the facts. You don't even make an attempt to describe how it affected you."

He looked puzzled.

"What have I been saying in class: about how to approach emotion and get to it without writing about it so directly?"

"But I thought I did."

I shook my head. "Hardly." I studied his face, its broad, angled planes, long dark lashes, soft straight hair, and saw a rugged delicacy. Then I went full throttle. "There are three other writing instructors here at the college. I don't think any of them has this writing about animals dictum, so you're welcome—"

"No," he interrupted, looking terrified. "I don't want to take anyone else's class. You're the one everybody recommends."

Although I was pleased to hear this, I said, "That's not true. In fact, I happen to know that one of my colleagues has better student evaluations than I do."

He looked genuinely discomfited. "I don't care about them, Mrs. Winslow." He leaned forward in his chair and, clearly shaken up, said, "The only other thing I thought I might write about was when . . . my dad left us. . . . For two years, he just completely disappeared." The last three words got out shakily. "But I don't want— I just can't—read that to the others."

"Don't worry, I won't call on you to read it."

Now finally he was worked up, breathing quickly, reminding me of ex-military guys who came to study with me after going to war: pent-up and uneasy fellows who often bridled at having to answer to a woman. Something told me even then that despite his willingness to comply, down the road he was going to be trouble anyway.

I said, "However, may I use your dog assignment, maybe even

read it aloud, to hammer my point about manipulating the reader?"

He groaned but then agreed.

"How about you do this: write about when your father left. . . ." I saw his look of pure horror. "Not for the class, but just for me."

"Okay," he said, "but only if it's just for you."

The piece he turned in to me was rather good, written with effective simplicity, and once I read it I understood why he preferred to keep his life story from other students. A sickly child born with his feet turned in, he'd had to wear leg braces for several years. To complicate matters, at the age of two he'd also suffered from meningitis, which left him with some nerve damage. His father, embarrassed by his son's physical weaknesses, neglected him, treated him like a maimed, mangled child. Matthew detailed long family car trips where his father barely even spoke to him and how his mother, whom he described as "traditionally subservient to her husband," a "born-again Seventh-Day Adventist," never backed him up, never confronted his father's criticisms, his cruelties, because she obviously feared sometime in the not-too-distant future her husband would leave her. And he did, for a time. "Interminable," Matthew called those two fatherless years; ten years old, he was virtually left to fend for himself by a mother who became so unstable she could barely take care of the household and spent many of her waking hours praying for her husband's return. Finally his father showed up back at home, offering little explanation for his absence, and yet was accepted by his mother unconditionally.

Matthew, in the meantime compensating for his early frailty and leg braces, began lifting weights as a twelve-year-old and taking up hockey—presumably as a way of proving himself to his implacable father. But even when he mastered the sport and grew physically stronger, his father never gave the approval he sought; and his mother was far too weak willed to provide any sort of encouragement. Against many odds, he turned himself into a fairly well-functioning, if brash, young man. A man I ended up falling in love with, a man over whom I suffered greatly and who suffered greatly over me, a man who comforted me and whom I comforted, a man from whom I resolved to part and could not part.

I wiped the tears from my eyes and was putting his letters away when I heard funny scratchy noises going on downstairs and hurried down to the first floor. Henrietta had once again chewed through the childproof lock on the cupboard in which I kept the garbage, and this time the kitchen was strewn with eggshells and coffee grounds and zucchini peels. After the impromptu meal, she'd managed to burst through the barrier that I used to cordon off my living room from all the animals and was hiding behind my grandfather's smoking chair, blubbering and shaking. There was a trail of piddle on one of my old Aubusson rugs. "You stupid f'ing pig!" I cried out, despite myself. "Who needs you anyway?" Her response: half grunt, half sob. "Oh come on, Henrietta," I said.

I'd managed to herd her into the kitchen and was just finishing cleaning the rug with rags and some stain cleaner when there was a knock at the door. Standing there with a brown-wrapped square under his arm, Paul was gazing at me with his huge, doll-like eyes.

"I heard you might stop by," I told him. "What's that under your arm?"

"Your birthday present," he said sweetly as I opened the door for him.

The gift clearly was one of his paintings. In the midst of my delight at his generosity, I wondered if he was giving it to me because lately he'd been worrying about dying, worrying that, in the event of his death, his close friends would be taken care of. A painting such as this could be worth $150,000—not that he'd expect me to sell it. He hugged me and, wishing me a happy forty-second, dutifully followed me to the kitchen and beamed when he saw Wade's cake.

"A chip off the old block," I said, referring to the fact that Paul was a superb baker.

Paul said, "Mom's recipe, actually."

"But your mom was Cuban," I pointed out. "Is carrot cake popular down there?"

"They—my family—used to make carrot cakes in Cuba before they emigrated," he said. "They did everything American. Anyway, this is for you." He held out the wrapped parcel.

I slowly unwrapped the brown paper and saw that the painting was based on a photograph he had taken of me half-reclined on a chaise in a very traditional polka-dot dress. The composition was clearly an homage to David's portrait of a famous beauty, *Madame Récamier,* which Paul knew to be one of my favorite paintings. The figure on the chaise was hardly an exact likeness, the woman's face is rounder and wider-eyed than I am, created in the tradition of Paul's more primitive-looking subjects; however, the arms, the long legs, the leaning-back posture was definitely *moi.*

In the painting I recognized certain objects from his living room: an imperial yellow Chinese vase, an incense censor dating back to the fifteenth century, an umbrella stand filled with peacock plumes. But he'd added an interesting feature, a translucent drape or screen of sorts that glows with illumination and is imprinted with the silhouette of a man. Paul had always been very much against my relationship with Matthew Blake, was disturbed by the amount of suffering it caused me, and I naturally interpreted this unrest in the sense of a masculine form looming almost malevolently over me.

"It's lovely," I said, continuing to study the painting. "Beautifully done, really. I'm so . . . well, honored . . . you made this just for me."

"Well, I didn't make it *for* you. I made it because I was inspired to make it," he announced to me with a bit of defensive imperiousness. "You just happened to be the subject. And then when Wade reminded me that your birthday was coming up, I just felt that I wanted to give it to you."

I hugged him tightly and told him how much his friendship meant to me and even apologized for being so cranky at times.

"It's okay. You've had a lot on your mind." Glancing around the kitchen he said, "If you want my opinion, there's a good place for it," pointing to a vacant spot on the wall that divided the open cooking area and the dining table. He took the painting, which fit perfectly between two crown moldings. "Got any picture hooks?" I went into my tool chest and found him a brass one as well as a hammer. Within minutes the painting was on the wall and seemed as though it was meant for just the place it hung.

We were both standing there admiring it when Paul turned to me, looking fretful. "You know they questioned Wade for an hour."

Choosing my words carefully, I said, "I think that they question a lot of people when this kind of thing happens."

Sounding annoyed, Paul said, "I told Wade I thought he was at home. I would have gladly gone on record. I mean, what I don't remember I don't remember."

"Yes, but it's not the truth, then, is it? And you don't want to mess around with lying. Because if and when they find out, it makes you look suspicious and possibly complicit."

"But he didn't do it. He's not the killer."

"Of course he isn't."

"You don't sound very convincing," Paul complained.

That's because I wasn't convinced. However, I said, "Well *I* don't think he did it. *I* don't think he has it in him. But I just hate the fact that he can't prove where he was."

Paul sighed and shook his head and said, "You're obviously not going to give me the reassurance that I want. So let's not talk about this anymore."

The moment had turned strange, terribly awkward in light of the fact that Paul had just given me an extravagant birthday gift.

"Paul," I said at last, "I'm sorry. I really don't mean to sound circumspect."

"I know you don't, and that's all right. But I'm getting too upset and probably shouldn't discuss it anymore," he warned, as though such a state of mind was a bad idea, bad for his health.

"Well then, let's just keep moving along," I suggested. "Are you still working on that painting with all the office workers?"

"Yes," he said, sounding somewhat relieved to be speaking of other things. "I'm thinking of calling it *The Bureaucracy*."

NINE

THE NEXT DAY ON MY WAY into the prison to teach my class, I noticed Prozzo getting out of his Jeep and Leslie Fullerton climbing out of the passenger side, his belly jiggling through his starched uniform. I thought of Matthew Blake at twenty-four, hockey solid; what a shame it was that this young Statie was already letting himself go. I also wondered why Prozzo had Leslie in tow. Surely he wasn't considering this not-the-brightest-bulb-in-the-box as an amanuensis of sorts.

I approached them, said hello, and then to Prozzo, "He your new protégé?"

"Assigned to me for a few days. He thinks he wants to cross over into my line of work." I shot Prozzo a look that meant "You've got to be kidding, right?" He actually winked slyly at me.

I said, "I hear you're keeping very good tabs on Cloudland."

Prozzo smiled strangely. "Your friend Wadey seems mighty shady."

"He's the nervous sort. And you're not exactly the guy who sets people at ease."

"On the contrary," Prozzo said with a tense smile. "But that's my job."

"I obviously understand that."

"And Wade *does* have a record."

"A juvenile record," I clarified.

"Okay, but he can't account for himself the night of the blizzard."

"He claims to have spent the night in his office."

"Curious alibi, don't you think?" Prozzo said.

"Not the best one I ever heard," interjected Leslie.

Annoyed, I turned to look at him and I'm sure my expression radiated "What do *you* know?"

Prozzo continued, "It just so happens that I have a woman who claims Wade spent the night with her."

"With *her*?" I asked, having trouble hiding my bewilderment.

"Did you think he was gay?" Prozzo looked bemused.

I backpedaled. "Honestly, with him it's been hard to tell. He always plays his cards close to his vest."

"Apparently," Prozzo said. "Because he lied to us *and* to you about where he was the night of the blizzard."

"Is this lady . . . trustworthy?"

Prozzo scratched his head and glanced at Leslie. "You tell me. Local landscape architect. Works for those swells up on Wild Apple Road, the people who live off of the salt mines in Utah, but who are so green they sell their excess solar-generated electricity back to Vermont Power."

"I know the woman you mean. She's around fifty? Light brown hair?"

The detective nodded. "According to her, Wade arrived rather late on the night of the snowstorm, between ten and ten-thirty."

I'd always had my suspicions, but never had been able to pinpoint Wade's sexual taste. "I admit it doesn't look great," I said. "Anthony obviously knows about this."

Prozzo nodded. "I told him I wanted to speak to you about it."

I opened my palms to him. "Here I am."

"Okay, so do you have any idea of why Wade might be covering up his private life?"

"My amateur armchair view? Fucked-up parents who made him feel unworthy. But you might want to check my theory with Anthony, your shrink on retainer." There was a moment of silent weirdness out there in the parking lot and then I said, "Have you gone back to Wade with what you found out?"

"A few hours ago I stopped by the town hall. He immediately admitted he'd been lying. But that doesn't necessarily implicate him either. As I'm sure you know, lots of innocent people tell stupid lies when they think they might be under suspicion."

"Do you mind if I confront him about this, the fact that he even lied to me?"

"Yeah, sure, have at it," Prozzo said.

"He actually made it a point to come over to my house and discuss the fact that you questioned him. He seemed very nervous. Now I know why."

We were distracted by some arguing going on in the prison, and one of the guards, presumably, yelling, "Shut the fuck up!" Then the detective resumed, "Now to the other item on my punch list . . . this book you were talking about."

"What about it?"

Prozzo looked speculative. "At first I thought: murdered women found by trees with religious material stuffed in their pockets is interesting, but not . . . bingo. Plenty of crimes have strange religious motivations, right? However, when I got in touch with the FBI in Washington, they couldn't find anything that matches this scenario." Leslie, I noticed, kept glancing at the entrance of the prison as though expecting somebody to appear. "So we basically have two victims with tracts found in their pockets. One dead and one alive."

"Angela Parker and Marjorie Poole."

"And if Washington can't give me anything, I need to know more about the book. Because I'm thinking: maybe we could be on to something . . . at least for these two killings."

"So now you're thinking there might be two murderers?"

"Hard to say. Perps will change up certain things to make themselves harder to pinpoint."

"What do you want to know about the novel: the plot; the rarity of the edition; the fact that it's a fragment with an outline?"

"Any and all," the detective said.

I hesitated. "Like I said, it's incredibly rare. In fact, mine might just be the only copy between here and Yale University. So . . ."

"If I have to borrow it I'll take good care of it."

"If you lost it, I'd have to kill you."

Prozzo smiled and turned to Leslie. "Well, at least then we'll have solved this particular case, right?"

Once I arrived home I called Wade at the town clerk's office. His assistant told me he was in a day-long meeting with the tax assessors. I left word for him to call me. Then sat down at my desk and was writing about places in Boston and New York City where one can go for the "re-tinning and repair of copper pans" when the phone startled me. It was a New Hampshire number that I didn't recognize, but then the name flashed: Hubert Parker. I stopped, for a moment uncertain whether or not I wanted to answer the phone call of Angela Parker's husband. Finally I grabbed the cordless and went to sit down in my granddaddy's smoking chair.

"Hello, Catherine Winslow," I answered at last.

"Hello, Mrs. Winslow," he began tentatively, and introduced himself.

"I saw your name on caller ID."

"Of course."

There was a terribly uncomfortable pause and then I said, "Let me tell you how sorry I am; how awful all this must be for you."

The lull continued. The man had either momentarily lost his nerve or succumbed to a tidal current of grief that made it impossible to go on. "Yes . . . it is," he said finally.

"A lot of people around here are thinking about you," I told him. I was even tempted to say "praying for you," but for me to say that would have been disingenuous.

"Oh, people have been . . . awfully kind," he said with flat affect.

"I've been meaning to write to you. Because I wanted to tell you a few things." I hesitated.

"Yes," Hubert Parker said.

If the coroner was correct and Angela Parker actually died in the orchard rather than in the parking lot of the rest area off the interstate, that meant she'd been stabbed several times, perhaps strangled into submission, had endured the ten-mile ride to Cloudland perhaps believing that her captor still had it in him to set her free, even imagining that being dumped off somewhere in a blizzard would locate her at least within a few miles of a residence whose inhabitants would surely take her in.

"She looked very peaceful when I found her," I told Mr. Parker. "Her face was relaxed and calm. I think . . . my feeling was that despite everything, she died quietly."

There was a sucking gasp on the other end of the line. I waited for a moment, sounding my thoughts for meaningful words. Finally, I said, "It's like carrying a huge sack of stones around on your shoulders, isn't it?"

"Especially when I get up in the morning."

"I know that feeling," I said, "that horrible feeling when you wake up. I know it from other things." I immediately thought of my husband's death and Breck's severe anorexia and the inevitable sense of despair over my disintegrating relationship with Matthew Blake.

"When she was missing . . . even after they found the blood in her car and figured that something happened, I never really ever gave up hope. There was a big part of me that . . . believed she was still going to come . . . home. I used to lie in bed and imagine she'd slip in right next to me while I was sleeping and that her cold side of the bed would suddenly be warm with her. And then of course—" He broke off and seemed to weep quietly for a few moments. "I know . . . I just can't believe that I won't hold her, not even one more time. That I have to accept that it'll be 'never.'"

"I hate that word, never," I found myself saying.

"If I held her just one more time, I . . ." He faltered. "I think . . . maybe I could finally let go. We were very close, Angela and me. We're almost the same age and now she's torn away from me and I've just been hanging there."

This was almost unbearable to hear. I remembered how my bed felt like a vast, empty plain when Matthew finally stopped sleeping in it. I remembered the sorrow of finding his orphaned socks, and certain possessions that he'd forgotten to take with him: a chinning bar that for months leaned against the corner of my bedroom, a pair of water shoes that he used for walking along the bottom of the Ottauquechee River. And I remembered one of the last things he ever said to me. "It's my doom, Catherine, that I love you as much as I do."

"So, Mr. Parker," I said. "Is there any way that I can help you with any of this?"

A few moments passed. He barely got the words out. "Well, I was actually hoping I could come and see you."

Oh no, I thought, why? How could I be of any help? "You can come and see me if you'd like," I offered. "Although I don't know if somebody who didn't know your wife at all will be able to help you. I'll certainly try, though."

"You *did* know her," he objected. "She took your blood at the hospital."

"But I hardly remember her more than that she was good at her job." I told Mr. Parker that his wife had been gentle with me, kind to me.

"But that's one of the few things that I find . . . I don't know, a little comforting. That somebody who knew her actually discovered her. . . ." His voice warped again; he was really trying to hold it together. "And if she was driven right by your house, then you were the last person to be near her . . . except, of course, *him*."

Angela Parker's last minutes of life elapsing only a few hundred yards away from where I was carefully setting out the ingredients for a cake I'd never made before and making a list of long-lost drugstore items that could be mail-ordered from Nebraska. During her short-term captivity on a slippery, fishtailing ride up blizzarding Cloudland, Angela Parker was probably fretting about her children and her husband, who'd long since expected her arrival. Did she wonder or suspect that the ending of her life was merely minutes away? Surely she still hoped something—the murderer's mercy at the very least—would intervene? She could probably feel the blood from the initial stab wounds pooling on the inside of her parka, and the pain that should've radiated from there might have been masked by shock. Anthony surmised that when they reached the orchard, the killer probably carried her like a death bride over a threshold of drifts banked like graves on either side of the road, dug her a shallow tomb in the freshly fallen snow, and laid her down, bleeding.

Mr. Parker resumed, "I try to remember that she helped people, how she was with others, how the nurses who worked at the hospital with her there felt about her. But of course I also . . . I wonder about how afraid she must've been and how much pain she was in, when he . . . when it was happening to her."

"Of course, you would. But now tell me, how are your children doing?"

"Oh . . . my children. They're too young to really get it. I guess that's a good thing."

"I hope it is."

"I've explained everything to them again and again—"

"When you say explain, do you mean—"

"I just tell them that she was taken to heaven. Before her normal time. That it wasn't expected but that sometimes people go there sooner. But of course they keep asking when she's coming back from heaven. And they think Mommy does everything better than I do." He drew in a sharp breath. "So I hear that from them too."

I found myself hating the fact that these tragedies tend to become even more painfully complicated and elaborate in their aftermath.

Mr. Parker went on, "Thing is, when they find him—if they find him—it's not going to make a difference at all to my girls."

"But it will to you."

"And . . . even though I want them to find him, I . . . I don't know if I'm ready to see who this person actually is."

"He stopped being a person a long time ago," I said. "He has less conscience than my animals. He *is* an animal."

"A calculating animal," Mr. Parker said, and then we both fell silent. Then the widower said, "Oh, Mrs. Winslow, I really shouldn't bother you with all my troubles. After all, it must be hard enough, living so close to where she was found."

He was right about that. "Well, it *is* weird and unsettling, but right now I'm thinking how it must be for you."

There was a significant lull before he spoke again. "Do you ever worry that one day he might double back? Back . . . to where you are?"

"Of course I do. I'm alone here, you see. Except for my animals. But if it's the same person who harmed the others, he's never . . . revisited any of the other places."

"Yes, that's true." Then he said, "Mrs. Winslow, maybe I should give this more time. You have your own difficulties to deal with. I . . . I actually feel better now. Sometimes . . . I hope you'll understand this . . . it gets so bad that I start looking for any way to feel better."

"Well, then, if it does again and if you'd feel better talking to me, by all means, call me," I said. "I absolutely mean that."

I gathered the rags drenched with Henrietta's pee dribbles and stepped outside for a moment. My tree peonies were just opening their dense pink pompom blooms. It then occurred to me that when Buddhists say "life is suffering" they don't necessarily mean that one suffers through life, but rather that suffering is what defines life, the pain that equalizes us, the pain that brings us together. I tried to think of all the months that Angela Parker was missing and how despite everything he'd been told that pointed to her demise, her husband felt determined to hold out some hope. Not that it bore any real comparison but I couldn't help thinking after Matthew and I had ended our relationship definitively, in full knowledge of all the reasons why it couldn't and wouldn't work between us, he still told me he went to bed every night hopeful that something would change the climate between us and the relationship would burst back to life.

We just don't want the good things in our life to die, and how and when the death bullet will strike and in what form becomes more and more of a preoccupation. When I think about dying, as I often have, I find myself musing on the forms of death that I could not bear: the slow, crippling shutdown of a body afflicted with Lou Gehrig's disease; being locked in the trunk of a car, and the meld of claustrophobia and bodily cramp and the panicking on how long the unbearable captivity will last, the desperation for any possibility of rescue. Or being high up in an airplane on a fatal journey and having to accept in a matter of moments the smooth glide transmogrifying into a lurching motion, the downward spiral toward a cold and pitiless ocean amid screams—or even the whimpers of those too stunned to cry out. Or a sudden collision on a motorway and the thunderous sounds of braking and colliding, the crystalline crack of shattering glass and the tangle of car wreck, the paralysis, the shock, the hemorrhaging blood. Those who die quickly, unforeseeably, are they given subtle presentiments that soon their light will go out? Did this nurse wake up the morning of her death wearing an inexplicable mantle of sadness?

Were her good-byes to her husband and children tinged with regret? Did she, on the way home from her skiing excursion, driving slowly and carefully through a blizzard, feel an emptiness? Or perhaps in the steady inner warmth of her car humming through the slush and grit of Interstate 91, she, for the last time in her life, indulged herself in a sense of brimming contentment for the family she had waiting for her at home? And what terrible divine intervention had made her choose one rest area as opposed to another in order to make her phone call? What decision sets people to make that fateful turn onto the avenue of their death?

I suddenly felt exhausted and decided I needed a nap, and slowly made my way upstairs. I fell into a deep sleep and awoke disoriented. I didn't even know what time of day it was because I'd drawn the shades. There was something wrenchingly familiar about this and I tried to remember what it was. Ah, of course: those last few days when my husband was dying and Breck and I were taking turns staying up all night with him (she insisted, refusing to sleep or go to school), when I became so weary and fatigued but kept pushing myself. I didn't want the father of my child to be alone with his suffering and was already missing him terribly, lamenting my decision to divorce him. I remember him telling me that as his body got weaker he began recollecting places he'd been to that he hadn't thought of in decades, street corners, single exchanges with people he'd met only once in his life, the fragrance of his mother's face cream.

One afternoon I took a reprieve from the death watch to sit down in my bedroom and inadvertently dozed off. I woke up to a strong burning sunlight intaglioed on my wall, and palpably feeling my husband in the bedroom with me while some voice inside my head kept saying, "I'm almost gone, Catherine, I'm almost gone." And then a split second later Breck calling me into the next room where we watched him take his last, laboring breaths.

More awake now, I wandered back to my earlier conversation with Mr. Parker, suddenly consumed with overwhelming hatred for the evil entity who waylaid his wife off Interstate 91. She was understandably too traumatized to be able to muster up the mettle that might have empowered her against him. And I knew that if this man were to come into my bedroom now, I would summon up my every resource. I'd reach into my night table for the dagger I'd brought back from St. Petersburg, and brandishing it at this murderer of women, of mothers, I'd cut him to his heart.

PART TWO

TEN

A FEW DAYS LATER, in late June, Hiram Osmond took a lie
detector test whose results were inconclusive. A group of
investigators (including Prozzo and Anthony) requested permission to inspect his arsenal of knacker's tools. A tightly organized
cortege of official vehicles drove up Happy Valley Lane and made
the turn onto the three-quarters-of-a-mile-long driveway that
led to a farmhouse dating back to the 1700s and whose founder-
ing, collapsing state was a reflection of the brokenhearted man
who lived there. Knowing they were coming, he'd done little to
prepare for his official visitors, and met them with hands permanently stained and cured from hauling beasts, from rendering
hides hung to dry all over the property, from butchering carcasses for bounties of bones. To their surprise they found ten alpacas, animals usually owned by more affluent people. Milling
in two different enclosures, the white Huacaya have long, elegant
necks and fluffy heads that look extraterrestrial, their large aque-
ous black eyes riveted to each of the visitors' movements.

When Hiram opened his workshop and showed the officials
his tools, they found long, thin knives that closely matched the
description of the weapon that had stabbed all the missing
women. They found grisly rags and blood-tainted garments, shreds

purportedly left behind by his wife and daughter. The detectives asked to collect the knives as well as the ensanguined rags to be tested by Vermont's crime lab in Burlington. The results were hardly surprising to me: the cloth was covered with the blood of steer and alpaca and goats and even dogs.

I decided that it might be best to confront Wade about his lie in Paul's presence. Knowing that they often gardened together in the late afternoon after Wade got off work, I stopped by around five-thirty on a very humid, overcast day.

Both men were wearing sun visors and canvas gloves, bent over and weeding the vegetable patch that had been put in earlier in the spring.

I decided not to waste words and to catch Wade off balance. After approaching and exchanging the necessary pleasantries, I turned to him and said, "So, am I on your side or not?"

He looked puzzled. "Come again?"

Aware that I now had Paul's attention, I continued calmly, "Are you trying to dig yourself into a deeper hole," indicating a patch of freshly spaded ground.

The furrowed look on his face slackened with recognition as it dawned on him what I was referring to. "My personal life is my personal life," he growled.

"Well, no longer, if it's got a bunch of cops and detectives crawling up your ass."

He shook his head with disgust. "I never thought she'd say anything."

"You're being naive, Wade. People cooperate in these sorts of situations because otherwise they fall under suspicion themselves."

"Well, I guess I'm different," he said. "I keep my yap shut whenever possible." In momentary frustration he tossed his trowel a short distance.

"To your own detriment," I remarked.

"What's going on here?" Paul demanded.

I gave Wade a look to mean "Does he know about any of this?" Wade shook his head. "Another brilliant move on your part."

"I'm just full of them, aren't I?"

"Keep it up and you'll find yourself occupying the glorious position of suspect number one."

Wade glowered at the ground. "I don't care anymore, if you want to know the truth."

I let a moment pass and then said, "I don't believe that."

"Let them suspect me."

"What are we talking about?" Paul persisted testily.

"Oh, we're talking about—"

Wade interrupted me and said to Paul, "I lied to the cops about where I was the night of the blizzard."

Paul looked dumbstruck and then managed to ask, "Why?" and "But you said you were at your office. Weren't you? I thought that was already a problem."

Wade barely shook his head. "I was in my office but then I left."

"Where did you go?" Paul's voice croaked.

"Visited a friend of mine in town."

"Who?" Paul said.

"Her name is Hannah."

"Hannah?" Paul said with incredulity. By the befuddled look on his face I could tell the fact that Wade had been with a woman took his adoptive father by surprise as well.

"Before that I was at the office."

"I don't understand why you didn't just tell them where you were," I broke in to keep the conversation on track. "At least somebody would have been able to vouch for your whereabouts."

Wade reminded me that he'd arrived at Hannah's house just after ten-thirty at night, which still would not account for his activities earlier in the evening.

"You're such an idiot," Paul blurted out crossly. "You do things that make no sense to me!" Had Wade perhaps misled Paul about the nature of his sexuality?

"I don't discuss my private life with anybody," he announced.

"No kidding," I said. "Where's all the shame coming from?"

He stared icily at me. "Nothing to do with shame. I'm just not comfortable divulging it."

"Why? We all want intimacy. We all want love."

"If I knew *why* I wouldn't be lying about it."

And it dawned on me that for Wade, lying was a knee-jerk response that went back to his blighted childhood. Unfortunately, as an adult this trait was hardly going to help him to diminish the level of suspicion that he'd already generated. Then it occurred to me that perhaps he was afraid that disclosing any relationship at all might threaten his adoptive father. Maybe he was paranoid that Paul might disinherit him, another subliminal reason why he didn't mention it to me?

Leaving that thorny thought and attempting to ease some of the annoyance they were undoubtedly feeling toward each other, I confided in Paul and Wade, "Well, you're not the only one they're looking into. Remember I told you—"

"Yeah, who is it, anyway," Paul said. "You can tell us."

"Okay, just keep it under your hats. Hiram Osmond." Although both men expressed surprise, they felt this suspicion made sense. I went on to say that Anthony's report of the visit to the farm portrayed Hiram as unnerved to the point of panic.

"I've known him for most of my life," I said. "And I feel bad. I'd like to go and pay him a visit." Turning to Wade with a smirk, I added, "I was thinking you should come with me. Both of you can't be the killer, so I figure that I'll be safe one way or another."

Wade considered the proposal for a moment and then said, "All right."

"How about after work tomorrow," I said.

"That'll be fine."

I picked him up the next day and we began driving along Route 12 toward the Osmond farm in the town of Hartland. It had been raining on and off the entire afternoon and the macadam road had taken on a glaucous sheen. "I have to be honest with you," I said to him. "The news of your affair took me completely by surprise."

He turned to me and I could feel his caustic stare. "How so?"

"I honestly didn't think you were into women."

"Why, because I used to be fascinated by Mother's dress patterns?"

"Not at all," I lied. "We're very good friends and you've never talked about your love life."

"Exactly. So why presume?"

"Because people who don't talk about their love lives usually have something to hide."

"But if I were gay, why would I hide *that*?"

"You might not hide it in a city but you would in a rural area like this. Anyway, *I* think you've sent out lots of mixed signals."

"Not true. I just play my cards close to the vest. And nobody— even Paul—knows me very well in *that* way."

"Clearly," I said, and thought, How sad. "For all I know, you could have children scattered all over the world."

"As if," he said.

We fell into a sullen silence and finally Wade said, "So what's the upshot with Hiram? You said he took the lie detector test."

"It wasn't conclusive."

"Great!" Wade exclaimed, crossing his pale, sinewy arms. "All I need to hear. They'll be asking me to take a lie detector test next. I'm sure I won't do any better."

"If you're so innocent why are you worrying?"

"Isn't Hiram worrying?"

Wade turned toward me, raising his lower lip and nervously

pulling one point of his flimsy mustache into his mouth. "Any kind of test gets me agitated. Even the driver's exam pushed me over the edge . . . and let's face it, I have a permanently guilty conscience left over from all the bad shit I did when I was a kid." He swiped his hand over my dashboard and disdainfully looked at the dust that collected. "Honey, you need to clean this sucker."

"Lay off me, will you?"

Wade burbled something inaudible in response.

We were now following the Ottauquechee River, whose rapids were low and brackish, passing a rope swing hanging from a tall tree high up on a bank. Just as we drove by, a shirtless boy was swaying out in an arc and then caroming into the water. "That brings back memories," Wade said wistfully.

"Good ones?"

"Not really. Getting teased for being scrawny. When kids want to be cruel, they are unmerciful." He reflected for a moment. "They did use to call me 'gay' when I was in high school but only because I didn't play sports or seem to date anybody, although I did." I could feel him glaring at me. "I just didn't brag about it like everybody else did." He cleared his throat. "I just never belonged in this place, in this town. If it weren't for Paul I'd be so gone from here." Then he explained that Paul's main dealer in New York City had recently called to request that Wade take over cataloging the artwork, because Paul, with his dimming short-term memory, kept losing track of his inventory.

"Well, one day you'll inherit everything and . . . the rest needn't be said." I looked over to study his expression.

Wade exhaled sharply. "We'll see. If he doesn't drive me crazy. Like that Prozzo guy who loves to keep in touch. He's like a shadow on my kitchen wall."

"You brought this on yourself by lying, Wade."

"How many times are you going to make your point?" I had nothing to say in response and finally he went on mockingly, "And you know, what the fuck . . . about *Anthony*?"

"What about him?' "

"Where was *Anthony* the night Angela Parker disappeared?"

I glanced over at him. "Claims to have been home with his wife and daughters."

"Convenient, don't you think?"

"I agree. I suppose if it came down to it . . . they could be asked to substantiate his story."

"Yeah, but now they're in North Carolina. Anyway, why did *she* leave if *he* was the one having the affair?"

"I've wondered the same thing. He said she'd been after him to move south. So in one sense he played into her hand." I paused for a moment. "But I concur it *is* rather unusual that a parent just lets their spouse move out of state with the children. There's something—I don't know what it is—about their whole separation arrangement that doesn't add up to me."

"Hiram let *his* wife move out of state," Wade said as we turned into the long dirt driveway of the Osmond farm.

"No, the court granted that. She screwed him."

We went around a bend and were able to finally view a mishmash of fading white outbuildings, connected to one another with awkward Quonset hut–like passageways. We crossed over a brook on a small wooden bridge that groaned under the weight of the car. "God, this place has hardly changed," I said, "from when I was a kid."

"I couldn't tell you because I've never been here. But it certainly looks like the dump that I expected."

"Believe it or not there are beautiful antiques inside. Or were."

Wade looked dubious. "Come on."

"I kid you not. Picture this: dirt floors with good Empire furniture perched on little wooden blocks."

"How many times have you been here?"

"Only a few. People—even Hiram's closest friends growing up—didn't come often. It wasn't exactly a welcoming place, although the parents couldn't have been nicer."

Back in the late seventies Hiram's mother worked as a laundress, and when her husband was out on farm errands with the family's only car, she'd walk a mile or more to pick up and deliver clothing. During the summers when my mother and I would spend July and August in Vermont, often driving we'd come upon Mrs. Osmond walking with bundles strapped to her back and stop to give her a lift. Once when we picked her up, Mrs. Osmond invited me to visit their farm because a pig had been born with two heads.

I was around thirteen at the time. I rode my bicycle down their long dirt driveway and on arrival had to pass through the door of a chicken-wire fence with which the Osmonds surrounded the entire house in order to protect their fowl from predators like fisher cats and coyotes. It was a surreal, bizarre farm: pigs and chickens milling around amongst the carcasses of cows and sheep and horses that were just open-air curing, waiting to be rendered.

On that particular occasion I'd been expecting Hiram to answer the door, but was greeted warmly by Mrs. Osmond, a diminutive woman with onyx-dark eyes who was said to be part American Indian. She ushered me into the parlor, where period antique chairs and tables were positioned on a raked dirt floor. She told me to sit down on a finely brocaded divan. I asked her where Hiram was and a moment later he entered the room grinning ear to ear, clutching a large pickling jar. Inside, maybe eight inches long, floating in formaldehyde, a tan-colored piglet body with two heads was delicately magnified in the solution. I was shocked and frightened by this diminutive monstrosity. "I thought this was going to be alive," I said to them. "I thought we'd be seeing it outside."

"A two-headed pig can't live," Hiram said in a patronizing tone.

I was nevertheless disappointed.

Mrs. Osmond offered me homemade molasses cookies; slightly nauseated by what I'd seen, I politely declined and waited an appropriate amount of time before saying that I needed to get home. Hiram ushered me out, but instead of bringing me in the way I came, he led me through a different entrance. Not ten feet away lay a dead black cow, smelly and festering with huge pink sores and swarming with flies. I stopped, afraid to walk past it. Hiram took my hand and was leading me when suddenly I saw a small young pig scampering out of the cow's belly.

"What's it doing there?" I cried.

"What do you think, it's eating," he said.

"That's really sickening!" Wade exclaimed when I finished telling him the story.

The main section of the two-story 1700s Cape was partially caved in, and a makeshift standing seam gutter had been built to overlay where the roof had collapsed. It was hard to imagine that this jerry-rigged contraption could completely protect the interior from rain or snowmelt. The chicken-wire fence once used to circumscribe the main house had been taken down. The farmyard itself was overgrown with tall, limp grass. There were no live animals wandering around as far as I could see; the place was a lot less chaotic than I remembered it. But then again, this man was living alone now, probably with more time to organize his life. From where we stood we could see several large, dark hides hanging from a clothesline, a collection of enormous femurs leaning against the thick trunk of an ancient, gnarled maple. There was a chemical tang in the air, something both acrid and metallic; I assumed it was whatever substance Hiram used for rendering. Then, on the far side of the property, I spied the alpaca pens and the strange-looking space-age creatures. "I wonder why he's raising those," I said.

"You got to be kidding," Wade said. "It's potentially huge money. But let's not go any farther. I don't want to see anything dead."

Hiram came out a moment later wearing deeply stained tan Carhartt worker pants and a grease-marked T-shirt lettered with

POMFRET PULL, advertising a yearly competition between local teams of oxen. He was tall and lanky and I could tell he probably ate poorly, the bare minimum to sustain the enormous physical labor of ferrying around dead carcasses. As he'd gotten older his bright red hair had darkened to silvery auburn and he wore it long and clasped in a ponytail. He had his mother's exotic-shaped Indian eyes, but they were pale and watery, the eyes of his Welsh father. His face was several days unshaven, his fledgling beard sun-bleached blond.

"Afternoon," he said, stopping a few feet in front of us, as though conscious of the fact that he might reek from working outdoors with dead flesh and probably not showering as frequently as he should. I caught a whiff of his deep and rancid smell. The next thing I knew a calico cat ran into view, leapt on his shoulder and, cradling its body against his neck, began to do that strange kneading foot dance cats do. The cat was glaring at us. "This is Squirrel," he introduced us. "She's protective . . . I guess like a dog. We don't get visitors much."

"At least not until lately," I said, trying to sound sympathetic.

Hiram grimaced and then remarked, "You haven't been up here since we were kids."

"I was just telling Wade . . . about that time."

"When you came to see the two-for-one pig?"

"Yeah."

Very gently, he grabbed hold of the cat and shooed it off his shoulder. Dusting his hands together, he said, "You won't believe it, but I had another like that two-for-one not even three months ago."

I looked around and didn't see any swine. He saw me searching and said, "Dead on arrival. Didn't preserve it this time, though. Just rendered it." He went on to say that he still raised a few pigs but they were penned and kept from roaming and grazing indiscriminately. He smiled, his teeth surprisingly white and straight; his forearms were vascular from all the heavy lifting he did. "It's funny, Catherine," he said, "in all these years since you been here, until the one recently, there hasn't been another two-for-one pig. And then you arrive . . . again. What do you think that means?"

"I think it means maybe I'm a porcine fertility symbol."

Wade guffawed and said under his breath, "Oh my God, here we are getting all woo-woo."

"Don't mind him," I told Hiram. "He's knee-jerk cynical."

"Haven't seen you in a while. " Hiram turned to Wade. "You look the same." Then his expression turned speculative. "You know, I heard somewhere that you were pocketing the money from Paul Winters's paintings."

"You got to be kidding me," I said.

Wade was hardly rankled by the rumor. "The tongue-waggers around here are so desperate that they'll invent something outrageous for their own amusement. It's absolutely not true."

"I didn't think it was," Hiram said. "God knows what the gossip is about me."

Neither Wade nor I said anything in response. A moment later Wade's cell phone rang. He held up his finger, excused himself, and walked several steps away and took the call. I heard him say, "Okay, *all right,* I'll be right there." He returned to us and said, "I have to get back to the office. The tax assessors are meeting right now and there's a problem that only I can solve."

I really dreaded being left alone with Hiram. I said to Wade, "Right away?"

"Seriously. Can I use your car, Catherine?" I bugged my eyes out at him, as though to say, "Don't leave me here." "I really can't stay."

"If you want to take her car I'll drive Catherine home," Hiram offered.

This was the last thing I wanted, but could hardly think of how to alter what seemed to be the most logical plan. With great reluctance I said, "I left the keys in."

You really have no choice, I told myself. Just get through this one and stay calm. This is your childhood friend, after all. Hiram and I watched Wade drive back down the long dirt driveway, my car leaving plumes of dust. The moment it disappeared Hiram turned to me, his face darkened and on the verge of tears. Seeing him in this vulnerable state made me relax a little bit. "I'm getting behind on all my accounts," he said in nearly a whisper. Then, "I don't know why the lie detector said what it said. I was relaxed when I took it. And I told the truth."

"I assume you did," I told him.

"I mean, you're friends with Dr. Waite, who was here with the rest of them. You can vouch for me."

"I already have."

"I might do what I do for a living because I can't do anything else, but I don't kill people one after another."

"Hiram, *I* want to believe you. *I* . . . think you're probably innocent."

"Probably?"

Reckless though it might have been, I made myself say, "Unfortunately, a few things add up against you. You were seen walking on Route Twelve pretty near where Angela Parker's body was dumped. You drive a rig with a certain kind of tire that matches the truck or the SUV that drove up Cloudland. And White River Junction has a record of a history of violence toward your wife."

Hiram's voice grew shrill and angry. "She invented that. The bruises . . . I don't know how she got them. I never hit her. Somebody else obviously did. Whoever it was, she was protecting *him*."

"So you're saying she might have been having an affair?"

He looked skyward for a moment, and when he looked at me again, his expression was hopeless. "She easily could have. I was out all the time working, trying to support her." He began scratching his beard. "I know she grew to hate being here." With a glance around the bizarre farm he murmured, "I guess I don't blame her for that."

"Okay, Hiram," I said, "but listen to me, if your wife arrives at the police station with bruises and marks of beating and, using them as evidence, blames you, it's a tough accusation to refute."

Hiram grew so annoyed he slapped his thighs with both hands. "So then you think I'm lying about this part."

"Let's put it this way, Hiram. I know Celia and the kind of background she came from and that she was a known liar, herself. And I told them, I told Anthony and Prozzo that. But it doesn't matter what I say or what I do or do not believe."

"I keep expecting them to . . . that one day they're just going to show up and cuff me and lead me away."

"One thing you should know, Hiram," I said. "You're not the only one they've got their eyes on. Several other people have been questioned more than just once." I wanted to say Wade but knew I couldn't.

"Jesus, do I wish I'd called a tow truck that night—"

I said, "Also realize they're under pressure from all sides, from the governor to civic organizations . . . to come up with a culprit. People who live up here and are used to leaving doors unlocked all the time are now locking them. I don't know if you've been reading the paper, but they've been warning anybody whose car breaks down not to knock on doors. Because people are afraid and they'll shoot at a shadow, let alone a stranger. They—people who live here—don't realize that in the rest of the world, there are plenty of murderers and thieves and in most places doors have to be kept secured."

This statement seemed to mollify him, if only momentarily. He launched into small talk, asking me about my column and Henrietta, whom he'd met a few times, and even wanted to know how Breck was doing. Then his face brightened. "Can you just stay out here for a minute? I have something for you." This request unsettled me. I didn't want him going inside and leaving me alone; who knew what he might bring back? But then he said, "Something my mom would have wanted you to have," ducking into the farmhouse. He remained there for a while and by the time he reemerged holding a small jar of pickled fiddleheads, I was terribly edgy. "Last batch she made before she died. Still delicious." I had no choice but to politely accept his gift. The brined fiddleheads looked like cochlea blanched to the color of dirty ivory. I didn't even think my Henrietta would be interested in eating them.

A moment later I noticed my car rambling back up the drive-way. Soon Wade pulled up beside us. "Before I got back to the office, the tax people called to say they solved the problem without me. Amazing!"

With great relief I said, "Well, we're done. You can move over. I want to drive my own car."

ELEVEN

THE NEXT EVENING I was sitting on the Waites' porch next to Emily's greenhouse, watching fireflies and luna moths hurling themselves against the screens. Despite the considerable heat, Anthony was wearing a long-sleeved cambric shirt. The drone of the insects was rowdy in comparison to the hush within the house: by now Emily and the girls had been gone for weeks, and with them gone was the din of chattering siblings and clattering pots and the sluicing of tap water. What, without the arguments about conflicting schedules, disputes over school permissions and sleepovers, and wrangles over whether or not to give in and buy a certain pair of designer blue jeans that all the girls at school seemed to be wearing, does a man like this do with his now voluminous free time, when he's solely occupying a house once inhabited by a family of four? I assumed he plunged more deeply into his love affair with Fiona Pierce.

Did he think I disapproved of this new relationship, a palimpsest over his doomed marriage? Was this why Anthony had been using the investigation as an excuse for his busy schedule? Lately I'd seen Fiona's green Volkswagen Beetle scurrying up and down Cloudland Road at all hours of the day and night. Meanwhile, the one time I'd spoken to Emily in North Carolina she sounded positively cheerful, filling me in on how she and the children were spending the summer, their tours of North Carolina's coastal areas and school enrollments for the autumn semester.

I was also determined to find out why Anthony so easily agreed to his children living in another state, something any compassionate family court judge would have forbidden.

I'd brought him a jar of sun tea and sprigs of fresh mint, and was happy to see that he was keeping up with the considerable gardening that was required by all the perennial beds of delphinium and phlox and mallow and echinacea Emily had planted when they first arrived on Cloudland five years ago. Sipping out of a tall plastic glass, he remarked that it had been nearly seven months since Angela Parker had been abducted.

"I keep hoping our murderer decided to retire ahead of the game."

Anthony shook his head. "No such luck. The vast majority of serial killers can't stop themselves. They're predatory, like lions who kill and get sleepy and content until they go hungry again."

He was looking out over the expanse of his just-mown fields, strewn with pinwheel bales of hay that resembled runes on a trestle table. The sky above us was a dimming chalky blue and the clouds streaking across it looked dense and corrugated, ponderous with moisture. "I think we'll probably see something from him fairly soon," he mused as though predicting a tempest.

I swatted a green-headed fly that was dive-bombing me. "That's comforting to know." How could he be so sure, I wondered.

With his fingers, Anthony carefully combed the hair off his forehead and tilted his head back and let loose a groaning sigh. "I detest this heat," he said. "We never used to get heat like this . . . where I grew up in New Brunswick."

"There's something called a short-sleeved shirt."

"I actually keep cooler this way."

"Must be a Canadian or English practice," I said, and then reminded him the newspapers were claiming this summer the

Eastern United States was more acutely affected by global warming than the rest of America. He nodded and wondered aloud if up in Canada they were enduring heat to the same degree.

"Speaking of feeling heat," I said, "I saw Hiram yesterday. Did you get enough blood samples?"

"Yeah. We took samples everywhere we could find them."

I waited for a few moments and then said, "He's sick over the fact that the lie detector didn't clear him."

Anthony pulled his shirt away from his body and flapped it so that some air could get in. "You believe his story?"

"I don't think he's a killer. And he swears up and down that he didn't beat his wife."

"That's the problem right there. I saw the photos of his wife. She looked pretty battered. Who else could've done it?"

"Somebody she was having an affair with, he claims," I said, watching for any change of expression on Anthony's face.

He looked dubious. "You know this kind of denial is older than the hills. Nice, sweet guys who keep it all in until they can't contain it anymore and let loose on the person closest to them."

"I understand that, but I've known Hiram a long time."

"Means nothing. Love brings out the worst in people. Love is war." He glanced over at me in a scrutinizing way. "As you well know. All due respect, I don't think you've seen enough profiles of killers who began their murdering careers by beating their wives."

"Or profiles of wife-beaters who don't go on to commit murders. But okay," I said. "Point made. However, even if he drives to the places where some of these women have disappeared, he's on such a tight schedule. Always hauling some dead beast from one place to another. Would he really have the time to spend trolling for victims, not to mention having a dead cow or horse in the back of the pickup truck?"

"He makes his own schedule, Catherine. He never got that frozen cow he was supposed to haul away," Anthony reminded me.

"But that was during a blizzard."

"Precisely, a blizzard and an excellent opportunity to abduct a woman making a phone call at a deserted rest area." Anthony pinched his shoulders together and looked at me wearily. "Gut-wise I don't get an all-clear on him, Catherine. And I don't think you do either. You just don't want the killer to be somebody you know and like. And who could blame you there?

"But let's put this all in perspective for a moment. . . . Do you know how many people we've questioned and have asked to take polygraph tests?" I probably looked bored. "I could give you a round number. Let's say we've questioned one hundred people in the Upper Valley, four of whom were asked to submit to the polygraph."

"Anybody else I know?"

"No, thank goodness."

"You've really questioned one hundred people?"

Anthony explained that something about each person matched up with some significant detail common to all the serial murders. It could be as simple as a man convicted to five years in prison for stabbing his wife, or a man accused but never proven guilty of strangling his girlfriend, or even a few men who stopped their cars at rest areas and unsuccessfully tried to lure women into them.

"And of course there are the known psychological histories of some of these people. If a once-convicted felon ever told some prison psychologist about being severely beaten by a parent, we check him out. If he ever confessed or implied that he hated or attacked women or presented a history of impotence, then we consider interrogating him."

I wondered, "Did you ever consider that instead of a local, it's just some flatlander? Somebody who came to the north country and made it his business to memorize all the old dirt roads with their ninety-degree turns and switchbacks, even the roads that lead to nowhere?" Somebody such as himself, I thought, now living alone.

"I consider everything."

"Every time I try to imagine who this person might be, I always come up blank."

The silence that followed seemed curiously long. Anthony decided to move on. "And now that you know Wade lied the way he did, what do you think of that?"

I grumbled, "How do *I* know about Wade? He's so mysterious and cagey. So how can *I* be objective? What I *do* know is law-abiding people often lie because they're petrified of being falsely accused. When I was working for newspapers we'd always come across these situations during a murder investigation."

Anthony nodded in agreement. Some distinct birdsong caught my attention. I glanced at my watch and saw that the time had gotten on to seven-thirty in the evening. "Do you hear that?" I said. "The wood thrush?"

Anthony tilted his head back, trying to detect the warbles amidst the dissonance of avian chatter.

"There it is again," I said. "Hear it?"

"I think so," he said, bringing his head forward again. "But not clearly."

"All this . . . music is what I love about Vermont summers."

Anthony glanced toward the empty blue house. "Hey, I've always loved living here. Obviously, it's a lot harder now."

Noting his sadness, I asked, "So, besides Hiram, besides the other four suspects you mentioned, have there been any other leads?"

"Just that homicide up in Burlington."

He was referring to the murder of a college coed abducted in the streets of Vermont's largest city at one o'clock in the morning. But she'd been sexually assaulted in a brutal way before she was killed, so there was really no strong forensic link to the women murdered in the River Valley.

Knowing he'd reached a momentary dead end, Anthony now explained that, in search of more information, he'd revisited the assault on Marjorie Poole, the drug-using potter attacked outside her studio who escaped with a stab wound. Knowing that she had been high on Vicodin and cocaine and alcohol during the attempt on her life, Anthony had taken it upon himself to try to improve her drug-hazed recall by hypnotizing her. He'd managed to regress her back to the night of her attack and suddenly she's standing in the doorway of the refurbished mill, bleeding, watching her assailant, bent over the stab wound she inflicted on him, staggering away to an old Ford Rambler, a vehicle whose tires do not match the tire marks found near the orchard where Angela Parker perished.

She's reliving the aftermath, standing outside in subzero temperatures, her breath billowing into dense freezing vapors, her nostrils crystallizing, and trying hard to read the license number.

Anthony naturally asks her to take her time, to let numbers float into focus, and she frowns and squeezes her eyes shut and finally comes up with a New Hampshire plate and the letter "R." Then three numerals, 8,9,2, and she sounds certain, definitive. And Anthony is thinking this could be a real break in the case, even if she misidentified the make of the car, they can plug the numbers into the New Hampshire system—even into the Vermont and Massachusetts systems. However, when they scanned the motor vehicle data of all three states, there was no exact match to the plate, and the close contenders were cars a lot newer than an old Ford Rambler—a BMW X5, a Saturn Vue, a Cadillac Escalade. And when a search was run on the car owners, none were linked to any prior criminal offenses.

"A Ford Rambler is not exactly a common car," Anthony said.

"Maybe Marjorie Poole once knew a Ford Rambler. And her memory of it barged into her hypnotic state."

Anthony frowned. "I can see the value you place on hypnosis. But it has been very helpful solving crimes."

And I realized I wasn't skeptical of hypnosis, but rather just skeptical of the idea of resurrecting Marjorie Poole's testimony.

"But more to the point, a Ford Rambler, being a two-wheel drive, could not possibly have made it up Cloudland."

"There were some four-wheel-drive models made, but few and far between and sold mostly on the West Coast, California in particular," Anthony pointed out.

"Whereas those gas-guzzling SUVs are as common as street trash."

Whatever it was, the vehicle had to have been able to make it up our road during that storm—presuming, Anthony said, that I actually did hear somebody barreling up the road long before the plow. I glared at him and he glared back at me and said, "Well, you weren't so sure when Detective—"

"I'm certain now!" I snapped. "One way or another I hear and see everybody and everything. I see people coming and going. I see Emily. And I've seen *Fiona*. Plenty of times."

A tight smirk tuned itself on Anthony's face and he sat back in his chair, gripping the handles. "So why haven't you just come out and asked me?" he said at last with a bit of irritation.

"Maybe because I believed in you and Emily as happily married, a paradigm for my own fucked-up romantic life."

Anthony chuckled cynically.

I couldn't help being a little catty. "But Fiona . . . she's so white bread."

"You're not exactly an exotic, yourself," he said with a bit of stridence.

"Well, you and I—we're not having an affair!"

Anthony's expression was momentarily dazzled with anger.

"Look," I told him, "it's not my intention to ask you what or when or how. I just want to know why?"

"Why does any relationship end, Catherine?" he implored me. "Or begin, for that matter?"

"Often because there is somebody else in the picture," I said. "So what's your excuse?"

Anthony took a moment to compose himself before continuing. "Okay, point taken. So let's look at the situation. In a forensic sort of way. Here's a woman, my wife, with a secure university job in nearby New Hampshire. She separates from me, wants to give up her *job* and move to North Carolina to be with her family. Why such an upheaval?"

"So hurt by the fact that you were having an affair that she just had to get out of here."

"Usually the person who's having the affair is the one to move out, right?"

"My thoughts exactly. Maybe you stayed because the land came through your family. And she wanted to move anyway."

"Did it ever occur to you that *she* might have been having an affair?"

Blindsided, I stared at Anthony. "So then you were both having affairs?"

"My affair, as you know through the grapevine, is relatively new. Whereas Emily has been involved now for at least a year and a half."

"With somebody in North Carolina?"

"Yes."

"Somebody she met visiting her family, or at a conference?"

"The latter."

"So who is he? Another academic."

"Bingo, you're hired."

I stared at him, gobsmacked. Anthony chuckled flatly, jostling his legs up and down, and leaned back in his deck chair.

"Emily didn't want me to tell you. I had to respect her wishes."

"Why was she embarrassed? Especially with me, of all people."

"You'll have to ask her why."

I stared fixedly at him. "And you have somebody, yourself."

Anthony looked aggrieved. "But I *didn't* for a long time. And I had to live day to day with somebody I loved who fell in love with somebody else. And stopped making love to me. And was very open about her feelings for this other guy, who I can't deny is great-looking."

"How old is he, do you know?"

"I believe he's two years younger than she is."

"And so what about Fiona?"

"Fiona is great, don't get me wrong."

With that, he looked back at the two-hundred-year-old house lacking its family, creaking with aged timbers settling on its foundation, mute with lack of life and activity. "But Fiona is one person, she's not a family. I miss my girls. It's so quiet in there now. . . . I can't get used to it. That's why I stay out all the time. That's one of the reasons why I've thrown myself into this investigation."

There was a gnawing silence during which I decided to be conciliatory. "You know," I said, "it's not like *I* haven't been in your position before. When *I* was married. And my husband started an affair. And then I had one."

"Exactly. I know you understand."

"Now that you've bothered to explain everything to me."

Anthony looked impatient. "Like I said, it was *her* decision to keep *her* relationship private. And mine too, because of the obvious embarrassment." He slapped at a mosquito that had landed on his wrist.

And then I recalled my visit to the Waites the morning Anthony was making pancakes for his daughters, who sat obediently at the dining table, drawing pictures while I was reflecting on what Granny had once said about him and his cruelty.

"I have to admit. I never thought that separating would be more Emily's decision than yours because . . . of something I just happened to remember Granny saying about you."

Anthony frowned. "Your granny was certainly opinionated, I'll give her that."

"She told me you were capable of cruelty. And I guess I made assumptions about yours and Emily's breakup . . . do you happen to know what I'm referring to?"

He looked positively stricken. "I think so."

I waited for him to continue.

"During med school I fell in love with another student who was doing research on the Ebola virus in a lab in Toronto. She caught the illness. Almost died. Then ended up blind in both eyes."

For some reason I thought of Dickens's Esther Summerson. "Did you leave her?"

He nodded. "After her illness she kept trying to talk me out of the relationship . . . now I realize she did it because she was afraid I'd leave her and wanted to at least have a hand in it. So things ended and she was . . . devastated." Anthony's voice quavered and tears flashed in his eyes.

I pondered his story for a moment and then I said, "Well, at face value it does make you sound cruel. But those situations are really hard. I can understand choosing not to marry her. And you were so young."

Anthony was momentarily too choked up to speak. Finally he said, "I've carried the guilt with me. Especially because she never met anybody else and still lives with her parents in Nova Scotia. And so when this whole thing happened with Emily I just figured it was payback."

I took this in and then said, "So you really loved Emily?"

"I *still* love Emily," he said just as a brigade of cyclists dressed in colorful spandex suddenly appeared, climbing the steep grade of Cloudland Road in a tight pack, their panting bursts of conversation preceding them.

TWELVE

WHEN I GOT HOME FROM ANTHONY'S that evening, before listening to the messages I scanned the list of calls that had come in: one from Burlington and the other Boston. The Burlington one was accompanied by the name Nan O'Brien, a name familiar to me but which I couldn't immediately place. When I began playing the message I realized this was the clairvoyant the Burlington police had consulted regarding the abducted coed who was murdered in a rocky gorge, as well as the young student who'd mysteriously gone missing at Middlebury College at the same time that Angela Parker disappeared. The message was very simple. "I am Nan O'Brien. I work to find missing people. I need to speak to you about something in particular. If you could call me I'd appreciate it." She left a number. It was nine-thirty in the evening, too late by Vermont standards to make a phone call, but my curiosity got the better of me.

"Hello, Catherine Winslow," answered a smoky voice. "I had a feeling it might be you."

Did she have caller ID? "I hope it's not too late."

"I'm a late one," she said.

"Your message intrigued me," I said. "How can I—"

"No, how can *I*?" she interrupted. "I've been having this vision over and over. A vision about you. And a book that you're trying to find. Does that have any meaning at all?"

"There *was* a book I was trying to find, but I found it."

"Oh, well then I guess I'm a bit late. This can happen."

"Late but at least not incorrect." I hesitated. "I don't believe in psychic phenomena but I will say this is pretty interesting. Funny thing is that I recently read about you working with the police."

"Trying to. With the Middlebury boy, nobody is really listening to me."

"So you have a theory as to what happened to him?"

There was a pause. "I'd rather not go into it, especially over the phone. Because it's not exactly a straightforward theory. I get this information, but I don't interpret it, necessarily. Anyway, I would love to meet you sometime. I'm a huge fan of your column."

"That might be something to hold against you."

She laughed heartily. "Well, I read you for pure pleasure. Your hundred-year-old recipes. Those sachets that keep mice away. But I will confess to you that I am a *terrible* housekeeper. I did try one of your recipes, though, a caramel sheet cake that was sent, I believe, by a reader out in Texas."

"Well, believe it or not, I'm not the greatest housekeeper myself. My daughter will vouch for that."

There was a short pause and then she said, "Look, I know you found the body. I read about it in the *Burlington Free Press.* If I was right about the book, I'd like to help you figure out who did it."

I felt suddenly woozy. "What makes you think *I'm* trying to solve it?"

"I just assumed you were. You're a journalist, right?"

I laughed. "Sort of."

"I'd offer to drive down to you, but I hurt my foot going on the search for the woman who was murdered in Burlington. I fell between some rocks when we were sweeping Huntington Gorge."

I was intrigued and suddenly got an idea. "The *Valley News*. They've been bugging me to do something else for them. I've gotten out of the habit of doing profiles, but maybe I can do one on you."

"I'm not really looking for publicity," the woman said. "I just would like to chat and possibly contribute."

"Why not try and make it official?" I suggested.

"Okay. As long as you don't mind trekking up here."

The caller from Boston had left no message. But just after ten P.M. the phone rang and the same number flashed again. I stared at it, at first determined not to answer any unidentified person, but then with the sense that it was a wireless call I felt an eerie compulsion to pick up.

I had no idea how I'd react when I finally heard from him. I guess it hardly surprised me when tears started and I had trouble speaking.

"Hey, it's okay, its okay," he said gently. "Sorry I surprised you."

"I thought you promised not to call me until . . ." was all I could say under the pressure of the moment.

"I've been worried."

Baloney, I thought.

"I'm here now at my parents' cabin. I arrived yesterday."

"When did you get back from Thailand again?"

"In April."

Two months before he'd written to announce his return and to wonder how I was doing after having found a murdered woman. I thought I could hear him stretch, or imagined him stretching. "So why are you calling me now?"

"I've been wanting to for ages. I have a feeling you've probably been through a difficult time."

Not nearly as difficult as the time I went through with you, I thought. "When I got your birthday letter I didn't know what to think."

"So I guess you know what's coming next."

I did, but said nothing.

"It's been over two years. I'm different now. In control of my life. I'm working pretty steadily. I have friends. You have nothing to worry about."

"I should not be alone with you, Matthew."

"I'll bring someone, Catherine, if that makes you feel easier, but who shall I bring?"

"Google 'rent-a-chaperone.' I'm sure there's a branch office in Boston."

He guffawed. "God, I've missed that humor. I've missed you so fucking much. Have you even missed me?"

I felt it would be wrong and encouraging to confess my terrible loneliness and how, plagued by the specter of the relationship, I still dreamed about him. So I said nothing.

"Look," he said. "I'm up here for a bit. I can get there in no time. Just say *when*."

Nothing in my head seemed to be stirring. "I need to think, Matthew. I need to get my wits around the idea. Please don't call me or come here until you hear from me? Can you at least promise me that?"

There was an anxious silence and finally he said, "I guess if I have to. Yeah, I promise."

"One way or another I'll call you within a few days."

"In a few days . . . you swear?" he persisted in the manner that used to unnerve me.

"I've got to get off the phone now," I said, and told him goodbye.

My students all knew that I liked to have lunch at the bar of a certain tavern in downtown Burlington that served good pub food. Usually I took a copy of *The New York Times,* read it in its entirety, judging the articles, feeling bitterly competitive with some of my former colleagues whom I'd worked with at various magazines, dreaming about resurrecting my flatlined career as a journalist that had reached its peak when I wrote a well-regarded op-ed piece about my experience with Breck's anorexia, something that generated bushels of compassionate mail. The burst of notoriety came at a price, however; Breck grew so furious at me for writing about her "disorder" that she barely spoke to me for six months. The *Times* continued to solicit me for mother/daughter articles and opinion pieces. Concerned about maintaining my relationship with Breck, I was forced to turn them down. The editors finally stopped calling.

One day, I was at my favorite tavern nibbling on a hamburger that had gone cold due to my rapt enjoyment of a friend's absolutely brilliant two-thousand-word piece on a professional tennis player when I felt somebody standing next to me. Matthew had shown up at the restaurant wearing an expensive-looking pressed white shirt with fine ribbing, tight jeans, and with his hair pulled back into a small hipster-like ponytail.

"What brings you here?" I said to him congenially.

"Months of waiting," he said slowly and clearly.

"Months of what?"

He looked at me fixedly and almost seemed a bit impatient. "May I sit next to you?"

"Sure, but I need to know what this is about."

"I don't see how I can be any more obvious."

I was afraid of this. The anger was rising but I willed myself calm. "Oh, you certainly can, Matthew, you're my . . . student."

"Former student," he corrected me emphatically.

"What's happening here?"

He sat down next to me, his leg just barely brushing up against mine. "I . . . I . . . I have this thing for you. I've had it ever since our first conference."

I moved my leg away from his, cursing myself for not trying harder to get rid of him early during the autumn semester.

"Matthew. Not only am I your professor, I'm at least fifteen years older than you."

"That's hardly anything," he said. "You wouldn't be thinking twice about it if the man were older."

I agreed that the older man/younger woman scenario was more usual. "Because not all, but many women don't want to be involved with men a lot younger. Too much of a risk for them."

"For some women I suppose it is," he agreed. Leaning a tad closer to me, Matthew went on. "So have you ever been involved with a younger guy?"

"I don't like this conversation."

"Please," he said. "Just talk to me about this. That's all I ask."

"Then quit leaning over me. Sit in your chair properly." He straightened up. I took a moment to calm down, trying to recall when I was his age, full of my own exaggerated self-confidence and swagger, the years when I was still emotionally unbroken. "I guess it depends on what you mean by younger. A few years, yes. More than a decade, definitely no."

I was aware of the wonderful angular cast of his jaw and that his face, often prone to acne, was for once clear. His shirt slightly yet deliberately unbuttoned, the fabric resting against his tanned, youthful skin. And I think I must've shaken my head because he said, "What's wrong?"

"I'm practically old enough to be your mother."

"First of all, my mother is way older than you. Second of all, I look older than my age and you look younger. If we were walking down the street together, nobody who saw us would think twice. So sue me for liking . . . mature women."

"I always think it's messy when professors get involved with their students. That's why I've avoided it for the five years I've been here."

"But I'm a former student. A consenting adult who graduates in two months."

"Call me up when you graduate." This was part audacity and still part brush-off.

And yet despite myself, I'd cracked open the door, admitting a sliver of light.

Matthew paused, dazzled by it. "I would have waited, but I just can't any longer."

"Wait for what, Matthew?"

Fixing his large, glossy, chestnut-colored eyes on me, he took a nervous, fluttering breath and spoke. "To tell you that you're inside my head." He floundered for a moment. "All the time. I know it sounds corny, but that's the only way I can describe it."

"It doesn't sound corny as much as it sounds worrisome."

"Don't worry, just try and get to know me."

"Get to *know* . . . you're really out of order here!" I snapped.

At first he recoiled from the impact of the words, but then, undeterred, dared to reach forward and put a roughened hand (probably from playing hockey) over mine and squeeze boldly. He shivered and I somehow knew that he couldn't help himself. It was a movement that seemed to have its own inevitability, its own sense of itself. While I worried that, at the bar of a restaurant I often frequented, we'd be seen by somebody who knew one or both of us, I felt completely disarmed by it, the way I did in class, the day he leaned back in his chair and stretched and I found my-self unable to admonish him to sit properly. His hand was large and there were a few dark hairs on the top of it. I merely stared at it, admiring without trying to dislodge it. And heard myself say as though from a great distance, "What are you doing, Matthew?"

"Just take me home with you, now," he whispered, trembling.

"I can't do that," I said in a not-very-convincing manner. "It's wrong."

"You have no idea if it's wrong until you see what it is."

And then something just gave way. In full knowledge of the risk I was taking, I couldn't find it in myself to rebuff him anymore. I'd been struck and conquered by how single-minded he was; no one since my late husband had been so sure of himself in what he desired, in what he demanded. All my protective sarcasm fell away like scaffolding. "Just like that," I said. "And then . . . what?"

Softly yet resolutely, he said, "I have a much better idea of all this than you do."

"What idea?" I said. "Wait a minute. Don't you have a girlfriend?"

He shook his head. "I was dating a girl for a while when I was taking your class. There's nobody really in my life now. Except possibly you," he said.

"I don't think you hear what you're actually saying."

And then he did the craziest, boldest thing. He touched me in a zone on the back of my neck that nobody but my philandering husband had discovered, the place that made every concern melt away. And at the time I think I must have equated the two men; caught up in the moment, perhaps, I was also afraid of what could certainly turn out to be the inevitable rejection.

And after I allowed Matthew to follow me home, to lead me upstairs to my own bedroom and shuck off his shirt with a single bold movement, after I closed my eyes for a moment because his body, though obviously young, was powerful and manly, I knew that I'd ventured too far out into the current and there was no returning to any pillar of safety.

And it was all compounded, heightened even, by the fact that he was trembling. At first I thought his nerves were making him cold, but then realized something was wrong and asked.

"I'm great. I'm fine." He seemed embarrassed suddenly. "I just get this way . . . remember how I wrote for you about having meningitis when I was a kid?"

I nodded.

"Well, whenever I get nervous, my hands and sometimes my chest begin to shake." For somebody who appeared so strong and forceful, he suddenly looked utterly vulnerable. And this touched me. My momentary pity for him changed into fascination. I was nearly able to forget my fear that he'd find me, a woman fifteen years older, less attractive with my clothes off; and to his credit, he was somehow able to sense this insecurity swirling within my hesitation. "No, no, no," he murmured in an almost paternal way. "You don't understand. Just let me," unbuttoning my shirt, then reaching behind and unclasping my bra and letting my breasts fall into his roughened hands. He was so gentle with them; feeling them, looking at them, he let out a pent-up groan, then looked at me, eyes sparking with fire. "You'll never . . . understand how for so long I've wanted to do this. I just never believed I'd ever get to." He sounded close to tears.

His jittery intensity was overwhelming and I felt somehow I had to dispel it. "I get the distinct feeling that you've done this sort of thing before. Seduced much older women."

He smiled and, shaking his head, continuing to caress me, said, "No. This is the first time."

We were together for two hours, our lovemaking veering between the slaking of pure hunger to interludes of erotic gentleness where we just stroked each other, marveling. In the end I rested my head against his chest and felt his strength and listened to the steady thumping of his heart. I sensed many things about him: a kindness yet an impetuousness, but also clearly an obsessive desire that made sense in a child of such (as he described it in the essay he wrote for my eyes only) remote parents. This provoked a tenderness in me, the impulse to try and heal all wounds, the wounds of wounded children, but also a wariness that was compounded by the ache of my own loneliness that had persisted since my husband died and throughout the intervening years, during my many brief relationships with men. Rearing up like a monster with a mind of its own was the clenching anxiety of desire that feeds on physical contact, while killing the appetite, destroying the ability to concentrate, requiring a daily druglike fix of the other person in some form or another. Did I really want this?

And what unlocked things between us even further was his remarkable self-confidence in lovemaking; our bodies fit together perfectly, and just as he'd inadvertently shown in the restaurant with his fingers grazing the back of my neck, time and again he divined exactly where to touch me—on the base of my spine, on the inside of my thigh, lightly and confidently nuzzling my cheek—that brought on a crush of emotion. I was the older woman but I had little to teach this twenty-four-year-old about sex. Thrilling though it was, it was also disconcerting, the compelling force of our physical love. I would battle against it, as well as his tenacity, throughout the entire relationship.

And when we were done that afternoon, we lay there holding hands, gazing at the ceiling, silent. I was stunned by the immensity of what had just happened. It was as though a cyclone had sucked us up into its funnel and dropped us into another country, into a place where there were no simple answers to our questions, where there were no paths leading away from a center of chaos and recklessness. All I could see before me was a landscape that promised the great possibility of pain. And so I was mustering the courage to say it was a wonderful afternoon but that it could never happen ever again, when Matthew turned to me. "Remember what I told you at the restaurant."

I thought I did but still asked him to be specific.

"When I said I knew more about this than you did."

"Well, I was just going to say that—"

He put his finger gently over my lips. "You are so, so beautiful," he said.

"Oh, come on!" How could he possibly mean this?

"Don't second-guess me. You're it for me. Just take what I'm saying. And believe me."

And I did believe him and I fell in love with him, the sort of dark, disturbing love that cuts deeper than anything and in so doing becomes its own justification.

THIRTEEN

E ARLIER THIS YEAR, around the time Angela Parker vanished, an eighteen-year-old freshman named Timothy Marek
disappeared from the campus of Middlebury College. An Arizona
boy who'd been spending January break at the school, living in
one of the residence halls that remained open during the holidays,
he went for an afternoon stroll and never returned. The article I
read about him in the *Valley News* called him "studious" and "re-
liable"; it claimed he was an avid lacrosse player who was tall and
lanky and had a palm tree tattooed on his left shoulder. After he
vanished one student came forward and said he'd been drinking. The possibility of his leaving town was quickly ruled out; the
bus that stopped in Middlebury en route to Albany did not pick
up anybody matching his description. Townspeople and shop-
keepers along Route 7 were queried about whether or not they'd
noticed anybody hitchhiking, and nothing out of the ordinary
was reported.

January temperatures are the most frigid of the year in Vermont, and the night Marek was gone the thermometer dipped
down well below freezing. As the next few days passed in an arc-
tic aura, the sleepy New England college town held prayer vigils
in churches, in huddled gatherings around bonfires, beseeching

the wintry fates to return him unharmed. In a small town the misery of an unexplained disappearance infects the mood of everyone. Both college students and schoolchildren woke up to nightmares of violence and abduction, and counseling centers were set up to help the distressed. Adult citizens reported feeling lethargic and unusually depressed, seasonal affective disorder notwithstanding; they were haunted by the idea of a young man with his life before him ripped out of small-town reality. Meanwhile, the police infiltrated the campus, interviewing people who'd had contact with Timothy Marek, meticulously combing through his clothing and belongings, questioning the skeleton crew of workers who maintained the boilers and the dining halls and the empty academic classrooms during the coldest band of winter. The available students who'd remained on campus (and some who'd received the dean's mass e-mail and cut short their winter holiday) and staff joined together with the townspeople into organized search parties, scouting the woods and riverbanks and snowmobile trails. Banners were draped in the center of town, COME HOME, TIM. WE LOVE YOU, TIM. One of his closest friends confided to the police that Marek had spoken of finding a cheap airfare to go and see Salzburg Cathedral, but neither his bank account nor his credit card (attached to his parents' account) was drawn down by the price of a plane ticket.

Then the January blizzard that buried the body of Angela Parker arrived and dropped two feet of snow. The alarm and hysteria only intensified as the natural barrier of winter made detection more difficult for the search dogs and for the rescue parties.

The FBI sent a few of its field officers to try to determine whether or not Marek might have fallen prey to the group of people marauding around North America, stalking college campuses for students whom they abducted, murdered, and mutilated, burying the remains in densely forested areas. In the case of each of these crimes a grafitto of a smiley face was painted in yellow on a building or a tree somewhere near where the abduction occurred. Soon enough a smiley face was found emblazoned on a fluted metal warehouse on the outskirts of Middlebury. When that news hit, Middlebury people who never locked their doors bought deadbolts, and the most liberal-minded, anti-gun citizens went out and purchased rifles. Unfortunately, due to the harsh extremities of the weather, the forensic experts claimed it was difficult to determine whether or not the paint of this particular smiley face dated back before Marek himself had disappeared.

He'd been missing since winter and here it was the end of June.

An eight-by-eleven photostat of his Facebook shot was plastered on the clairvoyant's refrigerator: a look of intelligence in golden-green eyes behind rimless glasses; a long narrow face that reminded me a bit of the actor John Carradine. Nan O'Brien was watching me studying Marek's photograph and then pointed to her arm. "See these goose bumps? That's because he's nattering at me right now. He won't stop talking."

"What's he saying?" Anthony, who was standing behind us, asked with a tone of slight skepticism.

She turned to him. "The usual. Just 'find me, find me'. . . . You have no idea. He is so insistent."

After I'd spoken to Nan O'Brien that first time, I contacted the *Valley News*. Explaining how she'd been working with the Burlington police to find missing people, I pitched the idea of writing a profile and managed to get an assignment. When Anthony heard how she'd helped locate the woman recently murdered in Burlington, he asked if he could accompany me on my first interview. And so together we'd driven one hour north to the shores of Lake Champlain and the largest city in Vermont.

Nan O'Brien is a woman in her late forties with soulful eyes, shoulder-length wheat-colored hair, her movements soft and graceful and exuding a peaceful intensity. She was wearing a gauzy top and loose black cotton pants, her exposed neck adorned tastefully with simple silver-and-enamel jewelry. She invited us to come into her living room, offering us places on a cushy sectional couch. Her injured foot was wrapped in a red Ace bandage and she limped along and sat down on the edge of the sofa and arranged it so her leg was propped up on a large cushion.

Notebook and pen in hand, I began. "So, Timothy Marek, do you think he was murdered?"

Leaning back against the couch, she shook her head. "No. My sense is there was a mishap, he fell down and died of exposure."

"So what about the smiley face?"

"My sense is some kids did that," she said, making a brushing-off gesture with her hands. "And are too afraid to come forward."

I realized that I was getting ahead of myself. "Let's just backtrack for a moment, shall we. . . . How did you begin all this work? Have you always done it? Or was there something specific?"

"I've always had visions. But it wasn't until I was living in Briarcliff Manor, just outside New York City, and heard on the news that a . . . twenty-one-year-old kid living in Fort Greene, Brooklyn, disappeared. I was watching it on television and then out of the blue, I get this vision of his body underneath the Verrazano Bridge. The vision repeated itself. Eventually I began hearing his voice, too, telling me that he was down there and that's where the searchers should look for him. I wanted to contact the authorities but didn't. Then a few days after this a tugboat passing under the bridge saw something. A bright orange tennis shoe floating along; he was wearing it when he was last seen. They started searching for him and eventually found his body in the shoals around the bridge. It was after that that I began offering my help."

"How many years ago was that?"

Nan swept the hair out of her face. "Around fifteen." Seeing that I was scribbling frantically, she paused. "How come you didn't bring a tape recorder?"

I told her I listened more carefully when I knew I had to take notes by hand, adding, "This practice, it's not for everybody. Anyway, so how exactly do you work now? What's the method?"

"Well, like I said, the first stage for me is like daydreaming. About missing people. The daydream or vision occurs at least twice before I pick up the phone and contact the authorities. I sometimes will call the families, depending on their request for help." She frowned. "I don't like to call myself a psychic, and please don't refer to me as one in your article. I call myself an intuitive counselor."

"Gotcha," I said.

"The point is, the missing dead always want to be found. You'd think it would no longer matter to them, that they'd naturally be drawn to higher realms, but they're concerned about the living, who are searching for them. They keep appearing in dreams to anybody who has the ability to perceive them." She paused for a moment and then said to me, "The woman you found, Catherine, for two months I kept seeing her, hearing her. I can show you the notes I made on my computer. I saved them so that the date shows electronically and nobody can say I filled it in later. You probably don't know this but she disappeared within a few days of Marek, so for a while I was getting stereo."

"May I ask a question?" Anthony intervened.

"Ask away," Nan said with a gracious smile.

"Angela Parker, how exactly did you see her in your . . . vision?"

Nan pondered for a moment and, sighing, said, "She appears to me swimming in a lake of snow, drifting through it. . . ." Her face scrunched up as she tried to extract the memory. "It's like she's weightless, and she looks really purposeful. To materialize like this requires a tremendous amount of paranormal energy."

"If you were having the vision, why didn't you make an effort to contact us?" Anthony asked.

"I did try. I spoke to somebody, a detective, or deputy detective who only heard part of what I had to say and then hung up on me."

Anthony caught my glance and looked startled.

Nan went on, "I had a similar vision about the woman here in Burlington who disappeared and ended up being murdered. I was seeing her through a video camera. I was planning to wait and see if I had the same vision twice, but then my good friend who works in the Burlington police department called me. I told him what I'd seen and he ran with it. Turns out I was right."

"And the Middlebury boy."

Nan's face lengthened and she said in low tones, "What I've been saying for months is, like the one under the Verrazano Bridge, he's in water. And like I told you, the authorities are not really listening." She paused, as if choking back some emotion, cast her eyes down at her bandaged, injured foot, and swung her straight hair forward. "My sense is, like that student said, he got drunk. But then he went for a walk. He slipped on ice." She looked up at me. "He could have fallen or broken his leg or his foot so that he just couldn't move. He was too far away from campus to cry for help. He crawled to a place where he thought he might be able to stay warm, and when the temperature dropped, just died overnight."

I felt suddenly woozy and had to take a deep breath to compose myself.

"Then the snow came. A few days later, that January blizzard."

"Hold on a second," I interrupted her. "The days before the blizzard weren't that cold." Thinking of Hiram's failed attempt to retrieve the dead cow, I said, "It was warm for January. The temperature was in the thirties."

"True," Nan conceded. "But if he was drunk and lying in the snow it was probably cold enough at night for him to have died. Anyway, when the blizzard came my sense is Tim got covered over in the drifts that melted some when it got warmer and then froze again, solid ice. I don't know why the search dogs couldn't smell him. But I'm assuming that when the snow finally did melt in the spring his body got swept into the river.

"There is a search-and-rescue group out of Maine," Nan went on. "They have this helicopter camera that can take photos way down into a lake or a river. They flew over the Otter Creek and imaged a body lying in the riverbed. They relayed the report to the police, who investigated the location and found nothing. In the interim he got carried farther downstream. My sense is he's lodged under debris."

The silence that ensued in the room was kinetic. At last Anthony broke it and said quietly, "Can we talk a little more about *our* situation?"

"How did you see the book?" I asked.

"I saw the book and sensed it belonged to you. And felt that it wasn't in your house. And saw somebody reading it."

"Can you remember who it was, who was reading it?" Anthony said.

"Just a man. Not young, not old. Nothing special about him."

"Well, it's a short book," I explained. "Doesn't have much of a storyline." Nobody spoke for a while and then I said, "Well, here's something else for you. I think I might have the only copy of this book for miles around. In fact, there might be only one other copy of it in the northeast."

"And where would that be?" Nan asked. I told her it was Yale University. "That's kind of far." She dismissively shook her head. "I mean, do you wonder if this person, this killer, could have read *your* copy?"

The question jolted me because I'd asked myself the same thing. I tried to think who else could've read the book and my mind went blank. And then I remembered the slip of paper that Breck claimed to have found. "Here's one thing." I turned to Anthony. "I didn't even mention this to you. But my daughter, who had the book for a year and a half, said she found a slip of paper inside it. Three words were written on it: 'you and her.' She claims it wasn't my handwriting."

"Ah, that's it!" Nan cried. "The key to what you're looking for!"

Both Anthony and I gaped at her. "What makes you say that?" I asked.

"Just popped into my head. As these things do. Those words, those three words, have something to do with the murders."

"That was eerie," I said, as Anthony and I were driving along the banks of Lake Champlain, busy in the summer with recreational sailboats and kayaks and Jet Skis. A double-decker ferry streaming with colorful flags had just left a terminal and was making its dutiful crossing toward the shores of New York State.

He nodded and then said, "Tell me about it."

" 'You and her.' Even if she is on to something, that doesn't bring us any closer to figuring out who it is."

Anthony said, "It's equivocal at best. But suppose for the purpose of argument, we could say 'you' might be the killer and 'her' might be somebody the killer loves."

"Or has murdered."

"Or has murdered," Anthony repeated.

We made a turn onto College Street, and now with the lake to our backs began heading toward the interstate. Well-kept Victorian houses lined the route, and as I looked around the city where I'd spent five years, I felt sad and bereft. I resumed, "She seems like just some ordinary lady, like somebody who'd send me a recipe or a question for my column. You know, the kind of person whose writing pen has a feather on top of it."

Anthony disagreed. "No, she seems too earthy, too grounded. Too crunchy to have a feather pen. She probably worries about her carbon footprint and sustainable living and is green as green can be."

I decided to defer to him. "You could be right about that. . . . I will say, her recounting of what might have happened to that student . . . as she was telling us, I could see it all so clearly."

"I went into this with skepticism," Anthony admitted.

"You and me both," I said.

"But I feel differently now. I don't know why exactly, but I do."

"So do I."

We'd just passed the halfway point in our journey home from Burlingon to Woodstock when his cell phone started ringing. He hated talking while driving and, grabbing the phone nestled against the outside of his thigh, handed it to me and asked me to read the number.

"It says private."

"Answer and tell me who it is?"

I announced, "Anthony Waite's line," and got a "Who's this?"

Recognizing the New Jersey accent, I said, "How ya doing, Marco?" and then told him Anthony was driving.

"I've been better, to be honest. Can I speak to him?"

I held out the phone, Anthony grabbed it and placed it over his ear. "Yeah, what's going on?" he said, and listened for a bit.

From where I sat on the passenger's side, Prozzo's end of the conversation was intermittently audible. I heard him say, "Back down here in our neck of the woods." And then something about, "But on the New Hampshire side."

I was delighted to hear Anthony reply, "Do you mind if I put you on speaker?" He fiddled with his phone and finally, after a bit of feedback and background noise, I heard Prozzo's voice blaring, "Doesn't matter who hears now. The reporters already know about it."

"Any idea how long the car's been there?" Anthony asked.

"Ten days or more . . . they didn't want to tell us about it, those New Hampshire fucks, pardon the French, Catherine," he said. "Anyway, when can you get here?"

"Hang on so I get Catherine up to speed." Anthony shifted slightly in his seat and was about to speak.

"Sounds like they found an abandoned car," I said, preempting him.

"Yeah, down in Charlestown, right next to the river. And New

Hampshire has been all over it for ten days," Prozzo fumed over the speaker.

"Maryland plates," Anthony informed me.

"And a trunk full of a woman's stuff," Prozzo added.

"Anyway, Marco, Catherine and I are driving back from Burlington. I need to drop her off before I head down there."

There was a significant silence and then Prozzo asked suspiciously, "What were you doing up *there*?"

"I'll explain when I see you."

"Come on, Ant, what's the big secret?"

"Okay, Catherine was interviewing a clairvoyant who helped find the body of that Burlington woman."

"The one who got shoved into Huntington Gorge," Prozzo said.

"I decided to go along so I could ask a few questions about our situation."

"I can't believe you'd buy into that crap," Prozzo remarked. "Whenever there's a murder those people always come out of the woodwork."

Anthony looked over at me and said, "Let me jump, Marco. As soon as I drop Catherine I'll head down to you."

"All right. And if on the way you happen to run up against any New Hampshire Staties, just mow 'em down."

"Will do." Anthony handed me the phone and I switched it off.

Anthony's car was traveling over an uneven section of highway and for a moment I listened to the tires thumping and thwacking. "So you think it might be another one," I said at last.

He nodded. "Out-of-state car parked by the river, a whole trunk full of a woman's clothes. Where is she? There have been other dead bodies found near the Connecticut." He cogitated for a moment or so. "Funny sometimes how you just get a few details, they aren't necessarily conclusive, but you know in your gut where they're going to lead you."

"A little bit like Nan O'Brien," I ventured to say.

"But I mean, surely what I'm describing happens when you're doing investigative journalism, right?" Anthony asked.

"Well," I said, "you might divine the truth. But everything has to be backed up with fact. No leaps of faith. You can get discredited. Or sued."

FOURTEEN

A N ARTICLE ABOUT THE ABANDONED CAR appeared the
following morning in the *Valley News,* stating that the Maryland owner was from the Dominican Republic, living in the
United States on an expired visa. It had yet to be determined if
the driver was alone or if there were other passengers, but certainly one of them was a woman: a battered sky-blue suitcase was
found when the trunk was jimmied open, and among the contents
were black spandex brassieres; a pot of iridescent eye shadow,
cherry-and-lime-green-colored panties, a box of tampons, several
pairs of low-cut blue jeans adorned with spangles, and one em-
broidered dress that seemed as though it were made by hand.
There was a copy of the Bible in Spanish.

I pictured the owner of the suitcase as a young woman in
her early twenties, lured to America, wide-eyed and hopeful, and
that the dress was perhaps something her mother gave her with
great ceremony on her very last night in Santo Domingo. I kept
thinking/hoping that the stranded car was just a coincidence
and had absolutely nothing to do with the River Valley murders.

Shortly after reading the article, I went to the prison to
teach my class. When I arrived, the inmates already knew about
the marooned vehicle—I assumed there was access to the

newspaper—and immediately asked if I believed there might be another victim whose body had yet to be found. I told them I knew as much as they did.

One-legged Jess was sitting in a fold-out chair holding on to his crutches, struggling to gain a standing position. "Why don't you put them down. Stay a while," I said. He shook his head and refused. Then Peter, my patricidal seventeen-year-old, explained that during outdoor activity people had been stealing Jess's crutches and pushing him around. The rest of the guys were sitting in a circle holding their copies of *Dead Souls*. They had seemed to appreciate Pushkin, so I thought I'd hug Russia and try them out on Gogol's fantasy of crossing social and financial lines with a scheme.

Raul spoke up. "Well, you know, buying the names of dead people is kind of like having a cell phone in here. No reception most of the time, but people who got 'em, even when they can't use 'em, still don't want to share with nobody else."

Very good analogy, I thought, and should have run with that but found myself floored by this incredible piece of information. "Cell phones?" I said. "You have cell phones?"

"Unofficially," said Jones, Anthony's former suspect incarcerated for sexual misconduct in a mini-mart. He was turning out to be one of the more vocal of the bunch.

"Shouldn't they be confiscated?"

It was explained to me that people visiting had managed to smuggle them to the inmates in spite of the security regulations.

"They some kinds that get through metal detectors and shit," said Travis, slumped down in his chair, bony shoulders pointing through his orange prison jumpsuit. I was surprised to hear him speaking; he hardly ever contributed anything much to a discussion.

"Good to hear from *you*," I said to him.

He narrowed his eyes at me and said, "You don't want to hear from me."

"Sure I do."

"He's talking about something else," Peter warned, and was then silenced by a malignant look.

"Travis." I attempted to further engage him. "Did you get a chance to read *Dead Souls*?"

"Hell yeah, I read it. Or most of it anyway," he said. "Guy's a fool. Buying the names of dead people so the world would think he was rich? What was he on?"

"Yeah, buying the names of dead slaves," Raul interjected.

"People find you bullshitting sooner or later," Travis pressed on. "But nah, didn't get to the end. Does he get thrown out of town or somethin'?"

I pointed out the man gets caught; however, the book itself was a bit inconclusive because the author died without having had a chance to properly finish it. Like Wilkie Collins and *The Widower's Branch*, I remarked to myself.

"Then why are we reading it?" asked Raul, crossing his tattooed arms over his chest.

Travis spoke up again. "Damn. I should write a frigging book. Could clean up with what I know." He thumped on his temple. "What I got in my head."

I took this in for a moment and then I said, "Maybe you should."

I always encouraged them to write down their stories and promised that I'd gratefully read them. Crude as the execution would undoubtedly be, embedded in them surely would be fascinating material.

"'Cause the shit I got to say you don't want to hear."

"Try me."

Travis looked at me as though I were an alien. "I know where this guy's head's at."

"Which guy?" Raul asked before I could.

Addressing the entire group, Travis said, "This killer fucker up here who's going around finding women and whacking them."

"Oh yeah, where's his head at?" Jones asked.

Travis was getting flustered and started waving his hands, his eyes raging. "I seen shit like this before. Somebody goes crazy. They start popping people in a certain way like warming up for somebody else."

I told him I wasn't sure I got his meaning.

"You better get it, lady. Because *your* ass is next in line."

"Pardon me?"

"I say this *mofo* will be coming for *you*."

Even though I knew what he was driving at, I felt I had to be sure. "But he did that already, came around to where I was."

Travis was losing patience and pinching his shoulders together and said, "Not talking about no down the street from you. Talking about right down your driveway."

"Oh Travis, shut it!" somebody said.

Looking thoroughly disgusted now, Travis said, "I'm just telling you what I know from what I seen."

Peter purposely lingered after class was over. In the midst of his chemically induced placidity, he seemed anxious to speak to me.

"Anybody in your family come to visit you last week?" I began, and was told that his cousins had. His older brother was a sophomore at Williams College; in the wake of the senseless murder of their parents, this boy refused to have anything to do with his younger sibling, a rejection that Peter tried to outwardly slough off in his late-adolescent way, but which I knew pained him terribly.

I asked if he'd been writing in his diary. In response, he gave me several pages that he'd been able to print out in the prison's computer room. With a quick glance I saw they were scantily filled with writing and larded with lots of juvenile drawings. Disappointed in his lack of effort, I folded them carefully and put them in one of the manila folders I was holding.

"He's not joking, you know." Peter was gazing at me steadily with his rheumy gray eyes.

"Who?"

"Travis." I could see that two pinpoints of color had risen to his doughy cheeks.

"He doesn't talk much but he reads the paper. He knows what's going on. And he told me you have to be careful."

"I *am* being careful."

Peter's face flushed even more when he added, "He just said it makes sense."

"That what makes sense?" I repeated impatiently.

Peter shook his head. "That the guy would come after you, too."

Perturbed by the bizarre, unforeseen warning, I found Fiona standing in the little office we shared. As soon as I came in, she smiled, said a cautious hello, and then settled back down at her desk to begin collating a bunch of very skillful drawings of the nineteenth-century brick prison building, the double-height chain-link fence, and the field beyond it populated by an old rusted hay thresher with huge, spoked metal wheels.

"Who did those?" I said, instinctively moving closer to her.

"Oh, this older guy I have who's a . . . molester, I guess you'd call him."

"His first incarceration?"

"I think actually it's his third."

"They're really lovely." I was glad to be drawn away from Travis's dire prophecy. Surely he was just trying to frighten me; the killer had yet to return to the same exact location. His radius was rather short but he'd kept moving.

Fiona went on. "I'm amazed that this man has the will to even do them. The other guys, they punch him, they torture him and push him down. He's got cuts and bruises all over him to prove it."

"May be his way of retreating and surviving," I said. "But don't the guards protect him?"

"Not really. Not somebody in for sexually molesting children. They're the lowest form of life in prison."

"Yeah, the whole prison pecking order." I sat down at my desk and swiveled the chair around so that I could face her. "Human nature. The strong punish the weak, and criminals in turn punish those whose crimes they believe to be worse than theirs." I reached toward her. "May I flip through them?"

She handed me the sheaf.

"I don't know if you've read the writer Primo Levi," I remarked as I began studying moody, detailed drawings of the prison from different angles, interior corridors and close-ups of grimy windows, barred cells, a parallax view of incarceration.

"I haven't," Fiona said. "But I've always been meaning to."

I went on to say that Levi writes movingly about the pecking order among the inmates of the concentration camp: the top of the ranking being political prisoners; next, Scandinavian inmates; then French; then English; then Poles; continuing down to the lowest rung, which are the Jews, Primo Levi among them. "According to him, each group of the incarcerated mistreats the group perceived to be just below it. He believed that such behavior is basic human nature."

Fiona was shaking her head and I could tell she was perturbed by the truth of this. "That's very depressing."

"I guess it's no surprise that Primo Levi killed himself. But not until years later," I added.

Fiona murmured something inaudible, and I returned to the drawings. It was sad to see such incredible skill demonstrated by somebody who'd lost control of his life. But then again, sometimes I felt as though I kept losing control of mine: my love, my resentments, fear of losing my daughter, fear of losing my life. "These are actually good enough to be exhibited somewhere." I handed the drawings back to her. "Don't know about you but sometimes I feel there is just a thin membrane separating me from my guys."

"Meaning?"

"I have plenty of criminal fantasies, for example."

Fiona smiled at me guardedly, enough for me to see her yellowed front tooth. She sat back in her chair, adjusted her skirt, and then said, "You really have it in for me, don't you?"

"Oh my God! I'm not talking about *you*!"

"No, but I mean you've been assuming I had something to do with Emily leaving."

I looked at her squarely. "Not at all. We're all adults, right? Perhaps you'll agree with me: sometimes as adults we make childlike choices that . . . I don't know, maybe because in some way we always remain children. But not in this particular case. As far as Emily goes, I don't think she should have taken her children out of the state. I don't think it's fair to Anthony. Beyond that, though, Anthony filled me in. He told me about her long-term affair."

"I wasn't sure if you believed him or not."

"Why wouldn't I believe him? Anyway, I've thought about it and decided it doesn't really matter who had the affair first."

"I think it does."

Well, of course you do, I thought. "Just so you know, I have no moral high ground to stand on."

Fiona blushed and pushed her hair behind her shoulders. "I just don't want things between us to be awkward."

"I know I've been frosty to you. And I'm sorry. I'll admit to you, part of it is jealousy. I wouldn't mind being with somebody *like* him. But obviously *not* him exactly."

Fiona smiled and said, "Well, I was a little jealous of your young guy, to be honest."

I chuckled. "I got that feeling. But just so you know, it came at a high price."

"I assumed it did," Fiona said softly.

When I arrived home from the prison there was another message from Matthew, asking if I'd decided when he could see me—hardly surprising. His being back in the country and now close by was making me feel terribly unsettled.

And then a message accompanied by an eerie sound of static: Anthony calling from the site of the abandoned car in Charlestown, New Hampshire. When I called him back on his cell, he told me that the registered owner of the car had not been driving it, but rather the owner's niece, to whom the suitcase presumably belonged. She was in the country illegally, spoke little English, and apparently had borrowed the car to drive up to Waterbury, Vermont, where she hoped to join a friend and be hired to pick strawberries and corn. Two DNA samples had been collected from strands of hair extracted from the car; one, the Dominican woman's, and the other yet to be identified.

"It's not the uncle's," Anthony informed me. "They ran one on him already. Now they're taxing the FBI's database to see if they come up with a match."

"So a DNA sample," I said. "That's promising news."

"If it leads somewhere."

Anthony went on to say that when the FBI showed up at the apartment of the car's owner in Maryland, the man at first had been reluctant to identify his niece or explain why the car was in New Hampshire. He'd also been afraid to try and trace the car, figuring she might have been detained by the INS and the car impounded.

"But that makes no sense. If she'd been detained, they have already located him from the car registration," I pointed out.

"Precisely. Anyway, we have an ID of the driver. Her name is Elena Mayaguez. She's twenty-four."

The name was melodious and lovely, and thinking she might be yet another murder victim left me sad and silent. Anthony explained that the woman's cousin had provided the FBI some of her clothing to see if they could match it to some of the DNA samples they found in the car. "Apparently her parents don't even know she's here."

"That's tragic," I said.

"There aren't a lot of people up here with dark complexions," Anthony went on. "A cashier at a local convenience store a few miles away from where the car was found easily remembered her." Beyond this, the New Hampshire investigators had coughed up two reports from separate motorists claiming to have seen a dilapidated Japanese car matching the one left by the Connecticut River screaming down the two-lane highway, tailed by a late-model American sedan with flashing lights. A motorist who'd observed the car chase choreography through a rearview mirror actually claimed to have seen the pursued vehicle swerve over to the side of the road—approximately in the same place where it was eventually found.

The deserted car held a full tank of gasoline, and it'd been construed that the missing driver probably stopped to refuel at the convenience store where she'd been noticed by the clerk and perhaps spotted by the killer at a pumping station. "Something else we've been thinking, Marco and I. If she was driving and being chased by another car flashing its lights, maybe she figured the car pursuing her was INS or government."

"Even if the car was unmarked," I added.

"Whereas most people would've tried to drive faster and escape, she probably thought it was better to pull over."

"That sounds plausible to me."

"Now, that aside, there's something else of an entirely different order going on down here."

"Oh."

"New Hampshire and Vermont are fighting over the sharing of evidence. It's crazy." I asked him to elaborate. "Well, Marco says New Hampshire sat on the abandoned car for a week before telling him. That's why it's already been published in the papers. He learned of it around the same time as the *Valley News* reporters did."

"So why is New Hampshire being so uncooperative?"

"That's the thing. They claim they haven't. I spoke to Prozzo's counterpart in Claremont, who says he passed along the data about the car as soon as they got it. Claremont alleges that during a phone conversation with Springfield, the car was mentioned, along with several other routine observations. They're obligated to pass crucial info back and forth, but Prozzo insists that the car was one of ten things Claremont summarized but didn't emphasize *where* it was found, just that it was found."

I also knew from experience that cooperating police departments were known for withholding information from one another when they were following a very specific lead, wanting to claim all the glory for a discovery that would help solve a case.

Anthony pointed out, "Poor communication like this is not the way to find the killer. Which is Marco's point. Hopefully they'll work it out, especially because now we've got something else concrete to go on." He paused, probably for effect.

"Which is?"

"One of the search dogs found a finger."

I felt nauseated. "Oh? Do we know it's her finger?"

"It went to Concord," Anthony explained, "to see if it matches the hair sample. The fact that the finger was found by one of the New Hampshire search dogs made it Concord's jurisdiction. They have their own forensic squad on it. I didn't even get a chance to see it before it was shipped off. That does make me wonder if they are deliberately keeping us out of the loop." He paused for a moment and said, "So we're feeling a little . . . let's call it the spirit of competition.

"And in that vein, Marco and I decided that we really need to pursue the Wilkie Collins connection. Because that bit is ours. New Hampshire knows nothing about it."

"But then you'd be withholding information from *them*."

"Well, let's see how relevant we decide the book actually is. . . . '*You and her,*' for example. Have you thought any more about it? Any ideas?"

"I know I lent the book to a few of my students, the ones I trusted to return it in good condition."

"Any idea when?"

"Probably during the last two years I was at Saint Mike's. I have to dig up the rosters of those classes."

"Yeah, maybe you should," Anthony said. I could hear him draw a deep breath and expel it.

"I'll do it right now."

After we were done speaking, I went into a storage closet and combed through several file boxes I'd brought down from Burlington. I found the file of my last semester at Saint Mike's and one from a year and a half before that. I scanned all the names and nothing jumped out at me. Somehow I knew that two of the writing files missing from the boxes were the ones for the students with whom I'd trusted the book. Momentarily abandoning my search, I sat in my study with a pen and notepad, trying to recall the names of some of the borrowers. No one immediately came to mind.

In the meantime, who also had read the book? Violet apparently had, but she'd never been to Vermont. Ironically, from the photographs I'd seen, this large-boned woman with a sheaf of tawny hair was, in terms of physical strength, probably a more likely candidate than Wade. And then I remembered something. *I* had gotten Wade into Wilkie Collins. He'd read quite a few, even borrowed some books from the library. Could he have borrowed *The Widower's Branch*? I had no choice but to check with him. So Violet and possibly Wade. Theresa, my college roommate, had given the book to me; being a Victorian scholar, surely she'd read it. But she lived in Connecticut and was small and mousey, the sort of person who ushered flies outside of her house instead of swatting them. Unlikely suspect. I had nothing to go on, but I just couldn't imagine the murderer being a woman.

Standing there in my study, I thought to myself: I've momentarily exhausted my resources on this particular conundrum. Besides, there was another one to deal with: Matthew's sudden reemergence in my life, the dilemma of whether or not to see him again after nearly two years and wondering, Wouldn't it be better to meet in a neutral place such as Joanie's Café? I knew he'd probably agree to it, I knew it was the right thing to do, but I found myself resisting what was right and wanting to see him alone. This desire frightened me but it also compelled me.

I went outside into the thrumming late-afternoon heat and deadheaded some of my day lilies. I turned my attention to the lawn, which was looking ragged and uneven. It never looked so good as it did the summer two years before when, from time to time, Matthew would insist on mowing it for me. Listening to the crescendo humming of the tractor blades, I'd sit in the cool sanctuary of my house researching and writing my columns: about how to best launder feather pillows; a clever extension duster for swiping cobwebs off high ceilings; or homespun recipes such as a marinade of garlic and sea salt, molasses and vinegar that made a tender melting morsel out of the toughest piece of beef. I'd contentedly watch Matthew through the same rolled-glass window where several years later I'd witness the blizzard that would bury Angela Parker in the orchard higher up on Cloudland. He'd work outside, stay for dinner, we'd drink wine, watch the wings of light fleeing the fields and the distant orchard full of gnarled apple trees, we'd make love in the lengthening shadows and he'd spend the night. And then wake up to blue bowls of milky coffee, crusty baguettes from the local bakery, and my homemade orange marmalade. Then he'd be off, back to his parents' cabin in the Northeast Kingdom, to some odd job or another.

Toward the end of this, his first postgraduate summer, Matthew traveled to Scandinavia with a student group organized by the university. His plan was to get lost in the adventure of roaming with a bunch of college friends; however, during that three-week period he called me every day on a cheap phone card he'd procured in Stockholm. He sent me long, rather boring travelogue e-missives from Internet cafés and seemed to be counting the days until his return.

It was while he was away that the chairman of the English department called to explain that the university had received yet another batch of anonymous letters leveling false accusations, including the sordid allegation that Matthew and I frequently had had sex in my office. Copies of these letters had been sent (by the anonymous writer) to several key administration officials and, apparently, to Matthew's parents, who were also informed of where the other copies had been sent and contacted the college to verify the complaint. A week after I'd learned about the correspondence, as if one had nothing to do with another, I received a phone call from the Human Resources provost saying that, due to budgetary constraints, one of the permanent adjunct positions in the English department needed to be eliminated and unfortunately it was going to be mine.

I was devastated by the news, but hardly shocked that, in light of the discomfort caused by the vicious letters, something like this could happen. Knowing that I was powerless as an adjunct, I told the provost that I loved teaching, felt that I had much to offer Saint Mike's. He informed me quite flatly that other adjunct professors had better student evaluations than I and ended the call rather abruptly, leaving me staring at the telephone as though it were an alien.

A few days later Matthew came straight to my house from Logan Airport, which meant that he had yet to be confronted by his parents about our affair. I was glad to see him, but knew my firing would be bringing on new complications. And for this reason I didn't want to spring the news on him immediately.

"I decided something," he said after we'd made love greedily and were lying in my bed together.

"What have you decided?" I asked, trying to hide my wariness.

Arms cocked behind his head, a lascivious look of conquest etched on his face, he said, "Well, life experience is as important as work experience. . . ." He looked meaningfully at me. "I think we should live together."

Knowing I now needed to launch into what had happened, I merely asked him, "But how?," knowing that his postgraduate plan (strongly endorsed by me as well as his parents) was to live in New York City with a friend on the Lower East Side and begin hunting for rent-paying work until he could decide whether or not he wanted to apply to business school. He now confessed he'd prefer living in Burlington and seeking employment there.

I let a few moments elapse before I said sadly, "I won't be in Burlington in the fall, Matthew." He turned to me, looking bewildered. "I lost my teaching job."

"You lost your *job*? How?"

"They said it was budgetary but I know it has nothing to do with that. They got a whole bunch more of those anonymous letters. Saying we had sex in my office, among other things."

Matthew slapped his hand against his forehead and lay back in bed looking defeated. "Oh no! So I'm the reason why they fired you."

"Do you have any idea or theory of who might have sent all these letters?"

His face cracked in pure misery. "No! I have no clue who could be doing this. Maybe the letter writer wanted you to lose your job, but they also really want to come between us. And we can't let them."

I could think of nothing to say at that moment and thought it best to keep silent.

He bolted upright in bed. "Is there no way to turn this

around? Can I go and see them, the administration, and tell them the person is obviously deranged?"

This is precisely where youth and inexperience get in the way, I told myself. "Matthew, I'm an adjunct. We basically have no rights. We're drones, in essence. At the university's beck and call. At the university's mercy."

"You're not going to break up with me because of this, are you? I mean, you love me, don't you?"

"Of course I love you, Matthew, that doesn't change. But I won't be in Burlington. I already gave notice on my apartment. So there is no other incentive for you to be there unless you *want* to be there."

"I don't want to live in New York," he told me emphatically.

Matthew followed his own instincts. He found an apartment share in Burlington, a job as a bartender at a very popular bistro that paid excellent money but required a commitment of more than forty hours a week. So naturally we saw a lot less of each other—maybe one day each week during his time off. He'd drive down to Woodstock to visit me, often arriving very late at night, and exhausted by his late hours, would sleep long into the following day. Sometimes when I was dressed and drinking my morning coffee I'd steal into the bedroom and watch his slumber, which was always still and deep. I'd look at him and feel sad, knowing that I was in effect pushing him away from me. But then I'd hear a voice in my head saying, "At least you've awakened him in ways and maybe that will be enough."

I had to go to Burlington one afternoon to finish gathering the rest of my belongings, mostly books, from the apartment I'd given up on Willard Street. I was standing at the bookcase, positioning volumes into moving boxes, when I heard knocking on the door. Knowing I was there, Matthew had arrived unannounced, smartly dressed in a white button-down oxford shirt, crisp khaki chinos, his face tanned from kayaking on Lake Champlain on a few days off, his shirtsleeves rolled up. I was holding Bulfinch's weighty *Mythology* under one arm when I answered the door; he gallantly reached forward and relieved me of it. "Why didn't you tell me you were coming?" I carped, as I turned around and headed back into the apartment cluttered with moving crates.

Handing me the book back, he said, "I assumed you'd be happy. We haven't seen each other in more than a week. I figured you missed me."

Of course I missed him, missed making love to him, but I merely said, "You should've just called. I have so much to do here and today is my last day to do it."

My words afflicted him, his face pinched up and he looked stung. I moved back to the bookcase and continued clearing it of books.

"I've seen so little of you lately," he pointed out.

"You've been here and I've been there."

"I've been waking up sick to my stomach," he informed me. "Because I can feel you moving away from me."

I would not even try to refute the truth. "How about something to drink?" I said, leaving the bookshelf and heading into my small kitchen, Matthew following close behind me.

I was thinking more along the lines of iced tea; however, with a peremptory gesture, Matthew fetched a flask of vodka from my liquor cabinet, took one of the remaining jelly glasses from a nearly empty cupboard, headed to the refrigerator, cadged a few ice cubes, and made himself an impressively stiff drink. He'd never done such a thing before. "Hey, don't quaff that too fast," I warned him. His eyes glittering with malice, he pounded the drink in two gulps.

"What's wrong?" I said, resting my hand between his shoulder blades, loving him with great despair.

He pressed his hands against his head and now looked at me with reddened, tearful eyes. "When we're not together, when

I'm seeing you so much less, my faith, *my faith* in you falls apart. I feel like . . . I have nothing to hold on to. I keep waiting for everything to crash. I go to bed and wake up several times through the night sweating, thinking about you. I feel like I've been cut off from your body. I go through all the photos I took of you. And read your letters over and over. I'm just a mess."

I told him I was suffering in my own way, that I'd been reviewing my decisions, the mistakes I'd made, both with my husband and Breck and the subsequent men I'd been involved with.

Reaching for his glass and draining dregs of vodka from the ice, he continued, his voice in tremolo, "That include me?"

"I don't know, Matthew."

"But my case is different from everybody else . . . because I've had this thing for you forever. And I'm so sick of people—like my parents—saying it's not valid because of the difference in our ages. It *does* matter because it's very real to me. You're my first love, Catherine, and I don't want to give you up."

I looked at him, sadly nodded my head, and said, "I understand."

"What about *your* first love, Catherine," he said. "Who was it?"

"I guess I'd have to say my husband."

I suddenly felt terribly conflicted: between wanting him with me and wanting him to leave. I wondered how many months it would take to recover from the druglike withdrawal for this lover. Beyond this, my relationship with Matthew had already harmed my professional life. That was no small thing. Then with great tenderness I saw that his hands were shivering, his beautiful strong hands that nevertheless were palsied due to the nerve damage of his childhood illness. I loved his hands. I loved them for their power and I also loved them for their obvious frailty.

"Why don't we go for a walk," he said at last. "Just stroll along Willard Street."

I turned to him. "Okay, Matthew, we'll go for a walk. But I want you to go back to your apartment . . . when we're done."

He looked baffled. "Why can't I come back here with you?" I slowly shook my head. "Why can't we make love?"

"I don't have time to make love, Matthew. I have to get the place cleared out today." I indicated the cartons and the duffel bags and the boxes for hauling books. "Surely you see how much more work there is to do."

"Let me help you."

"I want to do it on my own. This is my failure and I want to live through it without any company. So let's go for that walk, shall we?"

Matthew turned to me with fervent eyes. "I just can't do it," he said.

"Can't do it?" I echoed flatly, not knowing whether or not he was referring to going for a walk.

"Be the person you think I should be. Be the guy going off to make his life someplace and dating and eventually meeting somebody else and getting married. I just don't want any of that, Catherine. I want to be with *you*."

It was so simply and honestly said, and like a plaintive musical chord, struck surprisingly deep. In the resonance of it, I seriously considered giving in to him and, age difference notwithstanding, setting up the life of a couple, younger man, older woman, and just seeing how it went. But then I remembered my reservations, I remembered my husband's betrayal and my inability to forgive him. How would I ever forgive Matthew for his inevitable betrayal of me? But I'd have to and I didn't know if that would be possible.

"If we stay together, Matthew, I'll always be afraid of your leaving me. I'll be waiting for it, I'll be expecting it. And as time goes on I'll keep feeling older and older in comparison to you."

"Don't you think I know all this, Catherine?"

A change came over Matthew and he suddenly seemed almost calm. And then I admitted to myself how much I'd missed him during the last few weeks, his loping walk across my kitchen in a formless T-shirt, his hair all tousled, watching him sleep in my bed and the light creeping in from the edges of the shutters to fall in a muted cascade on his slack and unsuspecting face. He'd slept in my bed without a clue of how close to the end our affair really was.

"Let me stay here and help you," he insisted once more, his face now inches from mine, his breath sour from nerves. "And then we can say good-bye."

"I want to say good-bye now," I heard myself say. "I really think we've reached the end of this."

His expression changed once more and his eyes looked dulled and distant. And then slowly, almost gently, he put his damaged hands around my throat.

FIFTEEN

A SUMMER DAY IN LATE JULY, unseasonably chilly for Charlestown, New Hampshire, and Bellows Falls, Vermont. Goldenrod burgeoning in the fields, auguring the first frost, which could possibly come as soon as six weeks away. In these parts we can get the first twinges of autumn cold toward the beginning of August. There are those who will begin to dread perishing flowers, will dwell on the shorter lifespan of their domestic animals and, of course, their own mortality. At Dartmouth-Hitchcock Medical Center, some people will go for routine blood work that comes up abnormal, provoking a battery of tests, and bad news will arrive like a bullet shattering window glass while outside an unsuspecting world still exalts in warm-weather activities, knowing that before too long cold weather will invade and turn life inward. This momentary seasonal melancholy was particularly meaningful to the good townspeople of Vermont and New Hampshire who'd shown up to search the area around either side of the Connecticut River for the body of twenty-four-year-old Elena Mayaguez.

I volunteered for the search, too, my party led by a man, part Abenaki Indian, who tracked wilderness for the police, a man who knew how to recognize signs of disturbance in the forest, telltales of skirmishes and struggle that the rest of us would never notice. As I trekked along in his wake I felt strange and disembodied. It was as though the forest had swallowed me whole and I was wandering inside the cavity of some great beast, trees towering around me like the gargantuan ribs of a whale.

After we'd wandered around a designated area for an hour, our laconic guide sprang into motion and fell to his knees as though in prayer. He'd caught a glint of something in the dirt that had already been trampled by unobservant policemen. He bent down and, gingerly putting on a pair of latex gloves, extracted a small rectangle caked in mud. Without explaining what it was, he held it up to a fractured shaft of sunlight beaming into the forest. There was a moment where I thought I saw an iridescent flash, which turned out to be a small holographic emblem on a credit card. "Follow me," he said to everyone, and we marched dutifully behind him. When we reached the clearing, he handed the card to one of the forensic people dressed in yellow and said, "I can even read the name. It's Felice."

The first name of the man who owned the abandoned car, the man who now stood fifty yards away waiting by the torrential river, the uncle of the missing Elena Mayaguez.

The specimen was taken into a trailer, prepared, and examined. Soon several officials, including Prozzo, swarmed out; the detective's ear was pressed to his mobile phone as he was relaying the news to his New Hampshire counterparts. Then he began walking toward the small, wavy-haired sixtyish fellow overdressed for late summer in a battered ski jacket and tan slacks. Brought up from Maryland by the FBI for the purpose of identifying the body, once it was found, the uncle of Elena Mayaguez had been quietly watching the proceedings. What a burden this must be for him, I thought, just standing there waiting for the gruesome arrival of a niece's body, no doubt battered and brutalized by the river, bearing the fatal assault wounds that took her life. And having to make a phone call to the Dominican Republic, reporting on the recovery of the body of a twenty-four-year-old girl whose parents must look upon America as some fearful, wild, lawless place. Prozzo spoke to the uncle in excellent Spanish. When there seemed to be a break in the questioning and the detective headed over, I said, "You sound like a native speaker."

"I grew up with it. My mother was from Guatemala." Prozzo shrugged off the compliment. And then resumed his train of thinking. "Poor guy is really undone. He lent his niece the credit card so she could make it up to Waterbury no problem, without running out of money; people don't realize that Felice is a man's name. He feels responsible for this. Guilty. The problem for New Hampshire . . ." He paused with a self-satisfied look. "Is that his English is crap."

"Well, surely New Hampshire has somebody who can translate."

Prozzo shook his head and grinned smugly. "Nope. This time they have to rely on me. That's why they're being so cooperative and nicey-nicey." Then he said with a considerate tone, "You know . . . the thing I've never understood about a lot of these immigrants from Latin countries is why they don't make more of an effort to learn English. This guy says he's been here for twenty years. My mom was determined to master English so she went to language school. She spoke it near perfectly." He turned to me full on and I saw the compassion in his face and warmed to him in a way that I hadn't yet. "Could you do me a big favor, Catherine," he said. "Take this poor soul to lunch when it's time?"

"I'd be happy to."

"Good. I appreciate it." The detective turned his attention to the Connecticut. Crisscrossing it were several search-and-rescue boats that were open-ended and manned with divers, dog handlers, and trained Labrador retrievers who kept their noses close to the water, sniffing the air for that sharp molecular odor of decay traveling up a murky column of water to the surface. Several days of rains and runoff had bolstered the river's volume, and the motor-powered boats added waves to the melee of its current. The water in the places where the sun struck it turned the verdigris color of a tarnished chalice.

Scanning the river I noticed that on several boats, the trained crew of rescuers were taking long metal poles and jabbing at the depths. I asked Prozzo why the searchers were using poles and he began by saying that a few of the dogs had detected something in the air.

"They've alerted." He used a term from the search-and-rescue nomenclature.

"To a body?" I asked.

"Yes."

I looked downriver and saw a chocolate Labrador retriever wearing an orange vest doing twirls, hacking barks echoing across the currents. "I don't know if you can see it from here," he said, "but the river is boiling right where that boat is. Now they're trying to hit bottom with the poles because the dogs have narrowed it down. They're prodding now, to loosen the body from a place where it might be lodged so it can begin moving with the current."

And naturally I thought of the Middlebury student whom Nan O'Brien claimed was lodged under a pile of debris at the bottom of the Otter Creek. To think that after all these months he might still be down there: a victim of mishap or of murderous intent, out of his loved ones' reach.

Shielding his eyes with his hand, Prozzo seemed to calculate. "If they're closing in it would mean half to three-quarters of a mile she might have traveled downstream."

I glanced at Elena Mayaguez's uncle, whose narrow shoulders hunched forward. "So she might be found soon?"

"Appears that way."

I felt my stomach churning.

One of Prozzo's underlings approached, told him something, and he turned to me. "The uncle says, 'no eat.'"

"Makes sense," I said. "Wouldn't be hungry if I were he."

"Neither would I," Prozzo agreed.

There was an uncomfortable pause and then I went on, "Do you get much chance to speak Spanish?"

He looked at me askance. "Up here, in white land?"

"Why do you even live up here, in 'white land'?"

He laughed. "Because my wife is originally from here. I met her when she was down in New Jersey spending a week with her cousin. We got married before I got out of the academy. She convinced me here was a good place to raise kids." His tone was unmistakably sardonic. "So I found a job."

"It can be a good place, theoretically," I said, thinking, however, that Breck probably would have been better off if we'd remained in New York City.

Prozzo echoed my thoughts. "It is if your child fits in. And if not . . ."

"I remember you said you have a daughter. An only child, right?"

He nodded.

"I have an only daughter, too."

"Yeah, I know."

Almost as though on cue, Anthony showed up and informed Prozzo he was needed. Once the detective departed, Anthony scanned the welter of the river.

Then commotion. A flare rocketed up from one of the boats as the activity between the dogs and handlers became frenzied, as the shadows of the sun were moving across the water like crows. Shielding his eyes from the glare of the water, Anthony said, "Looks like they found her. They're just going to pull her out like she's been living down there."

And as we waited to see the bloated body surfacing, breaking the water's skin, I ached for the mother back in Santo Domingo, imagined her getting the phone call from the uncle. Of how she would let hurl this primordial cry that was . . . well, not recognition so much right away but rather a last-ditch attempt to deny the dreaded news that traveled more than a thousand miles in an instant, news of what had become irreversible, news that would plague the rest of her life. And with this howl of her desperation she would morph into all the mothers who come to grief over dead children, wailing with rage and protest at the world's cruelest turn of fate. If it would be my daughter's corpse borne up from the depths of the Connecticut, her body all water-engorged, her face eaten away, how could I possibly manage to go on when her life was torn from me?

PART THREE

SIXTEEN

"C AN YOU IMAGINE," Wade was saying to me. "This woman probably risked her neck to come to this country, spent all her savings on passage, gets a lead on a job, drives up into the boondocks and then . . . runs into a freaking lunatic!"

We were sitting opposite each other in Paul's living room. I merely stared back at him, wondering how to broach the subject of whether or not he'd ever borrowed my copy of *The Widower's Branch*.

"Did they find any literature on her?" he wondered.

This really threw me and I probably gaped at him. "Literature?" I repeated, thinking somehow he was referring to the Wilkie Collins novel.

Wade looked impatient. "Yeah, you know, the Seventh-Day Adventist pamphlets."

Of course, those. I told him dissolved papers *had* been found in the victim's pockets, but Anthony said it would be difficult identifying printed matter that had dwelled in river water.

Wade pondered this for a moment and then went on, "Why can't either of us get a eureka moment on who this guy is? He's got to be local. My bones are telling me. And I listen to them."

We were sitting in Paul's living room, surrounded by a few of the paintings that were the prototypes of his most famous museum pieces: haunting figures that recall the stalwart yet joyful Maya whose innocent features and protuberant, vulnerable-looking eyes one could say are exaggerated versions of Paul's perpetual childlike look of wonderment. He sets them amok in subway stations and in city scenes, naive, primitive countenances peeking out of crowds like ghosts. He had just been awarded a medal of achievement by the American Academy of Arts and Letters; that very evening Wade and he would be traveling down to Manhattan to accept the honor. From where Wade and I sat, we could peer down a long corridor into the greenhouse that doubled as an artist's studio. There Paul clung to his rigid eight-hour schedule at an easel in a big empty room that, during the winter, was staged with his beloved orange trees that cheered him through his seasonal affective disorder. Now the citrus were summering outside in a little semicircle fifteen yards beyond the farthest glass wall of the greenhouse that Wade liked to call the ice palace.

"I'm assuming the uncle went back to Maryland," Wade was saying. He shook his head and remarked, "Must've been horrendous for him the moment they found her."

"What about the parents getting the phone call? And their grief and even their rage."

There was a long, appreciative pause and then he surprised me. "Well, I understand rage. Rage almost ruined my life."

Looking around the living room, whose walls were crowded with the paintings of Paul's contemporaries, I said with some discomfort, "When you nearly destroyed this place."

"A place I've come to love," he remarked.

"Wade," I said, "I know how awful your parents were. I guess I never asked what made you do it. What sent you over the edge? Why did you come *here* of all places?" To ravage so many precious and beautiful things, I thought but did not say.

He rubbed his palms on his trousers a few times before he said, "I was so hateful of my life and everyone in it back then I didn't even realize what I was doing. It's not like I even chose this house or Paul. It was just a place nearby that belonged to somebody who clearly was a lot better off than we were. And wasn't my father's employer."

"So you would have drawn the line somewhere. You wouldn't have gone in and destroyed the employer's house."

Wade thought about it for a moment. "No, I was scared to death of the man. My father, who was so domineering normally, turned to mush around the guy. I didn't have the nerve to strike out at somebody I saw who was much more powerful than we were."

"But Paul?"

"I hardly knew Paul. I had no impression of him, really. Probably what made it easier." He paused for a moment. "I remember, though, when I broke in here, while it was going on I felt dead to the possibility of any consequence."

"So it *was* like blind homicidal rage," I said.

"I guess you could say that. Because I didn't feel bad afterwards. I felt numb."

Like a killer would, I thought but again didn't say.

"But when I was forced to meet Paul and reckon with everything I destroyed, especially all the sentimental objects he'd inherited from his mother, then I began to realize what I'd actually done."

I considered this and then said, "It's amazing he was able to forgive you, Wade."

"It was a grace I didn't deserve, really. And whenever I get impatient with him, I remind myself of that.

"But I will tell you . . . and this probably relates to somebody who commits serial homicide . . . even after I met with Paul and the priest and even after I confessed and apologized, it took quite a long time for me to take full responsibility for it. The regret kept growing and growing over a period of years. I was eventually able to atone for it by helping him, by devoting my life to him."

"Your rehabilitation," I suggested.

"Which prisoners, like the ones you teach, will probably never get. Believe me."

Paul called out from his studio to say he'd join us shortly. And so I knew I had precious little time to ask what I'd come to ask. "Wade," I said, "you've borrowed some of my Wilkie Collins, haven't you?"

He screwed up his face. "Yeah, several, why?"

"Did you ever read one called *The Widower's Branch*? It's his last book. Very short one."

He looked at me vacantly for a few instants, blinking rapidly. "Sounds familiar, but I don't think so. What about it?"

I distrusted his answer and without really thinking it through, I explained, "Oh, it's been missing for a while. It's the rarest edition of a Wilkie Collins that I own. Turns out I lent it to Breck but it came back . . . with pages torn out," I lied. "She claims the book was like that when she took possession of it. And . . . it was a valuable book."

Wade looked at me sternly and yet took the bait. "Well, even if I had borrowed it, I would have treated it with kindness. Treating things gently is second nature to me now. I'm constantly dealing with all those one-hundred-year-old records at the clerk's office; I have to be really careful because they can fall apart so easily." He paused for a moment, as though pondering something. And it occurred to me that he might have detected suspicion behind my questioning. Here was Wade, who once destroyed beautiful objects indiscriminately, now the steward of land and tax records, the gatekeeper of antique documents. His story, his confession about ransacking the very house we sat in, was illuminating, but who was to say definitively that he had been rehabilitated? Certainly not him. Could a substantial part of his psyche have remained corrupt, still demanding some sort of outlet?

At that moment we both noticed Paul standing at the entrance to the living room holding a cerulean bowl full of tempera paint, the medium he worked in and which he'd made himself from fresh eggs. Hanging from a carpenter's belt at his side was a large brush that presumably was creating a background wash. Glancing at a bulky plastic wristwatch covered in acrylic splatters, he announced, "We have to be out of here in an hour, Wade. You know that, don't you?"

"Why do you think I'm sitting here when I should still be at work?"

"Have you sorted out which suit you're going to wear? You can't get away with your normal sweater and blue jeans."

Wade rolled his eyes at me and then scolded Paul, "You don't think I know that? Jesus Christ!"

There it was, I thought, a glimmer of rage that might derive from a greater well of anger. To dispel the tension between the two of them, I threw something out that I knew would distract them. "Guess who I heard from?"

They both looked at me quizzically. And then Paul said, "The young 'un."

I nodded.

Wade looked down at his feet. "Doesn't surprise me."

Paul's huge crystal blue eyes were watering. "I suppose he's back?"

"For a few months."

"But have you seen him?" they both asked in unison.

"Nope."

"But you *will* see him?" Paul said with disapproval in his voice.

"He's up at his parents' cabin."

"If you see him you shouldn't see him alone," Wade told me.

"I know."

"If you did that it would be stupid of you," Paul seconded him.

In light of my immediate thoughts about Wade, I decided to be perverse and, knowing he'd decline, I said, "Do you want to be there when he shows up?"

"Why don't you get Anthony?" was his response.

"I haven't told Anthony about this. Anyway, I haven't agreed to let Matthew stop by. I told him I'd prefer to meet him in a neutral place."

"At least for once you're thinking," Wade said.

"And Breck, does she know about this?" Paul asked.

I gave him a look to mean "What do you think?"

Wade said, "I think she'll crucify you when she finds out."

"Everybody is just going to have to let me deal with this on my own," I told them.

Paul looked disgruntled. "I've heard *that* one before. Besides, I thought we all agreed that since it's just you and Wade and me and Anthony—I guess we can't include his family anymore—up here on Cloudland, that we're all going to look after one another."

"You're right. We did."

Wade asked, "So *where* is Matthew living? Is he *living* in the cabin?"

"No, he's living and working in Boston."

Paul went on, "Well, I just need to get this off my chest now. . . . Wade and I—we think you made a big mistake not pressing charges."

My hand instinctively traced the scarred divot on my neck that lingered from Matthew's desperate grasp, remembering how for days the skin was puffed and swollen, how difficult it had been to swallow. As it happened in mid-September, at least I could wear a light cotton turtleneck to cover the abrasions until they faded.

"I just couldn't bring myself to do it."

"That's because you felt responsible somehow," Wade said.

"The victim is not responsible," Paul added.

"I felt I could have handled it differently," I told them.

"We all think that about lots of things we could have handled differently, don't we?" Paul said with a trace of bitterness.

I called Matthew back when I got home from Paul and Wade's and he immediately offered to meet me somewhere neutral if that was the only way he could get to see me. "I've thought about it and it's okay if you stop by here tomorrow," I told him. "Late tomorrow afternoon. Paul and Wade will have returned from New York by then. I'll promise to call them twice during your visit."

There was hesitation and I knew Matthew was probably feeling ashamed to require checking up on. "Okay, that's fine," he finally agreed.

Wade and Paul returned home at two o'clock the following afternoon and called to alert me to their arrival. At four, the appointed time of my meeting with Matthew, I was sitting at my desk when an unfamiliar Volvo with Massachusetts plates pulled into the driveway. I felt a throbbing at the center of my forehead as I watched him climb out of the car and start strolling toward me. He didn't see me peering out the window, and I was able to observe that he'd finally buzzed his hair short and now there were a few filigrees of premature gray at the temples. When he glanced up, I could see that his face had grown more lean, cheeks slightly sunken in, and he seemed to have lost a good deal of his muscularity. When he finally saw me, he waved and I met him at the door.

By now the dogs were going mad barking at his arrival, swarming around his legs. Before greeting me, he reached down to give them reassuring pats and then spread his arms welcomingly wide and embraced me. He felt bonier and his scent was deeper, of the male body, slightly citrus, whereas he always used to have that wonderful young man's odor of light sweat and laundry powder.

I stood back from him. "You've lost so much weight."

"I know. And I feel smaller."

"Deliberate?"

He frowned and oddly made a vestigial gesture to rake the non-existent hair out of his eyes. "No, I got this lousy stomach condition. Probably from nerves. Took months to get over. I just couldn't eat very much for a long time. Stomach was tied up in knots." He raised his eyebrows. "As you can see, been having trouble gaining the weight back."

"Well, it makes you look more . . . mature. That and the flecks of gray."

He flicked himself at the temples. "I'm catching up to my elders. And only twenty-six."

"You poor old man," I said, standing aside so that he could pass. The dogs had quickly stopped barking and were nuzzling his hands, obviously remembering him.

"Still got Henry?" he asked, his own nickname for Henrietta.

"She's banging around. Under the kitchen table as we speak."

He walked in carefully ahead of me, his back straight. Strange to see the nape of his neck, as I'd been so used to his longer hair.

At one point he turned around and looked at me questioningly, and I said with a familiarity that distressed me, "The kitchen, obviously."

"Got any beer?"

"Do I know you?" I ribbed him.

His soft, puzzled look, the result of our rapid-fire exchange, of our former intimacy, would always bring a certain feeling of equality; and despite the terrible rupture in our relationship, I supposed we'd still find ourselves making the motions of . . . intimates. I invited him to sit down at the kitchen table. The moment he did, Henrietta, who'd been lolling underneath, sprang to her feet with a snort and one pig-eyed look at Matthew before hurrying out of the room.

"Nice reception," he noted. "She's got her business to attend to."

Sure enough, a moment later we heard her stream of urine pinging against the metal grate in the floor. He nodded. "Ah, some things don't change."

"Nope." I fetched a Magic Hat beer out of the refrigerator, opened it, and handed it to him.

His hands were trembling from his old affliction. He saw me noticing them and gave a shrug as though to say, "I haven't changed that much." "Will you have one?"

"I'm sticking to gin. Going to need it," I said, fiddling with a plastic lock that dog-and-pig-proofed a lower cabinet for a bottle of Bombay Sapphire. I sat down opposite him, we looked at each other, and then I poured a clear rivulet of gin over some ice cubes. "I can't believe I'm finally here with you," he said nervously.

I saluted him with my finger of gin as if to say, "Likewise."

He noticed Paul's painting, stiffened, and sat straight. Then got up from the table and went to stand before it. Recognizing its authorship, he said, "Did he just *give* this to you?" I told him for my birthday back in June. "Very generous, considering its value."

I agreed.

He turned to me, his face rapt, then reverted back to the painting. "That shadow behind the screen—" and then left off what he intended to say next. I wondered if he shared my theory on whom the shadow might actually represent. The atmosphere between us felt charged, and to dispel it I told him the painting was an homage to David's famous portrait of Madame Récamier.

Terribly anxious now, I began, "So, I know you just got back from Asia, but what . . . I mean, what will you do now?"

He went back to the table, sat down, tilting his head back to swig his beer. He explained that, having been certified as an ESL instructor, he was now able to live in Boston and teach students culled from the large, mostly Asian immigrant community.

"Did you just get tired of living over there?"

"More lonely, I suppose." He hesitated. "And then I had this . . . I guess I'd have to call it a bad affair over in Thailand." He glanced at me, his eyes darting and hesitant.

"Go ahead. It's okay," I said, hoping that there wouldn't be some inner detonation of jealousy.

"With an older woman," he said quietly.

"And?" I felt pinpricks in my face and neck, wondering what was coming.

"Her husband found out. One of those buttoned-up British types. He actually confronted me one day at a local bar. Told me off and said that if I went near his wife again he'd have me . . . taken care of."

"Jesus, Matthew. Do you think he could have?"

"Don't know. It gets funny in different parts of the world. You can't be sure. I didn't want to take a chance so I left."

"Probably a wise idea . . . Have you had any communication with the woman since?" I felt compelled to ask.

"No." He looked at me wistfully. "It wasn't love, Catherine. It was just a person who saw me and . . . she was the one who began it. Not like in our case. And I realized pretty soon that I was allowing myself to get into it because I was actually still . . . wanting you."

I was battling the raw feeling of jealousy when luckily the phone rang. It was Wade calling and I picked up. "We're back," he said in a singsong manner. This was a ruse, as he'd already called once to announce their return.

I played along. "How did it go?"

"It was wonderful. I'll tell you more later. . . . Is *he* there?"

"Yes . . . and everything should be fine." I aimed for a tone that wouldn't necessarily alert Matthew that Wade (of all people) was checking up on him. But that was fruitless; I saw Matthew's face cramping with shame.

"If I don't hear from you in two hours I'm calling back."

"Okay, sounds good."

The moment I put down the phone it rang again, thankfully, I thought. This time I recognized Anthony's wireless number. Excusing myself to Matthew, "Hi," I said. "I've been trying to reach you."

"When?"

"All last night."

"I was with Marco until late. And then I just didn't answer after I got home."

Which meant Fiona was spending the night with him, thought I. "So what news?"

"Get this. No stab wounds. No strangle marks around her neck. They did, however, match the finger to the body and they say it got torn off rather than severed."

"How would that have happened?"

"Bouncing around the river. Water-engorged tissue that softens."

I thought of the protagonist of *The Widower's Branch* finding the dead foot of a badly decomposed murdered woman. "So I guess nothing to link this murder to the others."

"Not really."

"So maybe somebody entirely different."

"That's what Marco thinks. That or the original guy is mixing it up now, finally."

"So what about the DNA sample they got from the car?"

"Nothing so far in terms of the national database."

"So where does that leave you?"

"In a state of frustration. Unfortunately we've had everything secondhand due to Concord's work. It was their boat that found her; the Connecticut River belongs to New Hampshire. Anyway, their preliminary says her body is bruised and mangled from passage over rocks and other detritus. Right now the only finding is drowning."

"So you mean, she . . . just went and submerged herself?"

At these words Matthew turned to me, watchful.

"Somebody could have pushed her in or forced her to get in. Probably with a gun or some other weapon. After coming all this way, looking for a job, it just wouldn't make sense that she'd drown herself. The uncle alleges she left Maryland full of hope and cheer."

"I see. That's really disturbing."

Anthony went on to say that the lack of cooperation and the rivalry between Vermont and New Hampshire had become even more polarizing. Marco was absolutely certain that his counterparts were harboring information and guarding their theories. "Marco says our chief coroner is better, younger than theirs. . . . I don't know."

Remembering the day I found Angela Parker, and the complaint I'd overheard Prozzo make about the coroner in Burlington, I said, "From what I saw he and the Vermont coroner are a bit at odds, aren't they?" I described how Prozzo ended up violating the protocol of waiting for the coroner to arrive and began his own investigation.

"Marco claims he was able to examine Angela Parker without touching her. And the coroner cut him slack because the guy wasn't reachable that day. My sense is that Marco respects the guy and the coroner respects him."

"Probably because they're both from around New York," I said snidely.

"You sound a bit preoccupied," Anthony pointed out. "Am I getting you at a bad time . . . playing with your chemistry set again?"

"I *am* in the middle of something."

"Don't tell me. You're trying out a flask of cat piss in your garden to deter the deer. "

I burst out laughing. "Actually, a friend of mine stopped by."

"Oh . . ."

I had no intention of letting him know Matthew was now wandering around the living room, knuckling the neck of his beer, glancing at the spines of books on my shelves. Henrietta approached him and he ran his fingers in a long scratch along her side. She collapsed on the floor, rolled over, and he began rubbing her belly just the way she loved it and just how he always used to do it.

Anthony went on, "There are a couple more things I want to run by you. Let's catch up in the next day or so. I'll be in and out a lot. I have to put in two heavy days at the hospital down in Springfield. I'll try you again if you don't reach me."

Once I put down the phone, Matthew, who'd been absorbed in reading titles on my bookshelf, turned to me. "Everything okay?"

"That was my neighbor, Anthony Waite. You never met him." I explained that Anthony was a psychiatrist working with the police on trying to solve the murders.

"You sounded a bit impatient."

I squinted at him. "Did I?"

He pivoted toward the bookshelf, as though purposely facing away from me. "Just my impression. But you always told me I was overly sensitive to your moods."

"Well, that was then. You're probably a different person now." I hope you are, anyway, I thought to myself.

"Yes and no," he said. Looking at him in profile, I could see how his face had colored with some emotion. Without even realizing it, I touched the divot on my neck that his fingernails had made. It occurred to me once again that perhaps I should have refused to let him visit without somebody else being there. Matthew, meanwhile, was slowly running his index finger over my long suite of Wilkie Collins.

"Have you read much of him?" I asked.

He turned to me, bemused. "After the way you went on about him in class?"

"I try not to think about the fact that you were once my student."

He smiled in silent acknowledgment of this. "I feel like I still am your student. I've read all the books on the lists you gave us: *A Sentimental Education, Slouching Towards Bethlehem, The Leopard, The Way We Live Now.* I've read all of Somerset Maugham's short stories. I've been keeping a journal since class. And of course, Wilkie Collins."

I let a few moments pass. "Which Collins *have* you read?"

"My first Collins was *The Moonstone,* which blew me away. Then *No Name,* which I almost liked even better. Then offbeat ones like *Man and Wife, My Lady's Money* . . ." He squinted and thought for a moment. "Isn't there one called *Guilty River*?"

"Talk about obscure." Ruminating for a bit, I then asked, "Ever hear of one called *The Widower's Branch*?"

With a look of bewilderment, he nodded his head and said plaintively, "Yeah, of course I have, you loaned it to me."

I shuddered inwardly. So he was one of the students who'd read it. "I did? I guess I don't remember. Breck once told me I read so much that it's affecting my memory."

"You appear pretty lucid to me."

"You can have a memory shot full of holes and still sound in compos mentis."

Matthew chuckled and said, "I'll try and remember that."

"Speaking of my memory, when did you actually get back from Thailand, again?"

"In April, right before I wrote to you."

"And you were there for how many years?"

"Two." He looked suspicious. "Why do you ask?"

"I was just trying to figure something out. . . . So you read *The Widower's Branch* right after we met?"

"Early on, before I . . . earned my stripes." I had to note he seemed totally relaxed. "One of the first times I came to your apartment in Burlington, I saw it on the bookshelf." With his prompting now I began to recollect. "And you were reluctant to lend it to me. Because you said it was so rare."

"But I also lent it to other students."

Matthew looked surprised. "Not in my class."

"Are you certain?"

"Absolutely," he said. "Do you know why I asked to borrow it? Just so I could . . . hold on to something that was dear to you . . . like a book. Because in the beginning I was afraid—I was sure—

that you'd change your mind about me and break things off."
He paused. "And if you didn't want to see me again, you'd have
to, at least once, to get the book back."

"Do you remember it at all?"

He thought for a moment. "I do remember it because it was
yours and especially then I wanted to remember it. . . . Isn't there
an outline that came after the text; it was for the rest of the novel?"
He turned from the bookshelf and faced me. "Doesn't this guy,
round about my age, I guess, lose everything: job, connections,
his beloved?"

I nodded.

Smiling weakly at me, he said, "The day you loaned it to me, I
remember going home and starting it and thinking it was the
perfect story for me at the time . . . for as long as it lasted."

"Why was it the perfect story?"

"Because I was lonely and because I was scared. Even more
so after we made love those first few times."

"Lonely?" I said. "Frightened? Wouldn't you feel . . . I don't
know, hopeful? Delighted?"

He shook his head. "You know I always obsessed about losing
you because of the age difference, because of the fact that I'd
been your student. I was always afraid you'd come to your senses
and suddenly refuse to see me again."

"I guess I did, finally, didn't I?" I found myself saying.

Looking crestfallen, he crossed his arms over his chest and
said, "After all this time do you think our relationship was a mistake?"

I wondered if Matthew had drawn some kind of parallel between his life and the life of the down-and-out, jilted Wilkie Collins character. After all, I'd jilted *him*. At last I said, "No." I had a
thought and took a moment to consider whether or not I wanted
to share it with him. "Relationships are odd," I said. "You don't
know how they come or even how they go. And suddenly they
start failing and sometimes fail so quickly. They remind me of a

recipe that I once got. Some far-flung North Dakota reader sent me instructions for a lovely cake that rose high into this beautiful shape. It almost looked like a golden hat, but then just like that it deflated into this miserable steaming curd."

"That's a depressing image!" Matthew exclaimed.

"But back to what I was saying before about the book . . . Here's an interesting fact you may not remember. So the protagonist in the novel finds this dead woman next to a huge fallen tree. She has some printed religious material in her pocket. And the outline suggests that more dead women will be found in a similar way, next to downed trees, their pockets lined with liturgical writings."

Matthew held me in a quizzical gaze. "I confess I don't remember that part. But why are you telling me this now?"

As matter-of-factly as I could, I explained the similarity between the plot synopsis in the book and the manner in which a few but not all of the women in the Upper Valley had been slain.

Matthew immediately sloughed it off. "Even with the printed matter found in women's pockets, it sounds a bit general, doesn't it, pinning this on an obscure book published a hundred and fifty years ago? Surely lots of religious fanatics become serial killers."

This reaction coincided with the opinion of Theresa, who, when I'd first e-mailed to ask her Victorian scholarly advice, felt that the detail of dead women found by fallen trees with, as she put it, "psalms in their pockets" could be argued as moot to the search for our killer. Beyond this, she claimed to be unaware of any widely publicized nineteenth-century murders on which Wilkie Collins might have modeled his final uncompleted fiction, but encouraged me to research it for myself. Which I did, to no avail. There was little written about *The Widower's Branch*.

"Another factoid that you might find interesting. The literature left in the pockets of some of these women was Seventh-Day Adventist."

Matthew groaned. "Oh God. Not one of us. Well, in that case he may be purposely leaving his victims by trees with lots of homilies hoping in his own perverted mind to convert them in the afterlife." Soon his gaze grew concerned. "This whole thing has really taken a toll on you, hasn't it?"

"Especially since I believe that my copy of *The Widower's Branch* is probably the only one in the Upper Valley."

Matthew shook his head. "Not necessarily," he said. "Even if somebody were patterning killings after an obscure novel, this particular book is well over a hundred years old. So surely there's a digitized version of it available on the Internet."

"There isn't," I informed him. "I searched with several different engines. There is just a brief synopsis. And nothing about bodies found near fallen trees or the religious material. Just a citation that *The Widower's Branch* was Collins's last, unfinished text, his most obscure and unknown work."

Matthew asked, "Do you still have passwords for JSTOR and Project Muse?"

"Nope. They were inactivated as soon as Saint Mike's gave me the boot."

However, I'd been able to use Theresa's Wesleyan sign-on for these two sites and had checked them all, including Boolean searches on Yahoo and Google. Then I explained how I thought my copy of the unfinished novel had disappeared, and forgotten I'd loaned it to Breck.

He looked startled to hear this. "You know, Catherine, *that* is really weird."

"What is?"

"That the book disappeared. I just remembered something—and obviously I was afraid to tell you this at the time—but when I borrowed your copy I put it in a very specific place on the edge of my desk. And then one day it just vanished. I looked everywhere for it. I tore apart the whole apartment. I was frantic. But then, even weirder, it just *reappeared* one night wedged in the bookshelf,

as though it had always been there. And I just couldn't understand how that could be because I checked through every single
book on my bookshelf at least a half dozen times."

"That kind of stuff with missing books happens to me all the
time," I reassured him.

"Yeah, but I almost had this feeling that somebody actually
took it away and then brought it back."

"Like who?"

Matthew shook his head. "Anyone who visited me, I suppose."

I decided to make light of this. "Literary elves burrow into the
pages of books you never crack. They come out at night and do all
kinds of mischief."

"For the purpose of a mind fuck," Matthew said, and we both
laughed. "So how *is* Breck?" he asked after a few moments of silence.

I told him she was fine and had become involved with an older
woman. "She won't be happy when she knows I've seen you."

"Who can blame her?" Matthew said with admirable equa-
nimity.

"None of my friends are happy that I'm seeing you," I felt I had
to point out.

"But that doesn't apply to you, hopefully," he said.

I endured his steady gaze for a moment or two. "I can't say
that I feel completely comfortable . . . with you here."

Matthew looked disconsolate. I was inadvertently touching
my scar again, this time in full view of him, and I could see it reg-
ister. He took a step forward, as though wanting to touch it himself, but then held back, momentarily at odds with himself. At
last he said, "Honestly, Catherine, do you think that I'm really
capable of doing something like that again?"

I panicked for a moment, unable to even speak.

"If you really thought so, then would you have invited me to
visit you?" He glanced around the house and turned his palms
up. "Alone?"

I had to respond even though I felt I couldn't. "It's not so simple, Matthew." I managed to control my voice. "Went . . . against my better judgment."

"I'm glad you took the risk. And I'm happy to leave right now just to prove a point."

Feeling a bit more composed, I said, "So you think if you left right now the next time I'd feel safer?"

"I'd hope so, Catherine. Certainly with time."

I knew I wouldn't.

SEVENTEEN

THE MORNING FOLLOWING Matthew's visit I got a phone call from Breck informing me that an article about the most recent body of "an illegal alien" being found had appeared in the Newark *Star-Ledger*. The paper reported that the forensics so far were not matching the latest victim with the previous one; however, the residents of Springfield, Vermont, and Claremont, New Hampshire, were once again fearful, locking their doors at night, while the purchase of guns kept skyrocketing at the local shops. In the Upper Valley of Vermont and New Hampshire, emergency town meetings were called to debate placing a temporary moratorium on women bicycling or jogging the roads alone. The paper even mentioned incidents of frightened homeowners shooting at suspicious shadows on their land.

"So people really *have* shot out into the dark," I commented. "I didn't read that one in the *Valley News*. Thank you, New Jersey, for telling me what's going on in Vermont."

"New Jersey has its virtues, Ma," Breck said. "Lots of them. Just waiting for you to discover."

"Could you be any more obvious? If you'd only stop sounding like an infomercial and find me a pig sitter, I'll throw my other two critters in the car."

There was a brief silence. "I was actually thinking of coming *there* for a short visit."

"I'd be absolutely thrilled."

"I'd have some time if I visit tomorrow. Would that work?"

She'd have some time? As far as I knew, Violet was the only one employed. "I'm not going anywhere," I told her.

As soon as I finished my conversation with Breck, I tried calling Anthony and got his voice mail. I left him a short message. I wondered what specifically he wanted to discuss with me.

The last time Breck visited me was in early January, just prior to Angela Parker's disappearance. When she arrived this time it was on a dry, cloudless Saturday afternoon. I told her to meet me at the Norwich farmer's market, one of her favorite venues, a once-a-week consortium of organic farmers and bakers and crafts-people that usually hired a nerve-grating fiddle band. Barely enduring the music, I was standing by a pyramid of mottled heirloom tomatoes when I saw Breck in a pair of pale yellow capri pants strolling across the trampled lawn holding a big straw shopping bag and wearing a matching sun hat. She'd gained some weight (much needed) and her face, though always augustly angular, wasn't looking so haggard. Before noticing me, she paused at a stand selling huge bouquets of phlox and dahlia and mallow and immediately set to putting together an arrangement.

"Those for me?" I said as I approached.

She dropped all the stems, threw her arms around me, and squeezed me tightly. "You look so grown-up," I said. "Like a young mother out shopping for her family."

"Not with this stomach," Breck said, pulling up her form-fitting cotton shirt and showing me a rippling abdomen. "Young mothers don't have this."

"Despite your six-pack you look like you're eating," I said.

"Eating like a horse," she said, reaching into her purse to pay the silver-haired, florid-faced lady who was wrapping the purchase.

"But probably exercising yourself to death," I said.

Breck explained, "Keeps me sane. What can I tell you. . . . May I ask you something?" Breck said as we began wandering among the stalls of local honey vendors and bakery "artisans" who offered golden loaves and pies and homespun macramé handbags. "Why do you think so many women in Vermont dress in formless clothes . . . even ones who are slender?"

"Rural people don't get dolled up for daily activities. You know that. But, believe me, a lot of us know how to throw ourselves together when we have to."

"Well, but look at you," she said. "In your black leggings and your sleeveless linen shirt."

"If I wasn't meeting you I'd be sporting tennis shoes and a muumuu."

"Baloney. You like to look good."

"I don't give it nearly as much thought as I used to." I reminded her of the wardrobe that I'd accumulated at deep discounts when I was on staff at several magazines. "Most of it just sits there. When we get home, you should go through it and see if you want anything."

"Okay, I will." Breck considered something for a moment. "Ma," she said, "I know you think fashions are heavily influenced by environment. But I never changed the way I dressed when I moved up here."

"That's because you were making a statement."

"At school they called me 'the dress-up freak.' The 'skinny minny.'"

"Well, you were a displaced city girl."

"Still am. New Jersey isn't exactly Manhattan. Even though we're twenty minutes away by *twain*."

We breezed by all the prepared food stands and found only one that Breck would consider; she bought us curried tuna salad sandwiches on baguettes and beet salad with chunks of chèvre. Just outside the perimeter of the market we grabbed an empty picnic table. Breck, who had run to put the fresh flowers in her car, returned with a thermos of herbal iced tea and a manuscript-page-sized Handi Wipe with which she scoured the table. "You certainly come prepared," I said. "A little anal retentive?"

She gave me a withering look. "Somebody in this family has got to be."

We unwrapped our sandwiches and Breck poured tea into clear plastic cups. After watching her take a few enviable bites, I remarked, "You're eating like a wolf!"

"Lunch," Breck said, jutting her prominent chin forward and waving her sandwich at me. "That's what happens at one o'clock in the afternoon." A stiff, sultry breeze came up and blew fine, shoulder-length hair into her face. She quickly reached into her straw grab bag and pulled out a tortoiseshell clasp to pin it back. She took another bite of her sandwich, chewed carefully, and then said, "So . . . Elena Mayaguez. Is she the first non-Caucasian?"

I nodded.

"Nice to know that he doesn't discriminate."

"I guess that's a point in his favor," I managed to say, sipping my iced tea. "If, indeed, it's the same guy, who has just changed his strategy."

Breck thought for a moment and then said, "You've been following this closely, Ma. Do you really think they're doing all they can? Rather than just investigating, are they trying to create a profile of this person, what he's all about and what he's after?"

"Why do you suppose they're using Anthony?"

Breck reminded me that with all the murders nobody had been able to get DNA samples.

I glanced at the scattering of people sitting at picnic tables around us and said quietly, "Just between us they *do* have a sample now. Though it's not public knowledge. So keep it to yourself. They found it in Elena Mayaguez's car. If it *is* the same guy, and it might not be, this is his first misstep, DNA-wise. Not on her, but they did find identical synthetic fibers on some of the women that would indicate he used gloves. He was wearing gloves when he attacked Angela Parker. Then again, it was the middle of winter."

"The middle of winter," Breck repeated dismally as she wiped her mouth. "So glad to be away from that endless Vermont dreariness."

"New Jersey ain't exactly the tropics."

"Well, we don't get walls of snow in Jersey. . . . Anyway, so this detective is down with the idea that the murderer is lifting his method from *your* book?"

"Just one of the theories being floated. There may be another copy around. We don't know."

Breck put her sandwich down. "Okay, so who else *has* read your book?"

Obviously, I would avoid mentioning Matthew's having read it. "I had several students who borrowed it. I promised Anthony I'd get him their names, but I haven't been able to find the right rosters of the classes they were in. Of course I have all the class rosters that I don't need. I could have sworn I lent it to Wade; though he claims not, I don't find myself quite believing him."

Breck's eyes sparked and she drew in a sharp breath. "Him again?"

"He always acts so innocent and open with me but I can't help being a little wary."

Breck added, "Violence toward objects can forewarn violence toward people."

"The thing is that he knows that, too, and admits it freely."

We both fell speculatively silent, and then I noticed her eyeing the half-sandwich I'd left on my plate. Pointing to it, she said, "Don't you like it?"

"I've lost my appetite." It was hardly the thought of Wade possibly being the killer, but rather the idea of broaching Matthew's visit to Breck, which I knew I had to do. She wrapped the leftover food in my napkin and carefully placed it inside her bag.

When we got home, Breck received a riotous greeting from the animals, particularly Henrietta, who'd always adored her. After slobbering all over her, Virgil and Mrs. Billy eventually went back to their favorite sleeping spots in my office; Henrietta shadowed us to the kitchen.

"Madame, where have you been all my life?" Breck said, scratching our darling behind the ears. Henrietta flopped down on the floor sideways, soliciting more. "You're shameless," Breck said, then combing through her purse, brought out my remaining half sandwich. "She knows where her bread is buttered," she added, leveraging a hunk of tuna and holding her palm out. Henrietta rolled the morsel off with her snout and snorted in momentary pleasure.

"Okay, now go under the table!" Breck ordered her. Henrietta listened, dutifully righted herself, and then muscled her way under. We heard the thudding sound of her collapse.

"You're the only person she really listens to," I marveled as Breck began rubbing the pig's belly with her toes.

"That's because she wuvs me," Breck said in a baby voice.

Over the next twenty-four hours I found it impossible to bring up the subject of Matthew's visit. On the second night of Breck's stay, I awoke at around three A.M., thinking I heard rustling sounds; the bedroom Breck had lived in throughout her teenaged years, and where she'd gone through her first serious bout with anorexia, was right across the hall from mine. Anticipating her arrival, I'd purposely exhumed her scrapbooks, stuffed animals, board games, and ribbons and costume jewelry. I got up, fully expecting to find her sitting in bed, sifting through her old trinkets and belongings as she had a habit of doing when she visited. Instead, I saw her standing in an expensive blue silk bathrobe (that Violet obviously bought her), scouring the upstairs bookshelves as Matthew had done downstairs two days before. I asked what she was doing.

Breck remained turned away. "Just browsing."

"At this time of night? What are you looking for?"

"Nothing in particular." She deliberately picked *Armadale* by Wilkie Collins out of the shelf and showed it to me.

"I just reread it," I told her. "I need to bring it back downstairs."

"To your Wilkie Collins shelf?" Breck sounded a bit sarcastic. "Is it any good?"

"Yes, quite." I told her many people put *Armadale* up there with *The Woman in White, No Name,* and *The Moonstone*. It portrays a very evil, powerful female character who was considered to be quite controversial when the novel first appeared. *Armadale* was also one of the author's more socially advanced novels.

"For one thing, the protagonist is half black."

"Oh, like Anthony's wife."

"Precisely."

"How is *she* doing?"

"Did I tell you she was having an affair for a year and a half before he found out?"

"Nope, kept that little tidbit to yourself."

"She didn't want me to find out about it for some reason."

"Maybe because the same thing happened to you. With Dad." Breck flipped the book over and scanned the back cover and said, "I might borrow this one if that's okay."

"You can, but only if you read it this time."

"I will." I could see a thought influencing her expression. "Mom," she said, suddenly plaintive, "I've been here nearly two days."

"Yeah?"

"Isn't there something rather important that you need to tell me?"

I waited for a moment. "First I'd like to know whether or not it was the reason behind your . . . impromptu visit."

"Obviously."

"How's *that* supposed to make me feel? You come here not to visit me but to check up on me."

"How do you think *I* feel when you never ask me how my partner is and refuse to come to New Jersey?"

I started getting irritated. "Okay, pig notwithstanding, I hate traveling."

"What do you mean, you hate traveling? You and I have gone all over the world."

"That was then. I wish you wouldn't take it so personally that I don't like going too far from home anymore."

Breck shook her head, exasperated. "Look, I'm really worried about you. God knows you used to worry about me."

"The *mother* is supposed to worry."

"It also happens the other way round!"

"Those jokers down the road!" I exclaimed. "I can't believe they'd have the balls to call you up."

"Believe it. . . . Look, Mom, we all want to protect you. You can't fault us for that. I mean, were you at least going to tell me?"

"Of course. I was working up to it . . . before you left. I've just been afraid of your reaction."

"So when did he get back from Asia?"

"April."

"How many times have you seen him, honestly?"

"Once."

"You know you should not have been alone with him."

"Bad move, I admit it. But Wade and Paul knew he was here and called during his visit. And it went fine. He behaved like a gentleman."

"Oh great!" Breck's tone was deeply sarcastic.

Ignoring her, I said, "We even talked about the incident."

"How evolved of both of you."

"I don't want you worrying about this."

Breck suddenly fumed, "What do you mean? The guy fucking ruined your life!"

"That's a bit melodramatic."

She looked disgusted. "Oh my God! Now you're downplaying what he *did*. It was directly because of him that you lost your teaching job."

"No, it was because of some letter-writing lunatic."

"Did you ever consider that letter-writing lunatic maybe was *him* trying to get you fired?"

I actually *had* considered this. "But the person also wrote to his parents. That was not what he wanted."

Breck was shaking her head. "Mom, I just . . . can't understand how you could have allowed yourself to be alone with him."

"I know it was wrong. But it's been a couple of years. I just . . . I went on instinct."

Breck looked at me warily. "Did you tell Anthony about this visit?" I merely stared at her. "No, of course you didn't."

"Anthony is not my guardian. He doesn't even know Matthew."

"But he keeps an eye on you."

"Wait a minute. How do you think Paul and Wade knew? Because I told them Matthew was coming here."

"At least you had the presence of mind to do that."

I leaned against the hallway wall. "You don't think it matters that Matthew and I have been apart for quite a while, now? Out of touch? Disengaged?"

Breck shook her head and looped a strand of hair behind an ear. Then she said, "Maybe you're not so involved with *him*. But what about *his* feelings toward you?"

"I think his feelings have changed, Breck. And that's why it's less complicated getting together with him."

Setting the Wilkie Collins novel down on a painted wooden chair standing right next to her, she said, "This is where you go so wrong in your thinking, in your judgment. Matthew will always be in love with you. And *that's why* . . . you'll never be able to trust him."

There was truth in what she said, and I didn't try to refute it.

Fighting to control her voice, Breck said, "You loved him more than you ever loved me."

"*That* is not true!"

"And you lost so much because of him and now you're . . . just going to let him back in again."

"Letting him visit once is not letting him back in."

She shook her head. "I know your pattern. You've gotten into bad relationships way too easily."

Despite my resentment at being criticized by my daughter, despite the urge to retort with something caustic, I swallowed the bitter commentary.

I remembered the time she came home one weekend during college without warning and found Matthew and me together. I'd previously mentioned him to her (in an admittedly scant description) in terms of his doing some yard- and housework and that, due to his estrangement from his parents, we'd formed an unusual "friendship." However, when she walked in the door and found me sitting on his lap, I believe she was flabbergasted, even though she hissed, "Why am I not surprised?" She was carrying an armful of textbooks, presumably to study in the sanctity of her bedroom. Glaring at us, she hurled them down on the floor; some of the spines cracked and perfect-bound pages came loose. She knew how much I revered books and her act of sacrilege was clearly directed at me. Then she cursed us and went upstairs to her bedroom, where Matthew was keeping his weekend bag. By then he and I had extricated ourselves from each other and were standing there waiting for the next bombardment. Finally we heard Breck bounding down the stairs and she burst into the room redfaced.

"Okay," she said to me. "One of us is leaving. Who is it going to be?"

"I'm leaving," Matthew said to her.

She refused to speak, not to mention look at him.

"But I'm going to have to go up there and get some of my things."

She flicked her head as if to say, "Then do it!," her eyes boring into me.

Now I moved toward Breck, stroking her hair and resting my hand on her shoulder. "For what it's worth, the visit went fine."

"It was the first one. His expectations were lower." An arduous silence followed. "Just one thing I ask of you," she said at last.

"What's that?"

"Don't hide from me the next time he comes. I want to know."

I found myself hesitating. "Okay."

"You don't sound sure, Ma. So is that a promise?"

"Of course it's a promise," I told her.

EIGHTEEN

THE PHONE RANG SEVERAL TIMES the morning of Breck's departure, and not recognizing the numbers, I let all the calls go to voice mail. I found it odd that I had yet to hear from Anthony, who claimed he'd wanted to confer with me—presumably about the investigation. I wondered if he'd somehow missed my phone message. When I finally listened there was just one voice mail, from somebody who spoke without identifying herself. "Hi, Catherine. This is all so very strange." Then she hesitated. I knew I recognized the voice but couldn't place it at first, annoyed that the caller didn't introduce herself. "It's like your visit did something to break the ice. I mean, not literally." Then she laughed a throaty laugh.

How could this person assume that I would identify her? But then just before she spoke her next sentence I twigged.

"He—Tim—stopped talking, completely stopped chatting to me not fifteen minutes after you and Anthony left that afternoon. Hasn't said a word to me in quite a while." Her voice cracked and when she spoke again, it was quavering. "His aunt called me earlier this morning. To tell me they found him. Under the pile of debris exactly where I said he'd be." Her voice regained some of its composure and she went on, "Now that my head is clearing, I'm hearing from other people. I have to say it's somehow meaningful that the woman who disappeared down there was found in the water just a few days before Tim."

The phone rang again as I was listening to the very last words of the message.

"Hi, Catherine, it's me, Nan again. I don't know if you got my first message."

"Just finished listening to it." I probably sounded snippy.

"I'm not calling about that anymore. I'm calling about Anthony."

About Anthony? What could she possibly have to tell me about Anthony?

"My contact in the Burlington police department just overheard a report and got in touch with me. He knows who Anthony is and that the two of you came to see me. Apparently, this morning Anthony had some kind of fall in a men's room in a rest area on Route 89. It happened twenty miles south of Burlington."

A fall in a men's room? Twenty miles south of Burlington? What was he doing up there? "Are you sure?"

"Positive. He—Anthony—has already reported it himself."

My chest tightened. I felt momentary disequilibrium and had to brace my hand against the wall. "Do you know if he's okay?"

"He's driving himself home. The state police advised him to go to the ER at Fletcher Allen, but he refused to and took responsibility for himself. I'm sorry to be calling you with all of this, especially because I don't have much information. But I thought you'd want to know."

I told her I appreciated it, promised to let her know when I found out more, and said good-bye.

I put the phone down, feeling bewildered. I wondered if Anthony's trip to Burlington had something to do with what he'd wanted to discuss with me. I hardly imagined I'd be able to reach him on his mobile phone but he surprised me by picking up, sounding very groggy.

"I just heard what happened to you," I said. "The Burlington police called Nan O'Brien. Are you okay?"

"I don't honestly know." Anthony sounded strangely breathless. "I stopped to take a leak. One of the urinals was overflowing. The tiles were slippery. I slipped and fell backwards. I woke up on the floor. I feel strange right now, Catherine, dizzy. I probably shouldn't be on the phone."

"You also shouldn't be driving!"

"I'm only ten minutes from home. Fiona is there, waiting. I'll be okay." There was a pause.

"Why were you going to Burlington?"

"I was on my way to see the coroner. I have something I need to talk to you about. But I'm feeling . . . I should really get off the phone. When can we talk?"

"I'll be here."

He clicked off without saying good-bye.

What was going on? Had I only spoken to him the night Matthew visited I would now know why Anthony had been on his way to see the coroner. I strongly considered calling Fiona and insisting that she drive Anthony to the hospital, but then stopped short, knowing she was quite capable of taking matters into her own hands.

Wade's office, normally as quiet as a catacomb, was filled with ornery taxpayers, Paul included, waiting on line for scheduled appointments with the tax assessors. Wade was answering the phone, directing traffic into the office where the tax assessors were conducting hearings. Even though Paul was standing close to his desk, the two men were barely acknowledging each other. When Paul finally went in for his meeting I noted to Wade that there seemed to be a hostile atmosphere between them.

Looking around to make sure what he said was in confidence, Wade whispered emphatically, "I'm in a very difficult position here."

I pointed out the obvious, that we all have to pay our taxes.

"I know, but he's not worried about himself per se. It's about those who just can't afford it, the increase itself." Indicating the room full of fidgeting, dyspeptic-looking people, Wade lowered his voice and whispered, "Many of these folks just don't have the resources." He reminded me that if an owner gets behind on taxes for two years, their home and land go up for tax sale to the highest bidder, who theoretically has the right to purchase the property for a fraction of its value by covering the owed taxes. "It's a sorry situation all around." He squinted at me. "Did you hear about Anthony?"

"Yeah. How did *you* hear?"

"I was in the corner store when Fiona breezed in looking for hydrogen peroxide and shit like that . . . for his wounds."

"So I guess she didn't take him to the hospital. "

"She told me he's been refusing to go."

"So typical for a doctor."

Neither of us spoke for a moment and then Wade looked at me askance. "So what can I do for you?"

"Am I not allowed to visit?" I heard myself say, still preoccupied with the news of Anthony's mishap.

He smirked. "Yeah, but what's on *your* mind?"

I asked if he had time to go to Joanie's for lunch. Wade looked at his watch and then the room full of waiting people and said it might be difficult to just leave.

At that moment, Paul emerged from his meeting with the tax assessors, flushed and fuming. Glancing at him, Wade exclaimed, "Oh, God, maybe I *should* leave."

As Paul was heading toward us, I said to Wade, "I'll invite him?"

"No!" he whispered fiercely.

But it was too late. "Come on to lunch with us, Paul. You can bend my ear all you want."

Wade looked exasperated.

"I don't need a sounding board," Paul said. "I need action."

"Oh puuuhleeeease!" said Wade.

"I hate these tax people," Paul said. "They're a bunch of idiots, except Barry Dean, who was a partner in a good Boston tax firm. Maybe I should move to *Boston* to get away from morons like them!"

"You don't think there are tax assessors in Boston?" Wade threw back at him. "In fact I'm sure taxes are a lot higher there."

"Well, at least they get some municipal services. Sewage and electricity and cable TV." He turned to look at the petitioners waiting their turn and then said confidentially, "These people are strapped with higher tax and they're getting nothing for it. Except possible bankruptcy. It's not their fault the state has no money."

Wade went into the records room where his part-time assistant was doing some research and announced that we were going to lunch. Wedged between them, I walked the short distance down the road and across the parking lot with the drive-up banking kiosk to Joanie's Café. To my great surprise, I discovered the café was under new ownership and was now called Midge's.

Gaping at the new bold-lettered sign, I said, "When did this happen?"

"Where the dickens have you been?" Wade said.

"Living inside my own head, clearly."

"You do read the paper, don't you?" Paul wondered.

Wade opened the door and held it for us. As we walked in Paul said to me, "Guess why the ownership has changed?"

Before anybody could answer we heard a sneering voice say, "Joanie became a tax refugee and moved to New Hampshuh." It was Sheila, everybody's favorite smart-assed blond waitress, referring to the fact that there is no state income tax in New Hampshire.

"At least some things stayed the same around here," I told her. "Like you." Then to Paul, "But there's your answer. Move to New Hampshire."

"No way in hell. I hate New Hampshire politics. I guess I'm not leaving my house until they carry me out."

"You folks need to chill and sit down," Sheila said.

"So how come you ended up staying on if Joanie got out of Dodge?" Wade asked as we followed her to a table that stuck out from the wall like a vinyl ellipse, one of the restaurant's new refurbishments.

"Because people *like* me," Sheila said with a disagreeable tone as she dropped three plastic menus on the table.

Under its new ownership, the café had been given a makeover of chintz curtains, new tables that were affixed to the wall, and shiny black-and-white linoleum floor tiles. A stainless-steel hood had been installed above the griddle, which was definitely an improvement over the previous nonvented incarnation that had given the café its characteristic burnt-bacon smell. The menu was only slightly different, gentrified, so that staples such as chicken salad and bacon sandwiches became chicken salad, cilantro, and pancetta sandwiches (or, alternately, wraps). Paul and I each ordered one, he asked for a vanilla milkshake, and Wade decided to have an omelette *au* Vermont chèvre. Once Sheila took our order, I said to Paul, "Imagine how much tax you'd pay if we all lived in Sweden."

"Can we move on?" Wade said to both of us. "I think we've worn through this discussion."

"Fine!" Paul said irritably, fanning himself with the menu.

Spying him, Sheila came over and snatched it out of his hands. "It's brand-new. I don't want you bending it."

"Listen to you," Wade said.

And then I told them, "Okay, guys, I got you here for a reason."

They both looked at me, a bit startled.

"Why did you have to call Breck and tell her about Matthew's visit?" Paul and Wade traded a glance and then looked at me again. "She just assumed that I was going to keep from telling her, myself. If I don't hide it from you, why should I hide it from her?"

Paul, who normally could be defensive and ornery, said, "You're right. I'm sorry. It was wrong of us."

"What you really mean to say is that it's none of your business."

"That's true." He gestured to Wade, who said, "We're out of order, agreed." As though needing an activity to ground his momentary discomfort, Wade grabbed my menu and his and called to Sheila, "Since you've appointed yourself as the menu police, why don't you take these, too."

Sheila smirked and made a beeline to our table. "Suit yourself, honey," she said, and walked away.

I addressed them both. "I will say that nothing happened between Matthew and me. And nothing is going to happen."

Wade reminded me, "Like Paul said before, we all promised to look after one another." The two men exchanged yet another meaningful glance.

"What's going on?" I asked them.

But they held back.

I was about to accuse them of harboring something when Sheila arrived with our plates of food. Once she set everything down, she turned to me, hands jammed on her hips. "Okay, gotta tell you something, Miss Catherine," she said. I braced myself for sarcasm, but then she surprised me. "Something's been bugging me for days."

I turned my palms to the ceiling, as if to say, "What could it possibly be?"

"Okay, so as we all know, I have a reputation as the biggest mouth this side of the Connecticut River. Keep that in mind. So just as I was getting off work the other day, I had myself an interesting visitor who was asking me lots of questions. Like how long I've known *you*. Like what do I *know* about you. Like do I know if *you* have any boyfriends. But hey, I didn't give him diddly."

"Who was it?" I asked, wondering if it might have been Matthew.

"That detective from down Springfield way."

"Prozzo?" I exclaimed, aghast.

Paul and Wade had fallen suspiciously quiet. "Prozzo," Wade said at last in a snide whisper.

A pall was cast over the table. We all sat there staring at one another, none of us eating. Without a further word Sheila began walking briskly toward the back of the restaurant and the clamoring kitchen.

Paul pressed both his hands on the table, as though he wanted to rise out of his chair. Then he looked at Wade. "Now we have to tell her."

"Tell me what?"

"Why we called Breck . . . because Prozzo came to see *us,* too. Asking questions about you, but mostly questions about Matthew Blake."

"About Matthew?"

Looking apologetic, Wade said, "And just so you know, I told him everything I knew, because to be honest, I was glad that for once he wasn't dogging me."

NINETEEN

W HAT COULD PROZZO possibly want to know about me
that he didn't already know? And why had he been asking
questions about Matthew? Why hadn't the detective just sought
me out? I called the general number for the Springfield police,
and learned that he was "out on an appointment." I left a message for him, then called to see how Anthony was doing (with a
dual purpose of procuring Prozzo's cell number), and Fiona surprised me by picking up the phone. She apologized for answering by saying, "One of Anthony's medical school friends should
be calling right back. He's a neurologist."

"How is he?"

"I'm about to take him to the hospital . . . finally. He's been
refusing to go. But then he had an episode in the shower."

She'd heard him cry out and found him slumped down in the
stall, leaning against the tiles under a deluge of water. She kept
asking what was wrong and all he could say was, "I can't think, I
just can't think!" When he recovered from this momentary fit, Anthony finally agreed to be driven to the hospital and gave her the
name of the neurologist he'd known in medical school, who happened to be affiliated with Dartmouth-Hitchcock Medical Center.

"I don't mean to usher you off the phone, but that doctor is supposed to be calling about meeting us over there. I already have Anthony in the car."

Now even more worried about Anthony, I knew it wasn't the time to ask him for phone numbers, not to mention find out why he'd gone to Burlington. I made Fiona promise to stay in touch about his injury.

I tried the Springfield police station yet again with no luck, and then realized my deadline for the latest column was four o'clock that very afternoon. Worrying that Prozzo now was focusing his suspicions on Matthew and perhaps on me as well, I decided it was best to remain occupied until I heard from him.

An archivist had written to tell me how to preserve newspaper clippings, in essence how to remove acid from the paper, which causes it to turn yellow and fall apart. I dissolved a milk-of-magnesia tablet in a quart of club soda and poured the mixture in a pan that was large enough to hold the flattened clipping, one of my op-ed pieces that I'd written for *The New York Times* on vanishing wildlife in Vermont, including the bobolink getting churned under by the hay threshers. Before putting the newsprint in the pan, I was instructed to put in a piece of nylon net that would allow me to pick up the paper without tearing it. I soaked the clipping for an hour, removed it, and just as I was patting it dry with the intention of allowing it to cure completely in the air, the dogs began barking madly: somebody had pulled into the driveway. I went and looked out my study window and recognized Prozzo's Jeep Cherokee. At last. He was swiping his signature Ray-Bans off his face and beginning a bowlegged walk toward the door. I went and met him. Tucking his sunglasses in his shirt pocket, he apologized for showing up without phoning beforehand.

"Got your message, Catherine. I didn't get back right away. I was actually hoping to see Anthony before dropping in on you. But he's not home. And hasn't been answering his cell phone."

"He's gone to the hospital." I briefly explained what I knew.

Prozzo appeared genuinely alarmed. "That sounds so bizarre, falling like that. Talk about bad luck!"

"You coming in?"

"Sure. Just don't offer me any dog biscuits." He patted his small belly. "I'm dieting."

The dogs, still barking, went up and sniffed at him and then shied away. Before going to sit down, he stood for a moment at the threshold to the kitchen, calculating something. "This is going to . . ." He stared at me. "Make things tricky. I need to get into the hospital to speak to him."

"Do you want something to drink?"

He raised his bushy eyebrows. "Yeah, maybe some water." While I fetched a jelly glass and filled it from the tap, he pulled out a kitchen chair and sat down, his bulk setting off a complaint from the wooden spokes.

"Careful," I admonished. "Don't lean back."

He chuckled at my petty concern.

I faced him. "So am I one of your new leads in the River Valley murders?"

Prozzo managed to laugh. "Who told you that?"

"A big-mouth waitress. And my neighbors. You should know that in a small town like this people protect one another, especially old-timers. And it gets back who's been talking or asking questions. I just want to know why you're questioning them and not *me*."

"Here I am," Prozzo said. Indicating the chair in front of me, he said, "Why don't you have a seat."

Feeling beleaguered, I said, "I'd rather stand."

"Okay." He paused, obviously for effect. "You had a visitor the other day."

"I get visitors all the time."

"Your former boyfriend."

I merely stared at him.

"You've been spending time together?"

241

"We've seen each other exactly once."

"So you've seen Matthew Blake only once."

I shivered when I heard the name pass his lips. "Matthew Blake," I repeated. "You do your homework, don't you?"

"You could say it's my job." He fell calculatedly silent, his flinty eyes once again riveted to me.

Remembering how he'd hounded Hiram Osmond to no real avail, I said with skepticism, "So *Matthew*'s the one you're trailing now?"

Prozzo was watching me carefully.

"It wouldn't be your first miscalculation."

I could see a flush creeping into his face and neck. "There's a lot of trial and error to this line of work, Catherine. It's not as breezy as TV."

"Do you happen to know that Matthew Blake has been abroad these last few years?"

At this, Prozzo reached into his breast pocket and pulled out an eight-by-eleven sheet of paper folded into quarters. "This is an employment contract with an ESL school in Cambridge that he signed a little more than two years ago. According to them, he's been steadily employed since the date of signature." He handed me a photocopy of a document with lots of fine print. A date was circled in black ink: April 5, 2007. I recognized Matthew's signature below it. Then Prozzo passed along a dot matrix printout of a Qantas Airways manifest: February 23, 2007. Marked in yellow highlighter: MATTHEW R. BLAKE and a corresponding passport number. "He did go to Thailand. This is the record of his flight home. He was out of the country for just over two weeks. And coincidentally, his return predates the first murder by one month."

I could feel my breath catch as I carefully placed the incriminating papers on the table. And finally sat down, my head reeling. So this meant that Matthew had lied about his life in Bangkok, had lied about his love affair with a married woman.

Marco went on. "When I stopped by to speak to your friends, I gathered he told you a whole different story."

My heart pounding wildly, I managed to say, "He told me . . . he was gone for two years and came back in April."

"That's pretty spectacular make-believe, don't you think?" The detective wrinkled up his face. "Why do you think he'd lie about that?"

I had no idea. My brain started conjuring up all sorts of questions and possible explanations and then, in the midst of the flurry, I remembered in a panic that Matthew had read the obscure Wilkie Collins novel.

I refrained from delivering this crucial bit of evidence right away, for I knew then I'd be damning him definitively. There was still something in me that conspired to protect him, to preserve his innocence, futile as this may sound. I was finally able to gather my thoughts enough to say, "Okay, the lie certainly makes him a suspect. But why is he a suspect to begin with?"

"As you know, we have several suspects. In his particular case, in 2006, he was arrested for assaulting a woman."

I was feeling dizzy now but managed to ask, "When?"

"While he was in college in Burlington."

But surely I would have known about this, about the accusation and the arrest. How could Matthew have hidden this from me?

"And presumably you know his mother is very religious?" Prozzo continued. I nodded. "That she was part of the Seventh-Day Adventist community? And that Matthew went to a Seventh-Day Adventist secondary school?"

"I knew the mother was a Seventh-Day Adventist. But there are plenty around here. The last part, about his attending a religious school, I wasn't aware of."

"So two omissions on his part," Prozzo said, making a temple with his hands. "But here's the third most important connection, which I'm actually surprised you haven't made yourself."

I shut my eyes for a moment, fully expecting him to mention the Wilkie Collins novel.

Instead he said, "All these women who have been murdered were strangled in the process. Didn't you ever make that connection?"

Obviously Paul and Wade had told him about Matthew's hands around my throat; I suppressed the impulse to touch my neck and found myself staring at Prozzo's garish pinky ring with a feeling of utter hopelessness. How could it possibly be: Matthew responsible for the deaths of all these women?

I managed to get out, "Of course I did. But I thought he was out of the country all this time. Surely you understand why . . . I wouldn't suspect him, myself?"

Prozzo nodded. "Absolutely. But confirming he lied to you about his return is a big piece of evidence that I need."

I heard myself sigh. "It's actually *not* the biggest piece."

Prozzo looked bewildered. "What are you trying to say to me?"

I rested my forehead on the kitchen table in complete and utter misery. "Matthew read that Wilkie Collins novel, *The Widower's Branch*. He knows the story." I now looked up at the detective.

Prozzo's eyes widened. "And . . . when did he tell you this?"

"Just."

"When were you going to tell *us*? About this?"

"I told you, I *thought* he was living abroad. Besides, I have had other students of mine who have read this novel. I've looked for the lists of their names and can't find them. And there's no way I could call the school for the lists. They'd see no reason to give them to me."

"But they would give them to me," Prozzo pointed out. "If I asked them."

"I'm sure they would."

The detective took out his pocket-sized notepad and jotted something down. His face wore an expression of calculation and the conversation dangled into an awkward lull. At last I asked, "Do you think I'm in danger now?"

"*I* wouldn't risk seeing him right away if I were you." Prozzo glanced at his watch. "As far as I know he's up at his parents' cabin."

"I believe he probably is."

"It's a little over an hour's drive. I think I'm going to head up there now to question him . . . about all these lies."

"And what happens if he's not there?" I said.

Prozzo glanced at his watch. "I'll call the school and see if I can get your 'missing lists,'" he said with an odd intonation.

"You think I'm lying about the other students?"

He looked at me askance. "Why would I think that?"

"Because you might suspect I'm deflecting you in order to protect him."

Prozzo shook his head dismissively. "Why don't you go spend some time with your friends down the road. I have their number. I can call you there. Do you have a cell phone?" I told him I did. "Let me have that too," he said, and jotted the number down on his notepad.

TWENTY

I WAS SHAKING WHEN PROZZO LEFT, could barely string together my thoughts or words. Impelled to call Breck, I broke down in the midst of explaining what Prozzo had told me. She wisely kept her "I told you so" apprehensions to herself and urged me to get in the car immediately and drive down to New Jersey.

"But he, Prozzo, will probably need me again. The way I left it—"

"Did he say he was going to arrest Matthew?"

"No, just question him."

"Look, Mother, I want you to be completely safe. Your cell phone will work just as well in New Jersey as it will in Vermont."

"Okay, but then I have to figure out what to do with Madame."

"She can't come to New Jersey. Violet's furniture is not pig-proof. No grate in the floor where she can piss to her heart's content."

"You don't think I know that?" I snapped.

"Just calm down, okay? You need to try and stay cool. You've got a lot to accomplish in a very short period of time."

"Then don't treat me like an idiot! Otherwise I won't be able to find an alternative." I racked my brain for several moments and then was blessed with an idea. "Hiram Osmond. He's got a bunch of pigs."

When I told her Hiram hardly ever answered his phone,

Breck suggested driving over to the farm and that I'd probably hear from Prozzo whether or not Matthew was at his parents' by the time I got back.

Hiram was standing near a pen of alpacas in the throes of being shorn of their fur. Squirrel, his cat, was sitting on his shoulder, marching her paws on her master, a disinterested observer to a racking routine. It was late July; from the little I knew, the shearing was happening at least six weeks late. Being in full fur during the summer months, male alpacas can suffer sterility and females can abort their eleven-month-long pregnancies. Hiram saw my look of bewilderment and quickly explained that in early June he'd had to cancel his appointment with his shearer, who, during the summer hiatus, had gone on vacation and had only just returned.

The shearer was a barrel-chested, grizzled-looking man helped by his two smaller-built sons who bent down and quietly tied ropes around the legs of each animal. Using a pulley attached to a winch, they slowly separated the legs until the alpaca was forced to lie down on a low table. One son placed his hands gently on the alpaca's head, while the other held and caressed the animal's body. There is a pure fathomless fear that glosses the eyes of animals when they perceive imminent danger. During that moment of frailty they appear almost human, their meek innocence never more in relief. It's a piercing sorrow one feels watching them struggle so defenselessly. With his sons holding it, the shearer climbed on the alpaca; the animal's body twitched and jerked as though in the last rhythms of life. Finally, it submitted and, petrified, went completely still.

I could see how watching the panicked animal upset Hiram, and it reassured me to know that the knacker felt compassion for living creatures. In comparison to my last visit, when he seemed unhinged by the incessant questioning of Prozzo and the other officials, today Hiram appeared rather composed. He was pretty cleaned up, too, recently shaven and didn't reek of sweat and blood and manure; today he just looked like any normal farmer wearing a fresh T-shirt, untarnished with blood. "This is a surprise," he said. "What's this, your third visit in twenty years?"

"Three's a charm," I said, and he frowned skeptically, as though my agitation was apparent. Looking past the piles of femurs and skulls and hooves in the knacker's yard toward one of his large white barns, I noticed the pigpen, which now enclosed two animals. I asked where the others had gone.

"Sold them."

"For slaughter?"

"No, to another farm. Now, I can't promise what the new owners will do with them."

I turned to him. "I've come to ask you a favor."

"Shoot," he said, his attention momentarily distracted by the hobbled alpaca engaged in a new bout of resisting the shearer and striving valiantly to free itself.

"How would you like to pig-sit for a few days?"

He smiled. "Do I have a choice?"

"Always."

"You got to go out of town?" Unfortunately, I told him. "She's a live-in, right? One of those potbellies? Somebody told me that."

I nodded.

"Wouldn't have taken you for one of those trendy people who keep potbellies in the house."

Glancing at the pen of alpacas, I said, "Wouldn't have taken you for an alpaca-raiser. I thought the profession belonged to the well-off."

He explained that several of the animals had been donated to him by a wealthy couple who'd lost their fortune in poor investments, and he was hoping that raising and selling alpacas would possibly supplement his dwindling knacker's income. "So what's your pig's name?" Hiram asked.

"Henrietta. She's a darling, for the most part. All I ask is that you don't accidentally send her to slaughter. Be more than I could handle right now."

He laughed and shook his head and told me not to worry: no pig under his care was headed for butchering—not anymore. "Good that we're in summer." He looked up at swollen rain clouds that were presently scudding in from the Adirondacks. "The indoor ones don't like staying outdoors, especially when it's colder. Lucky there are only two others right now. So, yeah, bring her on by."

"Hiram," I said. "You're joking, right?" He started laughing. "I mean, how does anybody shove a two-hundred-fifty-pound pig in the back of a Subaru?"

"Only one way I know of getting a pig to go anywhere," he said, with a devilish smile. "I'll show you when I come get her. When you fixing on leaving?"

"As soon as you can spare the time to drive over."

"Boy, what's the hurry?"

I told him family emergency, a daughter in distress. He didn't press me any further. "Okay, so what do you feed her?"

I told him I had a Pig Chow mash that I kept in a garbage can.

Back at the house the phone rang in the midst of my packing. The caller ID read that it was Matthew's cell. I glanced at my watch: forty-five minutes had elapsed since Prozzo's departure, so he would not yet have arrived at the cabin. But how could I be sure that Matthew was even at the cabin? For all I knew he could be nearby, calling with the intention of dropping in. I felt woozy and had to sit down. I wanted to confront him about his artful and shameless lying, but how could I speak to him now? Wouldn't I run the risk of drawing him to me? I just stood there listening to the phone ringing, importunate and jarring and finally giving up with one last little cry. In the clamorous silence that followed, I decided not to listen to his message, if, indeed, he'd left one.

Before I began the task of packing the car and getting the dogs settled, I phoned the hospital and learned that Anthony had finally been admitted. I asked for his room; when there was no answer I wrote the number down to check in with him later. The phone rang again just as I was about to step out of the door, and this time I saw it was Nan O'Brien. Wanting to get on the road, I figured I'd call her back on the way down to New Jersey.

Hiram arrived with his smaller pickup truck, which sported a retractable soft top that enclosed the bed in the back. "Better for keeping Henrietta in." He grinned and pushed a wooden ramp out of the truck and came strolling toward the house holding a quart container of vanilla ice cream. "Did you know this is a pig's idea of paradise?"

"Have they conducted a survey?"

"Just watch." With great confidence Hiram walked past me and headed toward the kitchen where Henrietta was lying on her side, eyeing him warily. He dipped a finger into the ice cream, pulled out a tablespoon's worth, and held it before her, approaching with soft cooing. The ice cream began dripping onto the floor. She clattered to her feet, slurping it up and then went bucking toward him for the rest. Hiram, in turn, began backing out of the house, holding the quart before him like an offering. "Any pig would chase me to the moon for this stuff," he commented, to which I replied, "I suppose you can catch more pigs with ice cream than you can with carrot parings."

Henrietta unabashedly followed him out of the house right to the wooden plank, scaled it without even a hesitation, and clambered into the back of the truck. Once there, Hiram dumped out half of the melting mass in a metal dog bowl, placed it down on the truck bed, and my darling wolfed it like ambrosia. Securing the soft top and closing the tailgate, he wrote a number on a scrap of paper and gave it to me. "My cell."

"You have a cell phone?"

"Yep."

"Your father is probably turning over in his grave."

"I certainly hope so," he said. "After bringing me into this dying profession."

When he drove off, Henrietta's head was still down, scarfing the ice cream. I noticed that Squirrel had accompanied Hiram in the truck and was now pressed against the rear window of the cab.

In a state of shock and numbness I drove for an hour or so down Interstate 91, until cell service was consistent. I left word for Prozzo at the Springfield police station that I was heading down to my daughter's home in New Jersey and included her phone number. As I pressed onward, Virgil and Mrs. Billy kept circling in the back of the car, unable to lie down and get comfortable. It was as though they sensed Matthew's lies and his predicament literally pressing down on me, my constant replaying of the conversation we'd had during his visit. Rewinding it in my head, I was particularly unnerved by how composed and earnest he'd appeared and how he so effortlessly transited the conversation about *The Widower's Branch* and the River Valley murders. Then again, wasn't this ability to detach from horrific realities and appear normal one of the characteristics of a killer?

I managed to reach Nan O'Brien, who wanted to know how Anthony was faring. I told her he'd been admitted to the hospital and that before leaving home I'd tried his room but there'd been no answer. While promising to keep her informed, a thought occurred to me. "Your friend at the police department . . . he'd have access to arrest records, wouldn't he?"

"Of course."

"Can you ask him to look and see if somebody named Matthew Blake was arrested in Burlington in 2006 . . . for assault?"

"Okay. I can do that. . . . Is everything okay?"

I considered for a moment whether or not I wanted to confide in her and then decided to say, "There are just a few complications with the investigation. Right now I'm on my way to visit my daughter in New Jersey. How about if you check with your friend in the police department and when you get back to me I'll be able to explain more." I gave her Breck's home phone number.

When I was driving past Springfield, Massachusetts, I tried Anthony's room at the hospital, and this time Fiona answered the phone.

"Thank God somebody is finally picking up," I said.

"We haven't been here very much. He's been having tests."

"So how serious *is* this?"

There was a short pause and then she exhaled. "He's got a pretty substantial concussion. They say it's not too bad but it's not mild, either. He's still disoriented."

"Oh God. I . . . can't . . . this is just awful."

"Actually, just a little while ago he told me he wanted to speak to you. Unfortunately, I can't put you through. He's still out with the doctors. It's going to be at least another hour. It might be best if you call back after seven and before nine? Where *are* you, anyway?" I told her I was driving to my daughter's house and they could expect to hear from me again later on.

Following Breck's scrupulously scripted instructions, Virgil, Mrs. Billy, and I arrived in Morristown, New Jersey, around five-thirty in the afternoon, did one promenade around the village square, and pulled into the driveway of a small but well-appointed Tudor house. Her Audi station wagon was parked in the driveway; I assumed that Violet was still at work in Manhattan so that I'd have enough time to get the children settled. As it turned out, she didn't arrive home until close to seven o'clock.

I'd forgotten Violet was nearly six feet tall—it wasn't often that Breck and I met women taller than ourselves—and I admit that she's a very imposing, alluring woman, with a pale blond pageboy, a crisp, energetic manner, an impeccable dresser. There had never been a discussion of her age; I suspect Violet is probably three or four years younger than I am. When she came home that first evening she was wearing a suit that I could swear was Chanel, which would have cost thousands and certainly the equivalent of a man's power suit tailor-made in Hong Kong. My great concern for Breck had always been that not only did she give up her life in Vermont for this woman, but that being jobless she'd also end up becoming the "housewife."

But I had to file this fear away, at least on the first evening; no sooner had Violet come through the door, greeted me warmly, and slung her Gucci briefcase on the old Spanish Inquisition table that lined a wall of the entry foyer, than she shed her Chanel jacket, rolled up her corporate sleeves, and without even putting on an apron, started culling ingredients for dinner: a pasta with a homemade sauce of radicchio and leeks in white wine. "Works a full day and then insists on coming home every night and making dinner for me," Breck boasted as she fixed me a gin and tonic with lots of ice and lime.

"So then what do you do with yourself all day?"

"I knit," Breck said snidely.

"Just love being in the kitchen," Violet immediately chimed in, to deflect any tension. "Really helps me unwind." Then to me, "I am so glad that you've finally come to visit. You even could have brought . . . Henrietta if you'd wanted."

Breck tsked. "Oh, come on . . . I asked her not to."

Violet waved dismissively. "Even if she peed on the rugs, there is something called Nature's Miracle. Works for dog pee. I'm sure it must work for pig pee."

I told her I knew all about the stuff and had even written about it in my column.

"I'm pretty sure pig pee has a higher concentration of urea that might permanently stain rugs," Breck opined.

Violet went and stood next to her. Although Breck no longer looked emaciated, she appeared quite lissome next to her big-boned older partner. "Don't be negative," I said.

"She just worries because most of the stuff in the house is mine," Violet explained. Turning to Breck, she added, "Now that Catherine has finally come to visit, I want you to pull up your shirt and show your ma your stomach."

"She's already seen it."

This woman is too much, I thought. In spite of my nagging distress over Matthew, I was momentarily amused and distracted.

Violet turned to me. "Think of a shallow bowl. That's what her stomach looked like before she put some necessary weight on." She returned to the cutting board and continued her dicing and slicing. "I guess I shouldn't be telling you anything about your daughter, who you obviously know better than I."

Appraising Breck, I said, "In the way that I *do* know her. But she does look a lot better. When you two first got involved I was worried that she'd neglect herself." I paused a moment and then added, "But I was never worried about the age difference."

"That would be the pot calling the kettle!" Breck said with appropriate sarcasm, and yet again Matthew's predicament detonated in my stomach. I checked my watch and found it strange I hadn't heard from Prozzo. Surely the detective would have questioned him by now.

Violet turned to me, her face completely animated. "I was concerned about her, too, trust me!" she boomed. "Now, get this. One day I actually suddenly saw something sticking out of her belly."

"Vi, do you really have to?" Breck moaned.

Much to my delight, Violet ignored her. "To me it looked like a tumor . . . but now don't worry," she assured me, "the story has a happy ending." Breck was groaning.

"So we get her into Manhattan to see my GP, who looks at it and orders a CT scan. What is it? No cancerous mass, but her large intestine sticking out of her stomach because she'd gotten so damned skinny."

"Okay, enough!" Breck said with true annoyance.

"I love your daughter dearly," Violet pronounced. "But when

this episode happened and we were riding back home I said, 'Girl, either you start eating normally or I can't go on.'"

"Don't think I haven't said similar things," I told her. "But it doesn't carry much weight when a mother threatens to disown a daughter over an eating disorder."

"She knows you'd never do it." Violet approached Breck, slipped an arm around her, and Breck collapsed against her partner and actually looked content. I was liking Violet more and more; however, she did strike me as being quite manic.

Violet had studied several languages (including Chinese) in college, and held a position at the World Bank. She was the point person who did a lot of meet-and-greet with her foreign—mostly Asian—constituents. Consequently she was out to dinner a lot in Manhattan, and Breck often spent her evenings alone. I would have thought this might have been difficult for my daughter but it hardly seemed to be. Maybe (and she certainly wouldn't admit this to me), although she clearly loved Violet, somebody with such a huge personality might be easier to stomach in smaller doses on a daily basis.

"She's great fun but a bit intense," I whispered to Breck during a lull in dinner during which Violet was shuttling some dishes into the kitchen. Too agitated to eat, I'd left most of my pasta on my plate.

Breck raised her eyebrows conspiratorially and said, "She actually reminds me of you in certain ways."

"Me? Oh please!"

"Okay, you on speed," Breck conceded.

Mrs. Billy and Virgil seemed to have settled down, each perched on either end of a leather love seat in the flat-screen-television room. The phone had rung several times after we started dinner, and when it did, I flinched, somehow believing Prozzo was calling me. Neither Breck nor Violet seemed concerned about answering. "We have to do this," Violet explained. "Otherwise my work people will never leave me alone."

"I'm just wondering if it might be for me."

Breck asked, "Doesn't everybody have your cell number?"

"I gave the detective your number, too."

"He'd call your mobile first, don't you think?" Violet said.

I remained on edge. Glancing at my watch, I saw that it was nearly eight-thirty. I needed to contact Anthony at the hospital before it got too late to call.

Breck gathered up the last few dishes and headed to the kitchen. A moment later she reemerged and said to me, "Ma, you were right. One of the caller ID numbers is Vermont."

"Damn . . . what's the prefix?"

"Hang on." She trotted back to the cordless phone and hollered back, "Four-eight-four."

"Springfield. Prozzo."

"So that *is* the detective?" Violet said as she got up from the dining table and went to the adjacent living room and sat down in an overstuffed armchair.

I yelled to Breck, "What does he say?"

"No message."

"What? Are you sure?"

"One hundred percent sure."

I hurried into the kitchen and grabbed the cordless that Breck had left on the counter and dialed my home voice mail. There were two from Matthew, the first of them ignored while I'd been preparing to leave town. "Catherine . . . it's me. I don't know if you're there, but I was wondering if I could drop by tonight and see you . . . again. Would that be okay? Give me a call and let me know." Then three hours later, him once more but sounding completely frantic, "Hi, it's me. Where are you? I need to get hold of you. It's critical. Just call me!" I could only assume that Prozzo had finally interrogated him.

Breck, who had been rinsing a stainless-steel platter, was

monitoring my face, and when I put the phone down, I knew that she knew. "Begging you to call, huh?"

"He sounds really upset."

"Upset? Uh, Ma, I've kept my mouth shut so far. But you must realize his life is probably *over*. And you better count your blessings that *you're* still with us."

"No, I will not . . . because honestly I just don't believe he killed anybody."

"Well, *I* hate to say it, but I think I was right all along about him."

Breck followed me out into the living room and sat down in another overstuffed armchair that was opposite the one Violet was sitting in. Strategically placing myself in a wing chair so that they were on either side of me, I glanced around the enormous living room, which was more like a great room: two long sofas arranged at a ninety-degree angle, armchairs in modern Italian design, geometric-shaped end tables filled with what I'd call *objets*: quartz obelisks and crystal figurines. Large glass cylindrical vases full of dried artemisia gave the room a slightly desiccated floral fragrance.

"You don't need to call him back, Mom," Breck repeated, this time for Violet's benefit. "I know you want to, but—"

"I'm *not* going to call him. At least not right now."

"Ma, look at me," Breck said. "You can't at all."

I flared up. "I'm not your daughter!"

"That has nothing to do with this!"

"My, my . . . Breck!" Violet murmured, warning her not to press me too hard.

It was time to call Anthony. My purse was sitting on an end table across the room. I hurried over and fished out my cell phone and scrolled through the numbers until I found the hospital exchange I'd dialed previously.

He picked up the phone, sounding very weak.

"It's Catherine," I said. "How *are* you?"

"Just okay. I'm tired. Glad to hear from you. They won't let me talk too long on the phone, though . . . okay, Fiona?" he said. And then to me, "She's on me about it."

"She told me you got quite a concussion."

"Yeah. Got to stay here at least until tomorrow morning." He hesitated a moment. "We got problems, Catherine."

His statement left me feeling winded. "What problems?" I glanced at Breck and Violet, who were sitting in their chairs motionless, trying to glean bits of the conversation.

"Well, I was going to Burlington, right—"

"To see the coroner?"

"Yeah. Because . . . a DNA match was finally identified to the second hair sample in the car." He broke off and the phone was muffled. "Wow . . . I'm really dizzy." Then I heard Fiona say, "I can give her the information."

"No," he resisted. "I need to talk just a little more. Just give me another minute, all right?" I braced myself for him to say the DNA match was to Matthew but he surprised me. "It's to some guy in Florida."

Flummoxed relief. But I knew the relief would be momentary. I said, "Prozzo came to my house—"

"I know. He was here at the hospital with his new theory."

"What do *you* think of his new theory?"

Anthony faltered again, the phone sounded as though it was being shuffled around. "Remember when I last called you and you couldn't really talk? The FBI agent assigned to us had just gotten in touch with me. He said he'd wanted to be in contact sooner but there'd been developments with that kid who went missing up in Middlebury—right before he was found. Anyway, he gave me some information, troubling information. I have my notes here." He stopped to confer inaudibly with Fiona. "All right," he said to her. "When I'm ready you can read the notes to Catherine, as long as you go slow. Real slow."

Anthony went on, "But the gist of my conversation with the

agent was that Prozzo has been in possession of certain facts that he has not shared with anybody else, including me."

"How does the FBI know what hasn't been shared?"

"Because he got the information from them. Not from this particular agent, but somebody down in D.C. with whom Prozzo has some kind of inside track. When our agent up here began talking about what I already should have known about and didn't know, we both figured out what was going on."

"Why didn't you confront Marco about that when he came to see you?"

"Two reasons. I was feeling rather ill when he showed up and I just wasn't up to interrogating an interrogator. And then I decided I want to try and find out on my own why Prozzo might be withholding information."

"Okay, I hear you. But now I'm wondering about Prozzo's claim that New Hampshire wasn't cooperating with him, that they were withholding information. In light of what you just said, I wonder how true that claim actually is."

"My thoughts entirely," Anthony said. He paused, muffled the phone, and then I could hear, "Okay, Fiona, take over."

She finally came on. "Hi, Catherine, I don't mean to horn in, but he's not supposed to talk too much or get worked up." She actually sounded annoyed. "When that detective barged his way in here he really wore Anthony out."

I reluctantly asked, "Should I call back?"

"No. As long as you don't mind my giving the notes to you."

"Not at all."

"So this is basically Anthony's shorthand of what the FBI told him.

"Two and a half years ago, before Tammy Boucher, the first victim, another woman was reported missing in Holyoke, Mass. Ann Marie Wilkinson, wife of a helicopter pilot who fought in Afghanistan back in '01. Apparently her husband, Christian, came home from the war with nightmares and his wife woke up once with his hands around her throat. Mother-in-law described him as overcome by memories. Like hallucinations. The couple had been living in Vermont but then moved to Holyoke shortly before Christmas in 2006. Once in Holyoke, the mother-in-law had trouble reaching them. For days on end. The daughter made excuses. Mother-in-law couldn't reach them either on Christmas Day or the 26th of December, 2006, and drove a hundred and ten miles down 91 to check on them. She had a duplicate house key, and when no one answered the door, she let herself in.

"There was a Christmas tree, gifts unopened. Nobody had been there for days. The house was really cold. Seemed to have been a hasty departure, clothes everywhere, scuff marks on the wall near the front door. She turned up the heating and called the police. The couple never returned.

"FBI was brought in, went on something the mother-in-law told the police, that her daughter warned her that Wilkinson might pick up and have them move somewhere else. They considered his possibly kidnapping her. Then, a few months later in the spring of 2007, Tammy Boucher, victim number one, disappeared in Charlestown, New Hampshire. Her body was found a month later in dense woods, stabbed and strangled.

"Wilkinson finally was located in Charlemont, the far western corner of Massachusetts, living alone. He told the police and FBI Ann Marie had left him before Christmas. Never bothered to contact her family. Claimed they'd been against the relationship and figured they were behind her leaving. He said his heartbreak caused him to leave hastily. Spoke fondly of Ann Marie, and blamed the war for his depression. He appeared distraught during the questioning."

I heard Anthony asking Fiona to give him the phone. "Hi," he said, "I'm on again. A little revived. So this guy has been a suspect for a while. They've been keeping an eye on him. And Prozzo has known about it and apparently been doing his own tracking of the guy and digging around." I heard Fiona muttering a protest in the background. "Anyway, the DNA sample found in Elena Mayaguez's car was matched to a sample found in the Wilkinson apartment in Holyoke."

I digested his declaration for a moment. "So then *this* guy is the killer."

"Mom, *what* is going on?" Breck interrupted.

"Can you just wait a second?" I hissed at her.

"We definitely have *a* killer. Problem is he can't be found and questioned because . . . *he's* dead."

"Dead?"

"Yeah, the reason why the FBI agent called to begin with was to tell us the guy died just over a week ago. . . . Give me a second." I heard Fiona once again objecting to his carrying the conversation any further. I wanted to be annoyed with her, but I knew she was right, that Anthony was probably wearing himself out and shouldn't be talking at all. "The FBI tracked him in . . ." He hesitated. "Florida, living with another woman and her daughter, but by the time they showed up at his house, Wilkinson was gone. Apparently he went to Abilene, Texas. That's where a man, a woman, and her daughter were found in a motel room dead of gunshot wounds. It was ruled murder and suicide. The man's DNA was digitized and sent to Washington and it too was matched to Wilkinson's.

"Prozzo believes there are at least two killers at large. And now his theory makes more sense than ever before. Because of the striking differences between the murders of Angela Parker and Elena Mayaguez. The Seventh-Day Adventist pamphlets were found in Angela Parker's pockets but not in the pockets of Elena Mayaguez. Or anywhere in her car. Angela was strangled and stabbed. Elena was not."

"But all the others were."

"Yes, so that means there are even more variables. One thing we do know, with Marjorie Poole and Angela Parker, it was obvious that the killer wanted to leave a signature, to leave pamphlets where they could've been found."

I was still hoping pitifully that Matthew somehow might not be involved in any of the murders. I heard Anthony take a deep, troubled breath and exhale. "I just can't understand why Marco would keep the information about Wilkinson's identity to himself. Anyway, he came to the hospital saying that because Matthew Blake comes from a Seventh-Day Adventist background, and because he lied to you about when he came back from the Far East and because he assaulted a woman in Burlington while you were having a relationship with him—all this is compelling evidence against him."

I sighed and then admitted to Anthony that Matthew had actually been at my house a few days ago, the night he called.

"Oh, really?" Anthony said. "So that wouldn't have been the time to talk to you about the case anyway."

Fiona stepped in yet again to admonish Anthony for being on the phone. I had to agree with her and reluctantly said good-bye to him.

When I was done with the call I explained everything, and to their credit, Breck and Violet listened carefully.

"No matter how complicated this is getting . . ." Breck began, "I'm sticking to Matthew. How can Matthew explain why he lied about how long he spent in Thailand?"

I knew she was concerned about my getting drawn back in by him, and so I purposely said, "Don't worry. I wonder the same thing."

"Yes, I'd want to hear what that reason was," Violet agreed.

"In the meantime, don't phone him," Breck seconded her.

Dismantling and reassembling and puzzling over my conversations with Anthony, I slept not a single minute that night. Prozzo's hoarding of information was nightmarish and incomprehensible and I couldn't help wondering if it somehow involved Matthew. Needless to say, my nerves were totally shredded by morning. I felt like a zombie when I wandered downstairs and found Violet dressed in a velvet bathrobe, holding a steaming mug of coffee. Through a pair of mullioned windows, she was observing Mrs. Billy and Virgil rooting around the backyard. "They're so lovely. . . . We really should find ourselves a dog," she murmured.

"Why don't you?"

"It's up to Breck," she said in a faraway voice, and then turned to me. "We do travel a lot, so that would be difficult, especially for a young one."

I told her that her foresight about possible neglect was admirable.

Glancing at her watch she said, "Okay, I'm about to get into gear. So you have everything you need?"

I told her I thought so.

"I don't know what Breck is planning today but we have charge accounts at the grocery store and the pharmacy and the dry cleaner, should you need—"

"Don't worry, I'll be fine."

While Breck was driving Violet to the train station, I checked my voice mail at home. Matthew had left two more messages. One said, "What is going on? Why haven't I heard from you? Catherine, please call me!" The second: "Okay, I didn't want to get into this on the phone, but this Detective Prozzo showed up here. There is something *really* important about him that I need to discuss with you. I know what he's trying to prove. Please call me as soon as you can."

I called him immediately, got no answer, and left a message saying I was out of town and to try me on the number that displayed, my cell phone. Breck returned a bit later and hung around the house for the rest of the day, as if to repress my urge to contact Matthew. The day seemed to trudge by while I waited for his phone call. I hadn't heard from him by the time she got a text message from Violet, who needed to wear something the following day that was still at the dry cleaners and asked her to pick it up. Breck agreed but seemed irritated by the request. When I politely declined her invitation to ride along, she left reluctantly. The moment she pulled out of the driveway, I checked my cell phone and realized with great annoyance that the battery had died. I plugged it into the charger and dialed voice mail.

This time Matthew had left a long one. "I can't believe you're not picking up, especially after the message you left me. I've tried calling you six times. Where are you?" He sounded aggrieved. "Okay, so Prozzo is coming back to see me again in a while. . . . Look, I'm sorry I lied to you about Thailand. I did go but only for a few weeks. I was embarrassed because I told you I was going away for a long while to get away from you and I . . . just couldn't stay very long. I was lonely. And I was really ashamed of this and having to tell you that it was the reason why I came home. Like when I went to Sweden. I guess I just hoped it would all get easier in my head and then I'd be able to contact you when I was feeling . . . different, less attached. But also I was afraid that when I finally contacted you, you wouldn't respond. Believe me, Catherine, there were so many times these last two years when I wanted to call you and almost did and I . . . but, in your heart of hearts do you really think . . . just because I lost it once with you. You know what happened . . . it was only because I just couldn't stand to . . . lose you," he garbled. "And I stopped almost as soon as I started.

"But here's the other thing, the more important thing. I am pretty positive this guy, Prozzo, is the father of somebody I dated very briefly at Saint Mike's. A girl named Stephanie Prozzo, who was not all there. There's a lot more of that story to tell. I'll explain to you when we talk. But please, please call me as soon as you possibly can."

TWENTY-ONE

BRECK ARRIVED HOME ten minutes later, burdened with plastic sheaths containing dry-cleaned suits and dark dresses, most of which I assumed belonged to Violet. She found me sitting practically catatonic at the kitchen table. She left the hangers up on the inside knob of the kitchen door, came in, and stood before me.

"You look freaked out." I relayed the message I'd received from Matthew. She asked if I'd actually spoken to him and I shook my head.

Breck sat down next to me and crossed her legs. "I'm so glad you're here with me and not up in Vermont."

I didn't answer.

She leaned toward me. "You need our help now."

I didn't need anybody's help.

Breck went silent, thinking. Then she said, "I'm sorry, but I just don't believe Matthew knows the detective's daughter. It sounds too coincidental. I think . . . he's trying to trick you into seeing him again."

"Trick me? Come on!" I pushed back in my chair, wishing I could escape somehow, not only Breck's company, but escape myself. I didn't know what to think or do.

"He's a liar, Mom. If his lies about Thailand are pathological, don't you think he'd lie about the daughter to try and discredit her father? Her father, who seems to be closing in on him?"

I looked away. "I have no idea."

"Let's face it, Mom, Matthew is manipulative. God help us."

I leapt up from the table, disconnected my phone from the charger, and found the number of Anthony's room at the hospital.

"Who are you calling now?" Breck asked.

There was no answer. I dialed the hospital main number, and they said he was no longer in the room and they weren't sure if he'd been moved or released. Then they asked if I were a family member, and this disconcerted me. I dialed his home telephone number and there was no response. I tried his cell phone and reached his voice mail. Where was he? Where was Fiona, for that matter? "He's totally out of contact!" I told Breck. "This is very unlike him."

"Complications? Maybe due to his concussion?" Breck wondered aloud.

I could hardly even consider it. My natural inclination was to try Matthew again. When I told Breck this, she said, "Mom, are you listening to yourself?" Then grabbed both my arms and, trying to sound compassionate, said, "If you're not listening to yourself, listen to me."

"I don't want to listen to you. I don't need you to save me. Much as I appreciate the effort," I added, hoping this would soften my statement.

Breck went on. "You're addicted to this man."

"I'm not addicted to him! I love him."

Breck gasped and looked stupefied. "You still love somebody who tried to hurt you?"

"Yes, I'm afraid I do."

"You love somebody who put his hands around your neck with the worst of intentions?"

"He stopped."

"He realized what he was doing and that he probably would go to jail for the rest of his life."

"Yes, exactly, he realized!"

"But he still did it, Ma. Which means he could do it again." Breck released her grip on my arms, wiped her tearful eyes with her wrist, and then put both hands gently on my shoulders. "All these women, Ma. All these dead women were *strangled* first. Strangled before they were stabbed."

And then a devastating realization hit me. If Matthew's hands in the end were too enfeebled by damaged nerves to strangle, then wouldn't he have to rely on other means, such as a knife, to complete a murder?

With that the phone rang. Breck picked up the cordless and read the number. "Vermont."

"Just answer it," I said.

I heard a woman's voice ask for me, and Breck say, "Who's calling, please?" She frowned and covered the mouthpiece. "Nan O'Brien?"

I grabbed the phone, my mind still staggering from the sudden reckoning, and it was all I could do to concentrate on what she was saying.

"Catherine," she began, "I spoke to my friend at the Burlington police department and have some information for you . . . can you talk now?"

"Yes . . . I can talk."

"Okay. According to him, my friend, somebody *did* place an assault charge against Matthew Blake. It was investigated and ended up being dismissed. It was a girl he apparently dated very briefly. Her name was Stephanie Prozzo."

"Stephanie Prozzo?" I cried out. "*She* was the victim?" and looked, horrified, at Breck.

Nan went on. "My police friend says she was unstable, her story didn't seem credible. Full of contradictions. They didn't end up pursuing her accusations very far."

"Hang on a moment." I turned to Breck. "Matthew wasn't lying about Stephanie Prozzo."

Breck threw up her arms in exasperation and left the room.

"Now, may I ask you what's going on?" Nan said. As overwhelmed as I was, I did my best to briefly explain everything.

"And I have a bit more. Apparently this girl has had quite a history of psychiatric disorders. She's been in and out of hospitals. She nearly died a little more than a year ago. Suicide attempt. Still living in Burlington when it happened, waitressing. She told the police and the people at Fletcher Allen hospital that she was in love with a man called Matthew Blake. Now, apparently, she's living at home."

Then something occurred to me: the anonymous letters received by the college, could Stephanie Prozzo have mailed them? Could she have been the one who helped derail my teaching career? I now filled Nan in about how the FBI found a DNA match to a man in Florida, who somehow realized they were trailing him and escaped, and how Prozzo had known about the man but hadn't shared it with any of his colleagues. We both fell silent for a few moments, each trying to sift through all the contradictions and recently revealed truths. "So what this means," Nan said at last, "is that this Prozzo guy is withholding some evidence and manipulating other information."

"He's trying to make the link to Matthew stick."

"So it would seem."

"It has to be because of his daughter. He must be beside himself over her."

She said, "I would agree. . . . So what are you going to do?"

"I don't know, Nan. But I have to do something."

"Whatever you do, Catherine, please be careful. And try and stay in touch with me."

When I got off the phone, I called Breck into the kitchen and relayed what I'd heard. She remained skeptical.

"I *am* now going to call Matthew."

"Well, I won't witness that. I'll be in the garden." Breck stalked out of the room.

This time I was able to finally reach him. "Where have you been?" he shouted. "I need to talk to you. It's about Prozzo. And who—"

"I know," I said, and told him what I'd learned from Nan, who had intimate contact with the Burlington police department. "Is he there now?"

"He showed up this morning and left and said he'd return in fifteen minutes. He never came back. When he arrived yesterday he told me I couldn't leave. He knows my car and the license plate. He said if I left he'd have the police track me down."

"This whole thing about his daughter . . . it's like he's trying to frame you. You can't answer any more of his questions. You've got to leave there."

"But how? Where do I go?"

"Give me a second to think. . . . Okay." There was one clear plan as far as I was concerned. "Matthew," I resumed, "you have to give me the truth now. . . . That was a big lie you told me about living for two years in Asia. A lie you supported with other lies."

"You got my message, didn't you? I told you why. And I *did* have an affair with that woman. It happened almost right away. That was one of the reasons why I wanted to leave the country."

"I *shouldn't* believe anything you say. And I'm going to tell you, no matter how you spin this, you're going to be thoroughly questioned and the truth will come out. If you lie to me now, I will turn my back on you forever. Which means if you end up in prison, I will have nothing to do with you."

There was a warbling sound and then he broke down and wept. Finally he said, "Then what do I need to tell you, Catherine?"

I heaved a deep breath and then asked, "Did you harm any of those women?"

I could hear him sobbing steadily now, and then his voice, in tatters, "The problem . . . is no matter . . . what I say, you're not going to believe me."

"I think I might be able to accept the truth and believe you if I . . . *can* believe in it."

"Okay, how about this?" he said, momentarily recovering his composure. "You're the most important person in the world to me. I *don't* want you to turn away from me. . . . I didn't kill anyone, Catherine. I couldn't kill anyone. I don't know what he has, or what he's cooked up, but I'm telling the complete truth. If I'm lying then I'd probably be angling to kill you, too," he pointed out. "So how can you possibly trust me, anyway?"

He sounded convincing to me, but of course I wanted him to be convincing. How could I really be sure? No, I had to choose; but hadn't I already chosen, already deciding to take the risk that everyone would say I was insane to take? At last I said, "Leave there and drive to my house."

"That might be one of the first places he looks for me."

"Not if you write him a note, attach it to your door, and say you drove back to Boston. *That* would make sense, because it's not his jurisdiction. He'd need to get Boston as well as the FBI involved, and that will take precious time. Just write him the note and go to my house. There's a key under the blue flowerpot next to the barn. Go in and wait for me. I'm coming home now."

"But he said if I tried to go anywhere he'd have the police track me."

"Have you looked outside your door?" He had. "Do you see any police cars?"

"Let me check again." He was away from the phone for a few minutes. "Doesn't look like anybody is out there," he reported when he came back.

"Then pray that he was bluffing and get going. You don't really have any alternative, as I see it."

Breck was still outside when I went upstairs, packed my suitcase, gathered the bags of dog kibble, the metal bowls, the stands the metal bowls fit into, and bundled everything into the big canvas bag I'd brought. I took out some dog biscuits, held them before Virgil and Mrs. Billy, and then secreted them in one hand so that they'd follow me. The dogs were incredibly obedient, almost as if they knew that their cooperation would hasten them back to their preferred environment. They dutifully pursued the hand clutching the treats just as Henrietta had shadowed the quart of ice cream all the way into Hiram's pickup truck.

I'd loaded everything into the car when Breck came around the side of the house, stopped ten feet away, and stared at me with her hands on her hips.

"Don't tell me. . . . You're going back."

"I have to."

"There is nothing you can do to prevent what's happening now. You can't get the detective to stop his weird investigation unless you get his superiors to stop him. And why should they believe what *you* say?"

"Because he claimed Matthew was once arrested and charged for assault in Burlington. And that was a complete lie!"

"He could easily claim to have said nothing about that to you, that you're making it all up. You spoke to Anthony. Why don't you let him handle it from here on in?"

I reminded Breck that my most recent attempt to contact Anthony was unsuccessful. And that he was still out of commission. And that time was of the essence.

"Okay, but Mom, if you can't be sure that either Matthew or Prozzo are to be trusted, you're taking a huge risk by going back to where they are."

"I have to do something, Breck. It's because of me that all this is happening. I have to find out why Prozzo never told me that the woman Matthew allegedly assaulted was his daughter."

"Why don't you just call and ask him?"

"He never answers his phone. Besides, Anthony and I need to confront Prozzo together. So if Prozzo happens to call, tell him I'm out or that I've gone to New York City, *not* that I've returned to Vermont."

"*I* don't like helping when you're doing something I don't believe in."

"You have no choice, Breck, you have to help, you have to protect me."

"I realize that, Mom!"

"I'm going to drive back, and if I don't feel safe, I will go immediately to stay with Paul and Wade, how about that?"

Distraught, she shook her head and said nothing.

I was leaving her again, the way I did when she was a child and I got distracted by the man who momentarily eclipsed her father, and later on by other lovers. I closed the distance between us and put my hand gently on her cheek. "I have to deal with this, Breck. I know it sounds mad, but I'm going on my gut. Prozzo's daughter was in love with Matthew and Prozzo is trying to implicate him in these murders. That is unholy."

Breck at last gave up. "I know where you're coming from, Mom. What more can I say?"

"I'll call you. I promise to keep you in the loop. But let me leave now."

I gave her a long, fierce hug good-bye, pulled out of the driveway, and began heading up the spine of New Jersey.

It was around three in the afternoon, very warm, and the sun was blaring at me through a hazy caul above the Watchung Mountains. I drove like an automaton. Early in my journey I reflected on how, like many New Yorkers and ex–New Yorkers, I downgraded New Jersey, which really has a lot to offer—a shoreline, mountains, and sweeping vistas of farmland—certainly topographically more interesting than Connecticut, which, in many quarters, has the reputation of being a more beautiful state. But neither of these places were a patch on Vermont. Even though

I'd only been away for two days, I missed the gentle landscape, the meadows being mowed in the second haying of the summer, round bales curing in the sun.

As I settled into the long journey, cajoling the dogs to settle down in the backseat, I began to ponder Prozzo's most recent actions. The more I thought about them, the more they baffled me. Here was somebody so completely invested in solving a crime suddenly veering off after a red herring. I understood that he blamed his daughter's mental breakdown on Matthew, but why go to such lengths for . . . well, there was nothing else to call it but revenge? How could he actually delude himself into believing his daughter's connection to Matthew Blake wouldn't at some point come to light? He was jeopardizing twenty years of a good solid career, subverting all the careful work he'd done on the River Valley murders by pursuing a ridiculous, quixotic theory.

I grabbed my cell phone, called Anthony, and luckily this time reached him at home. "Thank God . . . they released you," I said.

"Finally! It's so good to be out of there."

"How are you feeling now?" I asked.

"How am I feeling?" he repeated. "A little better. Still getting dizzy spells and feeling disoriented. Where are you, anyway?"

"I'm driving back to Vermont."

"Why are you doing *that*?"

I informed him what Nan O'Brien had learned.

"Are you sure about this?"

"The source is the Burlington police."

"Oh, Jesus. Well, I've just had a message from Marco. Saying Matthew tried to drive away from his parents' house and got as far as St. Johnsbury. The state police pulled him over and are holding him temporarily."

Oh no, I thought, he's in custody now, but said nothing.

"Marco wanted to come this evening and present his evidence

about Matthew, but I stalled him and made an appointment for tomorrow. I'm just trying to get a handle on what's going on."

I considered this. "Is there any way we can let Springfield know Prozzo has withheld all sorts of important information?"

"The FBI already spoke to them. I don't know whether or not Springfield will move on the information. Law enforcement agencies sometimes stick together and can be reluctant to rattle their own ranks over alleged irregularities."

"How unfortunate," I said.

"No, how stupid!" Anthony exclaimed.

There was a significant pause between us. "Catherine," he said at last, "I think when you get home you should just drop the dogs off and come to my house until we can figure this out . . . together."

"That probably would be a good idea."

I chose not to mention that Matthew would have been on his way to meet me.

TWENTY-TWO

I WAS DRIVING ON ROUTE 91 just outside of Hartford; steering the car with one hand, I managed to fish the scrap of paper with Hiram's number out of my purse. I punched his numbers in with my thumb, and while waiting for the call to be connected I noticed a highway billboard of a woman in a bikini leaning forward showing cleavage, advertising a day spa. As I was remarking to myself: yet another service or product sold through sex, I wondered about the relationship between Matthew and Stephanie Prozzo and if there was more to it than I actually knew.

Luckily, Hiram answered his phone. "It's Catherine," I said. "I actually left New Jersey a little earlier than expected. On my way back to Vermont."

"Okay . . . Well, I guess you'll want me to bring your little girl home."

"If you wouldn't mind." I told him where I kept the hide-a-key.

"To be honest, she's been missing you. She's been sticking to one corner of the pen, didn't even go inside the barn when it rained."

"Did you try ice cream?"

"Ran clear out of ice cream. Where are you right now?"

"Hartford."

"She'll be at your house by the time you get home."

"Thank you, Hiram."

"Glad to help, Catherine."

In Vermont, July daylight lingers until just after nine P.M. Brightly colored flowers harbor their glow, birch trees beam their whiteness, and the hush is filled with the song of locusts that starts up and trails off intermittently, leaving the throaty rattles of nocturnal birds. When I pulled into my driveway around 8:45, I could still see most of the familiar landmarks of my property: the sagging split-rail fence with a grayish silver patina, the old barn with a partially caved-in roof, its deep red stain. I pulled into my parking space, let the dogs free, and they gamboled around the lawn in gleeful circles. As I slung my overnight and computer bags over my shoulder, I could barely make out the rotund outline of Henrietta staring at me through the sliding glass door into the side of the house. Watching my approach, she trotted backward and forward, whimpering and grunting, terribly uneasy.

Passing through the door, I rubbed her head and her belly and then looked around for her garbage can of Pig Chow; it was nowhere to be found. Hiram probably had forgotten it. Luckily, Henrietta was not doing her usual two-step "I'm hungry" dance, so I assumed he'd already fed her. I wouldn't have to deal with fetching her food until tomorrow morning.

There was still enough light in the house to move around without switching on lamps, and I decided that I wanted to gather the gloom. I found myself thinking had Matthew not been detained and was still expected I might have gone around the house lighting candles for him. Or perhaps not. Perhaps that would send an ambiguous signal to him. I had the dogs' bedding and food still left to bring in from the car but wanted to let Anthony know I'd arrived home. I picked up the phone and could hear the pulsing dial tone that indicated messages.

Fiona answered. I said, "I just got back. I'm unloading some stuff. I should be leaving here in five minutes."

She told Anthony and then came back on the line. "We'll be expecting you," she said.

Then I checked messages; there was yet another one from Matthew. "Catherine," he began, "I just tried your cell. I guess you're out of range. There is something else that I just remembered. Recently, when I told you about *The Widower's Branch* and how I couldn't find the book . . . and then I found it . . . now I realize Stephanie Prozzo actually visited me while I still had it in my possession. She knew the book belonged to you; I'm pretty sure I mentioned it to her. I now remember I discovered it missing right after she was there, but for some reason I never made the connection. And it just happened to reappear again around the next time she showed up at my apartment." He sighed jaggedly and sounded stressed. "Anyway, I guess I'll see *you* soon." This was obviously left before he'd been detained by the St. Johnsbury police. This revelation only added to my confusion. It made Prozzo's actions and his allegations even more curiously one-sided. What exactly did this detective hope to achieve?

Then I thought of the piece of paper Breck had found jammed in the Wilkie Collins novel, scrawled with the words "you and her," the fact that Nan O'Brien reacted with alarm to its existence the first time I met her. Could this phrase have been written by Stephanie Prozzo?

As I went and fetched the traveling containers of dog kibble, as I gathered up their baggage and was transporting everything back to the house, the din of the locusts seemed to increase. I rounded up Virgil and Mrs. Billy, tossed their beds down in my study, and was just getting ready to leave and drive up the road to Anthony's, when the motion detector lamps switched on. A car was pulling into the driveway very slowly, the way cars do when the driver is lost, looking for somewhere else. When I glanced out the glass studio door, I saw Prozzo's Jeep Cherokee idling next to my car.

I froze and stood there, barely breathing, watching him get out.

In the glare of the spotlamps, I noticed he was wearing a tight sweatshirt that showed his paunch and a baseball cap, his face looking haggard and worn. He didn't see me. There was a bulge on the right side of his chest that I assumed was a gun. I wondered how much he knew of what I knew: that his daughter had fallen in love with Matthew Blake, that she was unable to contain her passion, that she committed acts of desperation that probably included writing anonymous letters to Saint Michael's College. With the dogs braying like banshees, I grabbed my car keys with the idea of sneaking out the back door and moving through a field of ferns to the dense woods. I'd slowly make my way around the perimeter of trees that began where the freshly mown field ended and the tall grasses began, head toward the barn; thus concealed, I would move along its flanks until I came within ten feet of my car. I'd jump in and lock the doors and drive off to Anthony's.

But I wasn't quick enough. Amid the commotion of barking dogs, Prozzo didn't knock, just barged in, and appeared in the kitchen looking harsh and annoyed. Startled and afraid, I greeted him by saying, "What are you doing here?"

"I came to talk to you."

"Not a good time. I'm leaving for Anthony's. I just got off the phone with him. They're expecting me."

He squinted at me. "Why did you come home? Why did you take such a risk?"

I couldn't think of a response so I said nothing and just watched him, aware that his stance seemed defensive and menacing.

"I need a word," he told me with flat affect, then walked to the kitchen table, pulled out a chair, and sat down.

I had the urge to turn around and run out the back door. But I knew he'd stop me. Prozzo was strong and resolute. How had he figured out that I was on my way home? Maybe from Matthew, who was now being held up in St. Johnsbury? My heart clattering against my rib cage, I could barely manage to say, "If I don't get to Anthony's in a few minutes, they'll be coming down here to find me."

Ignoring this, he said, "I need to ask you more questions."

"What do you need to know?"

"About the book that describes the women by the fallen trees."

Without even strategizing, slightly calmer now in the frantic hope that he'd shown up merely to further interrogate me, I said, "Go ahead."

Prozzo folded his arms over his chest. He looked bigger in casual clothing than he did in his cheap suits, and I figured he must have weighed close to two hundred pounds, nearly seventy-five pounds more than I did. "Before I get to the book, I'd like to know why, since we're supposed to be in contact, that you didn't tell me you were coming back from New Jersey?"

I met his accusing stare and said, "Because everything changed. And you know it changed. There's a DNA match now that throws the whole investigation into question."

"That may be. But that doesn't mean there is only one murderer."

"I understand your theory, Marco."

"But you don't realize that my theory involves you."

"What, that *I* killed all these women?"

"Don't be absurd." Then the detective's eyes narrowed as though he were looking down a gun sight. "When exactly did you give Matthew Blake a copy of that book?"

"You questioned him. Why didn't you ask?"

"He says he doesn't remember. But that if I asked you, you would."

I wondered why Matthew would have lobbed the answer

back at me. And then inspiration struck. "Obviously before the first of the murders occurred."

"Well—"

"That's what you're after, isn't it? The final piece of the puzzle, as you told me two days ago . . . Now *I* want to ask *you* something. You told me Matthew was arrested for assaulting a woman?"

"Correct."

"In Burlington?"

"That's right."

I waited a moment, waited until he was looking directly at me. "But Burlington has said the charges were bogus and got dismissed." He shook his head. "I'm a journalist. I naturally check my sources. Let's say I'm giving you a chance to revise what you said."

He averted his eyes. "No revision." I watched him for a moment, the way his massive shoulders went into a slump, his face wearily intent. A fierce wave of protectiveness toward Matthew came over me. I believed with even more conviction that he had committed no crime.

As I stood there, waiting to see what Prozzo's next gambit was going to be, it occurred to me that despite the detective's efforts to maintain stability within his own family, his daughter had tried to kill herself. Her state of mind must have been akin to Breck's self-destructive refusal to eat until her body began shutting down. Both Prozzo and I believed we'd failed our children.

The kitchen was darkening. I needed to put a light on. My white enamel refrigerator and stove still faintly glimmered in the broadening shadows. I took a step back and switched on a floor lamp whose shade glowed with Parisian street scenes. It warmed Prozzo's dismal face.

I resumed. "When you came here the day before yesterday to tell me about Matthew, why didn't you mention your daughter knew him and that she dated him? Don't you think that was a big omission?"

I watched him struggle for several moments before managing to reply, "Whether or not he knew her doesn't affect what he did."

"Agreed, but knowing he dated her and that he broke off the relationship has to affect your attitude toward him."

Prozzo considered this for a moment and shook his head. "He hurt her," he said with malice.

Curious reply. He'd been adept at concealing this volcanic resentment on previous visits to my house, as well as when I saw him at the prison and while the search-and-rescue teams were trolling the Connecticut River for the body of Elena Mayaguez. He'd maintained a tough exterior all along except for when we briefly spoke about our daughters or when he'd shown compassion toward Elena's uncle. I'd found him touching in those moments. I'd believed him to be a rational being who'd made his career out of sifting carefully through evidence, making deductions, spurred on by a hunch or a divine insight. He was a different man now. He was a broken man, he was an enraged man.

I continued, "My understanding was they only went out on a few dates."

"They slept together."

"That's what happens. In college, kids fall easily into bed. And relationships can be . . . flimsy. I can't tell you how many of my students have cried in my office when their love affairs suddenly went south."

"He made promises to her!"

"That's what she tells *you*. But who knows what the truth really is?" I thought for a moment and then said, "When you drove up to the Northeast Kingdom to find Matthew, when you questioned him as thoroughly as you questioned me and everybody else around here, why didn't you bring up the relationship? As a father concerned for his daughter's well-being, you could've spoken to the man she's been fixated on. And yet you said nothing."

"How do you know what I said and didn't say?"

"Obviously Matthew told me."

Mrs. Billy and Virgil sauntered into the kitchen at this point, and I shooed them away. The spotlamps outside hadn't gone off yet. Perhaps there were small animals moving around out there and reactivating them. I thought of Anthony, hoping he'd begun to worry, that he would drive down Cloudland Road to find out why I hadn't arrived.

"Stephanie *still* loves him," Prozzo capitulated at last with a note of ongoing surprise at his child's obsession. His voice cracked. "She's never been able to get over him. And then he left her for you—"

"He didn't leave her for me, Marco. He was never really with her."

"That's what he tells you, but it's not what happened. He loved her, too."

Maybe Prozzo knew something about their relationship that I didn't. I told him, "We may never know the real truth about them."

"If you hadn't been around, if you didn't exist . . ." He left the sentence unfinished.

So he really was blaming me for his daughter's breakdown. I had no choice but to try and reason with him. "Marco," I said, "this is a romantic obsession. It can happen to all of us. Sometimes all we need is a face and then we fall victim to it."

Prozzo began squirming in his chair. He held the sides of the table and began leaning perilously back. The chair was reacting to his weight, the wooden spindles creaking and straining. I felt a flash of terror; the room itself seemed to tilt with his movement. I heard myself say, "I've told you before to be careful. You're not a welterweight."

The detective grudgingly brought his chair forward. I had the impression that he had only partially listened to me, because he reverted back to his earlier argument. "You need to understand that you're the final piece of this investigation. And that Matthew Blake has been copying what's gone on in that book."

"I don't need to understand anything, Marco. I haven't seen any evidence at all that backs up what you're saying. But I did get a phone message from Matthew right before you got here. According to him, your daughter took the Wilkie Collins novel out of his apartment without permission. She took it, she brought it home, she looked at it, and then she returned it—all without asking his permission."

"That's a lie!" Prozzo said through clenched teeth.

I held back for a moment, trying to gauge whether or not I should continue, but then heard myself blurting out, "You've known all along what was in that book. You've known all along because you read it yourself. You figured out who Wilkinson was. You figured out that he left the area. First you recognized the co-incidence of fallen trees. Then you realized you could take the religious angle from Wilkie Collins and link it to Matthew's background. And then you attacked Marjorie Poole. And then you attacked Angela Parker. You brought Angela Parker up here to Cloudland and you let her die. But then when Wilkinson came back and murdered Elena Mayaguez—*that* was something that you didn't expect."

There was a short explosion of silence as the accusation soaked into the old bones of my early-nineteenth-century house, becoming just one more ghostly ache in its long history going back to when trees were split and hewn to the original frame, going back to when the forest was filled with clusters of homesteads inhabited by toiling, reverent Seventh-Day Adventists. Then, making a fist, Prozzo pounded the kitchen table, startling me. "No! That fucking guy was supposed to be in Florida." I looked at him, bewildered. "That's what the FBI said. But he was in Massachusetts. That's why he was able to come back so easily and do it again. And I just fucking figured he was two thousand miles away. That he was gone for good and that he was done. Angela would've been the last one." Then he stopped himself.

"But with the DNA match to this other guy and no DNA match from Matthew, you really think an arrest is going to stick?"

"Matthew was coming for you next. That's what you still can't realize."

I played along. "Coming for me because I jilted him the way he jilted your daughter?"

He shook his head, and now tearful, said, "She lives at home now. She's never been the same. He made love to her and then broke up with her. He was the first man she ever loved."

This was probably true, and I gave his statement a few moments of quiet dignity, of respectful silence. Finally, softly, I said, "I heard about her . . . illness. And I know . . . I can relate to that. My own daughter almost died of anorexia."

This final comment was eclipsed by an explosive scrambling underneath the kitchen table as my hefty Henrietta surfaced. Jamming her flank against my leg, she was panting, and I could tell she was in a state of high agitation. Less domesticated than my dogs, she dreaded large strangers. She stood there, warily eyeing Prozzo, clearly attuned to something wrong.

"What does she want?" he demanded.

"She's worrying . . . about me. She knows you're not welcome here."

The detective leapt out of his chair and nearly knocked it over. He hurried around the table, went and stood by the threshold to the kitchen. Patting the lump of a gun in his sweatshirt, he glared at Henrietta and said, "I want you to get this thing out of here." Then he walked a few steps to one side, presumably so she could pass.

"Henrietta!" I could barely speak from fright, and slapped her taut rear end. She had gone stock-still now, her eyes riveted to the detective. I whacked her again, but she'd locked herself in place, on critical alert.

"She weighs two hundred and fifty pounds. I can't budge her."

"You'd better! Or I'll put her away."

Feeling breathless, I pushed her rump forward. She moved a few steps and then backed up again and anchored herself between me and the kitchen table. "Why don't you forget about her. She's not going to do anything to you." Then, glancing at my watch, I tried one last time, "I really need to get on my way."

Prozzo laughed. "You're not going anywhere."

"Well, then Anthony—"

"Let him come here. I'll get to present my evidence about Matthew Blake to him tonight instead of tomorrow."

I placed my hands on the kitchen table and leaned toward him. "You *have* no evidence," I insisted.

The detective shook his head. "You're wrong. I have everything I need. Your boyfriend is on his way right now. He told the St. Johnsbury police he was planning on coming here. That's why I had them release him."

So even though his plan had been uncovered he was still going to try and execute it.

Prozzo resumed, "Don't you want to stick around until he shows up? Don't you want to be in on the final questioning? Because whether you like it or not your boyfriend is going to fry."

And then came the breaker of rage that I couldn't stop, even realizing it might bring me to harm. "No, Marco," I snapped, "you're the one who is going to fry!"

Prozzo forgot his fear of Henrietta and lunged at me, knocking me off balance. Grabbing me by both arms, he pinned me against the door that led from the kitchen to the back deck, pressing himself against me so it was impossible to move. I tried to wrench my way out of the wrangle but he held me like a vise. His eyes had a glint of extreme distance in them, almost vacancy, when he let go of my arms and grabbed my neck.

I'd never known such frantic fear, fear that my life had just one short measure left to it. He was squeezing and strangling and I was desperately clawing at his hands and trying to breathe. Though my head was pounding, the thought trickled through that being choked like this was my destiny, this surreal panic, fighting to get air, the pair of hands around my neck resolute, not Matthew's hands that once caressed and made love to me. These were angry, adrenalized hands that could kill me in a matter of moments. I was thinking that the whole world has to help me if I'm going to survive, something outside myself must make me strong enough to fight back, to resist. And then miraculously I managed to yank his hands away, just enough to suck in a few huffs of precious air. And then I heard Henrietta's scream, agonizingly human, and Prozzo bellowing. And the dim thought, Surely he's going to shoot her, as I felt his hands slacken and gasped the freedom of air.

Looking down, I saw her gaping mouth clamped onto his thigh and blood pouring from it. I knew how powerful and relentless her jaws were, that he'd have to kill her to make her let go. He moved back from me, scrambling to get his gun out from under his shirt, when I managed to knee him in the thigh. He pushed me away, bent over, and started banging both hands on Henrietta's head. But it did no good. Her jaw wouldn't release him.

By now I was feeling faint, fading, seeing explosions of color, only dimly aware the dogs were barking. I thought I was hearing the unearthly mournful sound the tied-down alpaca made—the last thing I actually remember before passing out.

I'd reached the dimension where souls appear to you, and you dream about all the things you wanted in your life but never got: elusive lovers, houses on the sea, unforeseen financial windfalls, forgiveness from alienated friends, forgiveness of late husbands, forgiveness of estranged children. And once you've greeted all of the beings you were meant to find, once you're blessed with the love you've always yearned for, then you pass into the realm that, except for the lucky ones who've had a preternatural glimpse, for most of us remains a mystery.

Matthew was cradling me and I realized we were in my bedroom. My first thought: What a luxury to be breathing again, to be lying there with my chest rising and falling effortlessly.

"How did I get here?"

"I carried you."

And then I remembered Prozzo had been strangling me. Matthew gently guided my hands to my throat, which I could tell was raw and inflamed. I looked at him, and he looked at me, and we both silently acknowledged the irony. And then he began, "When I got here somebody named Hiram had just arrived. He came back—"

"I know why."

"Then I saw Mr. Prozzo's car. Hiram was standing outside your door listening and telling me something was going on. I ran inside and he followed me. You were lying on the floor, you were moving but I had no idea what he'd done to you. Henrietta was mauling his leg and he was whaling on her. Hiram saw him reaching for a gun."

There were noises of cars pulling into the driveway, the screech of brakes, and doors opening and slamming shut, the dogs barking. Matthew went to the window. He turned to me. "The police are here."

"But where's—"

"Mr. Prozzo?"

"Yes."

"Downstairs. Listen to me, Catherine. Mr. Prozzo is dead."

"What?"

"We thought he was going to shoot us. Hiram had a knife on him. He stabbed him. In the back."

"But how will *they* know? How will they know that Hiram didn't come here to kill me and found Prozzo instead?"

Matthew looked at me, perplexed. "Because I was here. I'm a witness. And Hiram is a witness, too." Then his expression relaxed. "Look," he said gently, "you're not yourself yet."

"I am myself!" I insisted.

"Don't talk, just try to rest. How's your neck feeling, anyway?"

"It hurts. But at least I can breathe."

"Good, that's good."

There was banging on the downstairs door. "I have to go let them in," Matthew said. "Be right back." He started walking toward the hallway.

"But Hiram didn't kill any of them."

Turning around and looking puzzled again, Matthew said, "Of course he didn't kill any of them."

The dogs continued baying and Matthew left me alone. As I listened to him running down the stairs, I couldn't help thinking there was a certain spring to his step, his youth and his determination. I even allowed myself to wonder what it might be like if he stayed on with me for a while at least, and that I wouldn't care if either Breck or his parents objected.

It seemed quite a long time before I heard somebody climbing the stairs: Anthony, looking pale and unsteady, appeared in the doorway. "How are you?" He sounded out of breath.

"Neck hurts like hell. But at least I'm breathing. How are *you*?"

"Still getting these splitting headaches." He plopped down next to me and exhaled heavily.

"You look terrible," I said.

"So do you," he said with a grim smile. "Look, Catherine, I'm sorry about all this. I'm sorry I couldn't unravel it earlier."

"He wouldn't let you. But he's dead now . . . isn't he? That's what Matthew said."

Anthony nodded. "Yes, he's dead. I told the police to give me a little while with you. Do you think you need to go to the hospital?"

"No. And please don't call an ambulance. I'm going to be all right."

"You're going to have to get checked out. But it doesn't have to be right away."

"That's what I told you when you fell and got hurt. But did you listen to me?"

Anthony scowled and didn't respond. I heard people filing into the house downstairs. I heard their voices beginning to thrum. The dogs had stopped barking. I realized it was probably because of Matthew; he always did have a way with them.

Anthony rested his hand on my arm. "How much do you think you can hear now?"

"I don't know. Try me."

"Okay."

Prozzo's supervisor in Springfield had just contacted Anthony. The IT staffer at the police department had been instructed to comb through the detective's files and his computer, and confirmed that there were detailed entries indicating he'd been tracking Wilkinson well before Marjorie Poole was attacked, notes confirming he strongly suspected Wilkinson was the murderer. "But then Prozzo misread some data. He assumed the killer had moved a thousand miles away to Florida, rather than to Florida, Massachusetts."

"Ah. The town of Florida, Massachusetts. That's what he meant."

Anthony paused for a moment. "My theory: he figured he could copy the crime, using strangulation and the same kind of knife Wilkinson used, and strew the bodies with religious pamphlets the way they were done in the Wilkie Collins novel."

But Prozzo never reckoned that Wilkinson would come back.

That he'd cross the state line from Massachusetts into Vermont, that he'd drive up the Connecticut River Valley, stop at a gas station/mini-mart in Charlestown, New Hampshire, and pick out Elena Mayaguez. That he'd wait until she climbed back in her car and then follow her down the road, flashing his lights until she pulled over. That he'd drag her out of the car and chase her into the Connecticut River.

Anthony went on. "Luckily Wilkinson left behind the DNA sample. My hunch is that as soon as there was a DNA match, Prozzo probably figured he had only one chance to nail Matthew Blake as the copycat killer. And so in the end, when he told the St. Johnsbury police to release him, Prozzo counted on him arriving just after Prozzo murdered you. He probably planned to hide somewhere and just wait for Matthew to show up, and then arrest him."

"But I guess my Henrietta wouldn't let him."

Anthony turned his head toward the window and was quiet for a moment. Then he said, "I just went into the kitchen to see the body. Prozzo brought one of those Seventh-Day Adventist pamphlets with him; it was lying on the floor. He had a long filleting knife in his pocket."

"I guess we're lucky Matthew and Hiram were here together. To be witnesses . . . that it was Prozzo all along, Prozzo waiting for his opportunity to kill me."

Anthony nodded. "I'm pretty sure his tires will match the tire tracks we found up Cloudland, the ones that got frozen before the blizzard."

Lying there, I thought of the detective who tried to strangle me now lying dead in my kitchen. I thought of his poor daughter, whom he'd been tragically trying to avenge, a daughter whose insanity made her unable to live in the everyday world, a daughter whose life became undone for the love of a young man who never loved her in return. Or at least Matthew claimed he never loved her. I wondered how true this was. I wondered about Prozzo's belief: had I never entered Matthew's life, might he have been able to love this girl?

The voices were closer now. I could hear the policemen beginning to climb the wooden stairs, the hollow sounds marching toward me. Preparing myself to answer their questions, I wondered if, like a butterfly beating its wings and precipitating a hurricane, I'd started a chain reaction of despair that began with Stephanie Prozzo and moved on to Matthew and then to me and, finally, to her frantic father. Perhaps the death of Angela Parker might somehow be linked to my difficulty believing in love; and if so, that would be impossible to share, much less even to explain.

ACKNOWLEDGMENTS

I owe a great debt to the excellent reporting of Philip E. Ginsburg, whose book *The Shadow of Death* (Scribner, 1993) chronicles the events surrounding the serial murder of six women in the Upper Connecticut River Valley of Vermont and New Hampshire, as well as the search for the killer, who was never found.

I am grateful to Joan Harvey Cook and Nancy Anderson, who shared their stories about a famous knacker man.

I am grateful to Anne B. Adams and her account of finding one of the murdered women as well as for telling me the life story of her pig, Henrietta Rosewater, who appears in this novel under the same name.

I'd like to thank Lynne Barrett for her careful reading of an early draft of the manuscript and her triage of suggestions that made all the difference in the final draft.

I'd like to thank Ruth Sternglantz for her careful reading and her encouragement.

I'd like to thank my UK publisher of Arcadia Books, Gary Pulsifer.

I'd like to thank my U.S. editor, Keith Kahla of St. Martin's Press.

ACKNOWLEDGMENTS

I'd like to thank my agent, Mitchell Waters of Curtis, Brown, Ltd., for believing in this.

And I'd like to thank Bob Braunewell for being such a challenging muse.